Issued to the Bride: One Sniper

Cora Seton

Author's Note

Issued to the Bride One Sniper is the third volume in the Brides of Chance Creek series, set in the fictional town of Chance Creek, Montana. To find out more about Brian, Cass, Connor, Sadie, Jack, Logan and Hunter, look for the rest of the books in the series, including:

Issued to the Bride One Navy SEAL
Issued to the Bride One Airman
Issued to the Bride One Marine
Issued to the Bride One Soldier
Issued to the Bride: One Sergeant for Christmas

Also, don't miss Cora Seton's other Chance Creek series, the Cowboys of Chance Creek, the Heroes of Chance Creek, and the SEALs of Chance Creek

The Cowboys of Chance Creek Series:

The Cowboy Inherits a Bride (Volume 0)
The Cowboy's E-Mail Order Bride (Volume 1)
The Cowboy Wins a Bride (Volume 2)
The Cowboy Imports a Bride (Volume 3)
The Cowgirl Ropes a Billionaire (Volume 4)
The Sheriff Catches a Bride (Volume 5)

The Cowboy Lassos a Bride (Volume 6)

The Cowboy Rescues a Bride (Volume 7)

The Cowboy Earns a Bride (Volume 8)

The Cowboy's Christmas Bride (Volume 9)

The Heroes of Chance Creek Series:

The Navy SEAL's E-Mail Order Bride (Volume 1)

The Soldier's E-Mail Order Bride (Volume 2)

The Marine's E-Mail Order Bride (Volume 3)

The Navy SEAL's Christmas Bride (Volume 4)

The Airman's E-Mail Order Bride (Volume 5)

The SEALs of Chance Creek Series:

A SEAL's Oath

A SEAL's Vow

A SEAL's Pledge

A SEAL's Consent

A SEAL's Purpose

A SEAL's Resolve

A SEAL's Devotion

A SEAL's Desire

A SEAL's Struggle

A SEAL's Triumph

The Turners v. Coopers Series:

The Cowboy's Secret Bride (Volume 1)
The Cowboy's Outlaw Bride (Volume 2)
The Cowboy's Hidden Bride (Volume 3)
The Cowboy's Stolen Bride (Volume 4)
The Cowboy's Forbidden Bride (Volume 5)

Visit Cora's website at www.coraseton.com
Find Cora on Facebook at facebook.com/CoraSeton
Sign up for my newsletter HERE.
www.coraseton.com/sign-up-for-my-newsletter

Prologue

"GENERAL?" CORPORAL MYERS leaned into the small, sparely furnished office at USSOCOM at MacDill Air Force Base in Florida. "We don't have a lot of time, sir."

"Be there in a minute. You got Powell out there?"

"Yessir, should I send him in?"

"Give me a second."

General Augustus Reed wasn't surprised by Myers's anxiety. He knew without being reminded that hot spots all around the world had gotten hotter in the last month. After all, he'd been with the Army for over thirty years and he'd seen his fair share of trouble. Unlike the corporal, he wasn't worried, though. In fact, he'd never felt better. Trouble energized him. Made him sharp.

Distracted him from the mess he'd made back home with his daughters.

The General didn't even want to think about that. But he supposed he had to, with Powell heading to Montana today. He was sending the man on a special mission. Had pulled a lot of strings last spring, plucked him out of a Navy SEAL team when he'd gotten into a bit of trouble and forced him into a special cross-branch task force with the sole design of using him for his own purposes. Luckily the General had amassed the rank—and, more importantly, enough favors—to get away with that kind of thing when no one else could.

With a grunt of dissatisfaction, he pulled open the bottom left-hand drawer of his battered wooden desk.

He supposed things weren't such a mess at Two Willows anymore. Not like they'd been before, back in his daughters' teenage years, when his girls had seemed to need to rebel against him constantly. They'd spent the last eleven years trying to shake off any restrictions he'd put on them, including the men he'd sent to run the cattle operation on his wife's ranch after Amelia had died, and the women he'd sent to finish raising them. Now they'd all grown up, and he couldn't send guardians to watch over them anymore.

So he'd started sending husbands.

He'd found two fine men for Cass and Sadie, and he was about to send a third to Two Willows to woo Jo. Hunter Powell, Navy SEAL sniper. Those girls might think they'd given him the slip, but he'd proved the old man had a trick or two up his sleeve. And a sniper would come in handy given the trouble hounding Two Willows these days. Some drug running outfit had tried to grab his land to use as a base of operations. His girls—and the men he'd sent to marry them—had fought them off. Twice. Time to send in reinforcements.

Still, he couldn't squash the uneasy feeling in his gut

when he reached into the drawer and pulled out an envelope.

It wasn't that he was worried about his daughters, although he was; he had a feeling those drug runners would be back.

It was that there weren't many letters from Amelia left, and when he'd read them all, he wouldn't get any more. The General had come to depend on them, and he didn't know what he'd do when they were gone. Only someone like Amelia could have foreseen her stroke and written so many timely messages for him to receive after she left him behind. Amelia was special. She'd always had a sense of what was coming next. The General hadn't realized how much she'd foreseen until she'd died. Her warm, loving notes had guided him through his daughters' teen years and into their twenties. Then she'd brought up the topic of their marriages.

As the General slit open the envelope, he knew she'd have more advice—more instructions—for him.

Knew he'd follow them to the letter.

Probably.

Lately she'd been telling him it was time for him to go home. He wasn't ready for that. Not yet.

Dear Augustus, she began like always, and the General settled in for a comfortable read.

Her next words straightened his back again, however.

You have got to be kidding me. You didn't go to Sadie's wedding, either? It's bad enough you skipped Cass's. Is there still time? Can you book a last-minute flight and make it? Tell me that's what you'll do.

The General swallowed hard, fighting the knowledge he'd disappointed his wife—again. She was right; there *was* still time to get to Sadie's wedding, but he wasn't going to get on any flight to Montana. Amelia had to know why he'd stayed away.

> *It's no use. I know that you won't. And my heart is breaking—for my girls and for you. You have to make this right. You have to—*
>
> *Oh, why bother telling you what to do? Since when have you listened to anyone? Fine. Stay away, but keep sending those men. Jo is next, and she's in desperate need of someone to love her—and to understand her. I hope you picked a saint for her—*

The General swore. Hunter Powell was as far from a saint as you could get. A Navy SEAL. A sniper, no less. A man as haunted by his decisions as the General was haunted by his demons. He'd hand-picked the other men for his girls with an understanding of exactly why they were meant for each other. Hunter, he'd chosen because his gut told him to. It was as if he'd had one of his wife's supernatural hunches about the man.

The General didn't like that idea at all.

Especially given the reason Hunter had been kicked off his team and handed over to join the General's unit of cast-offs. Normally, he'd send a man like Hunter packing, but something about his story didn't ring true. Hunter was hiding something—the reason for his actions. He was a stubborn one, but the General's gut told him he was stubborn in a good way.

—remember that saints often masquerade in sinner's clothing. I know you'll choose well. Jo always has been the apple of your eye. She used to follow you everywhere—a daddy's girl through and through.

Amelia might as well have stabbed him in the heart. The General half crumpled the letter in his hand. He remembered those days—remembered tiny Jo trailing after him—and always some puppy or kitten—and on more than one occasion, colt trailing after *her*. Jo had loved two things in life—animals and her father. Not necessarily in that order. Back then all his girls had been affectionate toward him, but Jo had been his staunchest ally. He could do no wrong in her eyes.

And then he'd done the worst thing imaginable.

Left her for good.

Walked away from the church after Amelia's funeral, before her casket was even lowered into her grave, got in his rental car and kept driving all the way back to Florida, where he'd been stationed—and where he'd stayed ever since.

He could not go home. Could not set foot on Amelia's ranch. Not anymore.

It killed him to know that he'd never been defeated in battle, but he'd proved himself a coward all the same.

He missed his girls. Missed Jo. Missed her open-hearted enthusiasm for life. He didn't talk to any of his daughters much anymore, but Jo was the one who'd changed the most since Amelia's death. Gone were her open smile and love for him. Now he saw wariness in her eyes when they talked via video chat.

Loss. Heartbreak.

Swallowing against the old pain, he smoothed out the letter and finished it.

Send Jo a husband. A good man. Someone who will take the time to get to know her, Augustus.

And start making those plans. You have to go home.

Love,
Amelia

"General?" Corporal Myers opened the door again. "We've got to go—"

"Send Powell in."

"Yessir."

The General nearly smiled at Myers's obvious exasperation. If the corporal was losing his cool, then time was tight. He'd have to make this fast.

"You wanted to see me, sir?" Powell stepped into the room. The General stood up and went to meet him.

"That's right. You're leaving soon?"

"Fifteen minutes, sir."

Powell's Southern accent was as thick as syrup, but somehow it didn't detract from his sharp, watchful awareness. When he entered a room, people knew to leave him alone. There was something coiled inside him—something that snapped like a whip when necessary. He was a dedicated man, too, with plenty of commendations in his record for outstanding service to his country. Why had a man like him done something so out of character?

The General stopped himself. He knew as well as anyone how strangely a man could behave when those he loved were involved.

"You treat my girl right."

"Will do." Powell had taken on this mission without protest. The General thought he knew why. The man needed a new start. Somewhere no one knew how he'd let his team down.

Somewhere he could reinvent himself.

"She's got to love you—not just agree to marry you." He had no idea why he'd said that. Love wasn't a term he bandied about. That was Amelia's territory.

Powell's eyes narrowed. He nodded once, but the command had troubled him.

The General clapped a hand on his shoulder. "You've got what it takes. You might not think so, but it's in there."

"If you say so, General."

A hard man to read. A man with secrets.

Wounds.

Just for a moment, General Reed wondered if he'd made a mistake. If he'd read the situation wrong. What if Powell was exactly the man his record said he was? What if he didn't have what it took to stick with this particular mission? Marriage was forever.

"I'll do my best," Powell added suddenly.

The General's fingers tightened on his shoulder,

then released. "Good."

He hadn't made a mistake. Had someone else? Why had Powell stepped so far out of character when he'd gotten into trouble? He searched the SEAL's face for answers but felt Amelia's approbation even though he got none. This was the man meant for Jo. He knew it.

Somehow.

"Go marry my daughter."

"Yes, sir."

Chapter One

"**A**LL RIGHT, I'M off," Hunter said. He took one last look around the square office dedicated to the Joint Special Task Force for Inter-Branch Communication Clarity. He'd spent nearly five months working here, a strange end to his career as a Navy SEAL. The task force had accomplished nothing during all that time—a sham posting for a man who'd committed a shameful crime as far as the Navy was concerned. He and the other men were supposed to make sure information flowed freely between the various branches of the Special Forces. Instead, they'd marked time doing make-work projects until the General had revealed their real mission.

The room itself was the strangest he'd occupied in all the years he'd served. It contained the usual charts and maps you'd find anywhere military men were working. Interspersed among them were photographs—of General Reed's family.

Five young women stared out from frames hung on the walls around the room. Five collages were scattered around, too, each of them focused on one of General

Reed's daughters, depicting them at various activities. The maps on the wall weren't of foreign territory; they described General Reed's ranch—Two Willows. A fine piece of property, as far as Hunter could tell, located in Chance Creek, Montana.

The maps, charts and photographs had fooled him at first. All the others, too. They'd judged the General as an eccentric old man obsessed with his family. They'd dismissed the room's decorations as artistic. Unimportant.

They couldn't have been more wrong.

It had taken them weeks to see what it all really was.

Intel.

The General had been planning an invasion all along—of his own family's ranch. When he'd left his girls behind after his wife's death, they'd gradually come to see the place as theirs. The General had decided to take control of it back. Not by attacking it, but by marrying Hunter and the others to his daughters.

A strange assignment. A lifetime one. To his surprise, Hunter had found he didn't mind. Anything to clear his name and have a chance for a fresh start. Even if he had to marry in the process. He figured he'd never made any progress on that front on his own, and he was thirty-four. The thought of being settled didn't bother him. He'd always wanted to retire to a ranch. This way he'd get one. Maybe this whole strange state of affairs was a message from the universe to get his act in gear.

Besides, Jo Reed was… well… *something*.

His eye caught the photograph that had hung by his

desk these past few months. In most of the pictures in her collage, Jo's hair was tugged back into a ponytail and she was working with animals, but this was a more formal photograph, and he hated to think how much time he'd spent staring at it. Her auburn hair was arranged in waves around her elfin face. Her hazel eyes stared back at him, clear and forthright. Her features were sharp, but her lips were full. There was something alert about Jo—something that suggested she knew more than she was letting on.

Something amazingly sexy.

Every time he looked at her, Hunter got the feeling his life was about to change for the better, which was crazy given the circumstances, but still—

There it was.

Jo looked like the kind of woman Hunter had always wanted to find. Someone forthright. Someone intelligent. Happy. Natural.

Someone who knew how to laugh.

Someone he could depend on.

He turned to go just as Logan Hughes stepped through the door, crossed the room, whistling, and sat down at his desk. His chair creaked under his heavy frame. The marine was a large, muscular man, with huge biceps and an even bigger personality. He thunked a tall take-out cup of coffee near the monitor of his computer.

"Hello, baby girl!" Logan kissed the palm of his hand and slapped it against Lena Reed's photograph. Then he pulled a breakfast sandwich out of a paper bag and began to eat.

"Don't let the General see you do that," Hunter said automatically.

"Don't let him see me eat?" Logan asked in mock confusion.

Jack Sanders sprang to his feet so fast he knocked over his chair. "The last time! That's the last fucking time I ever have to hear this damn routine!" He pumped a fist in the air, caught himself and shoved both hands in his pockets. "Come on, Powell," he said to Hunter. "You can't blame me for celebrating. He's said the same damn thing every single morning since we landed here. And it's been months!"

Hunter, caught off guard by the blond man's un-characteristic outburst, chuckled. "You're right; I can't blame you at all." Logan Hughes *had* done and said the exact same thing every single morning since they'd all landed at USSOCOM. Connor O'Riley, a pararescueman in the Air Force, had been the first of them to play straight man to his routine. When he'd left for Montana, Hunter had stepped into his shoes. He wasn't normally one to joke around like this, but it was worth it to rile Sanders. If the man was a spook—and Hunter thought the chances were good, given his refusal to answer any questions about his past—he deserved it.

"Come on, Sanders," Logan said to Jack. "You know you've been dying for a chance to join in. Starting tomorrow it'll be just you and me left here. No one will have to know."

Jack's curses made Hunter join Logan's laughter.

"All joking aside." Logan became serious. "You'd better get going, Powell. Don't miss your flight. You're supposed to be there for Connor and Sadie's wedding. Say hi to Brian and Connor for me when you get there."

"Will do. And don't worry; I'll get the job done."

Brian had married the General's oldest daughter, Cass, a month and a half ago. Connor was marrying his second youngest—Sadie—today.

"Classic Powell. Look at him—he's not nervous at all. He figures Jo will fall hook, line and sinker the moment she lays eyes on him," Logan said to Jack.

Hunter didn't answer that. It wasn't true, for one thing. He had nothing in common with Jo. He'd searched her photograph a thousand times for any clues as to what kind of woman she was—and why the General had paired him with her. He could only be grateful none of the men in their group knew why the Navy was quietly spiriting him out of its ranks. They'd hate him if they did. Military men could forgive a lot of things.

Not desertion.

Jo wouldn't be able to forgive him, either. She was a general's daughter, after all.

"A mismatch if I've ever seen one." Jack echoed his thoughts.

"Opposites attract," Logan said, but he didn't sound too sure about that, and Hunter knew why. Hunter was more than a decade older than Jo; a battle hardened warrior to her fresh-faced country girl. He was as worried as the others that the General had made a mistake.

"Get her to the altar, Powell," Jack said. "A lot is riding on it."

More than they knew. His own self-worth was riding on it. When you joined a Navy SEAL team, you made a promise to the men you served with. A promise you'd give everything to the job at hand—to them. A promise you'd always be there.

He'd let everyone down. He'd done what he'd done out of desperation, of course, making a devil's bargain to fulfill one promise while breaking another. Still, he couldn't help feeling a better man would have found a way to keep all his promises without breaking any.

All he could do was grasp this chance the General had offered him to leave the Navy in good standing. It wouldn't erase what he'd done, but it would wipe the slate clean as far as his record was concerned. And it would give him the chance to start a new life—a good life. Better than he deserved, probably. Maybe he could finally leave the past in the past.

He knew what Jack meant, though. The General had made it clear: either they all married, or no one inherited Two Willows. Hunter wanted that ranch as much as the rest of them, and he owed it to his wife-to-be as much as anyone else to make it happen. But he wanted his record cleared, too. He'd committed his crime for the best of reasons, but still the charge struck too close to home.

If willingness counted, he'd be free and clear already, but he had to make Jo Reed love him, and he didn't know if that was possible. He was too old. He'd seen too much.

She was too young. Too new to life.

Uneasiness washed over him again as he nodded first to Jack and then to Logan. "See you soon."

Jack pinned him with a sharp look. "You're going to have to dig in. Make Two Willows your home. Find the places you and Jo overlap. Make it clear you intend to stay. If you aren't sure all the way about that, she'll know—and she won't buy in to the idea of marrying you."

Hunter was taken aback. What did Jack know about him to make him word his message like that? *Make it clear he intended to stay?*

"What Jack's trying to say is you can't be a loner if you want a wife," Logan told him. "Get in touch with your cuddly side, Powell."

His cuddly side.

He didn't think he had one of those.

Didn't think that was what Jack meant at all, either. The soldier held his gaze. "Get to Montana. And stay there," Jack said, confirming Hunter's suspicions.

Hunter gave him an ironic salute and headed back out the door. He'd go to Montana, and he'd dig in deep. That didn't mean Jo would fall in love with him, though.

When his phone buzzed in his pocket, he pulled it out, noted the caller and hesitated. This wasn't a call he wanted to take. Sighing, he accepted it and lifted the phone to his ear.

"Powell here."

"Hunter. What a greeting."

"Mrs. Frank."

Her swiftly indrawn breath told him how much his formality hurt. "You used to call me Sue-Ann."

Every word she said brought back memories of his childhood. The Franks had been his salvation back then. His ticket to belonging in the tiny Alabama town where he grew up. His mother had lived in Finley almost all her life, but that hadn't helped when it came to fitting in. Gwen was pretty, and had dated the quarterback in high school, although when she talked about those days, which wasn't often, she did so with impatience in her voice. There'd been a falling out, that was clear. Over the years Hunter had got the feeling the quarterback had proposed to his mother, and she'd turned him down. The quarterback left town. Gwen got an associate's degree as a court stenographer. She moved two towns away, worked at the county courthouse—and became pregnant, much to everyone's surprise.

His mother had refused to name the father. Had refused to give up her baby, either. In the end, she'd moved back into her childhood home, transferred to Finley's court, and Hunter's grandparents helped with child care until they died in a boating accident when he was eleven. In her spare time, Gwen wrote poetry, and had even published a small volume of verse that was well received. Poetry didn't put food on the table, though, she always said. She worked full time all his life.

Over the years, his mother had kept to herself out-side work and her monthly trip to Georgia to visit his elderly great-aunt Minnie. Hunter had realized early on that their family wasn't like the others in the community. They didn't attend church. Gwen didn't volunteer at the school or in Scouts or sports. There were whispered conversations between grown ups that hushed sometimes when Hunter came near. His childhood could easily have been a nightmare—if it weren't for Marlon Frank and his family.

Hunter's home sat on the edge of Heartfelt Acres, and once he became friends with Marlon, the Franks had adopted him like he was one of their own. Over the years, he spent far more time around Sue-Ann's dinner table than at the one in his own small house nearby. He loved his mother, and he knew she loved him, even if she wasn't a demonstrative woman, but she hadn't seemed aware of how hard things could be for a child like him. Or how lonely it was to grow up the only child of a mother who kept her thoughts so shuttered all the time.

When Gwen took her monthly trips to Georgia, Sue-Ann stepped into her shoes as his second mother— a doting, happy, traditional Southern woman who kept so busy with her home and family she never thought of taking on a career. The few times Sue-Ann had travelled away from home, she'd taken everyone with her— including him. Looking back, he was sure his mother had breathed easier knowing someone was watching over him. Her long hours at work left her little energy to parent him.

His relationship to the Franks had continued into

adulthood. When he visited Alabama, he still spent as much time at Heartfelt Acres as he did at home. Probably more. Sue-Ann had kept mothering him all these years, texting and calling him as often as she did her own son.

He owed Sue-Ann respect—and love.

But could she respect him now? She thought he'd committed the worst of crimes, and he couldn't explain his actions without letting Marlon down. He refused to do that—not after everything Marlon had given up for him. Still, it was hard to know she must think badly of him. How many times had Sue-Ann told him he didn't have to take on any of his parents' traits he didn't want to? "You are your own person, Hunter Powell," she'd said over and over again. "You get to choose how you'll act and what you'll do."

He was trying his best to follow her dictates, but it wouldn't look that way to anyone else. According to his record, he was as bad as his father when it came to sticking around.

The silence on the phone drew out until Sue-Ann broke it. "Hunter, I don't know what happened to you, but I do know that what a man sees in the service can change him—can give him terrible demons to battle. And no one blames you for what you did."

He choked back the words that crowded his throat; he hadn't done anything—

But that wasn't right. He'd made a decision. He'd let down his team. He had to own up to that, even if he'd had the best of reasons. He had to keep those reasons quiet, too. Even if it meant enduring Sue-Ann's censure. He'd promised Marlon.

"Hunter, we all love you. You can make this right. I know you can. You've given the Navy sixteen solid years of service, and maybe they'll make you pay for a while, but you can come back from this—"

"I've got to go," he made himself say. "Got a plane to catch."

"A plane? Where are you—?"

He cut the call. He'd thought he could bear the repercussions of his decision, but this was too hard. He'd never wanted to disappoint Sue-Ann Frank. Not after all she'd done for him. In her eyes it must seem like he'd deliberately ignored all the advice she'd ever given him.

He hadn't, though.

He'd followed it to a T. And that's what had gotten him into this mess.

Jo Reed had just deposited a stack of dirty dishes on the long plank table in the kitchen at Two Willows when her sister, Lena, joined her. Both of them were dressed in the same spring-green bridesmaid dresses they'd worn to Cass's wedding. Now they were wearing them for Sadie's. Jo felt ridiculous in the girly outfit, and she figured Lena felt even worse. Lena had always been the tomboy of the family, after all.

"Brian's being as skittish as a newborn colt. What's with that man?" Lena asked. "He and Cass have only been back home a couple of days—he can't be bored already."

Jo knew why Lena was snappish. With Brian home, and Connor O'Riley newly married to Sadie, two men would now live permanently on the ranch. And that was two men too many as far as Lena was concerned.

"I haven't noticed," Jo said. She bent down to pet Tabitha, her white cat who liked to pretend to be standoffish but really loved a good cuddle.

Lena leaned against the table and watched Jo stand up again, rinse her hands and begin to scrape the plates. Both of them should have been out entertaining Sadie and Connor's wedding guests, but while Jo was thrilled for the happiness Sadie had found with Connor, she found it hard to keep her spirits up when she thought about recent events. Her counselor had cautioned her the wedding could be difficult. Only a few weeks ago, Grant Kimball had taken her hostage in this very kitchen—

And she'd stabbed him in the back with a carving knife.

No sign of that struggle remained. There was nothing to show that she'd killed a man—first stabbing him here, then shooting him with his own pistol out in the carriage house where he'd cornered them again.

But she'd done it.

Ended a man's life—with Connor's help.

Jo fought to slow her heartbeat, which still raced from time to time when she remembered that day. Now here she was cleaning up from a wedding as if nothing had happened at all.

The weird thing was, after her initial shock and grief,

she'd settled down far more quickly than she'd thought she would. She kept running through what had happened—what Grant had done and how she'd reacted. Each time she did, she came to the same conclusion: she'd done exactly the right thing.

If she hadn't killed Grant, she'd be dead right now. Her sisters, too.

It was that simple.

She'd read Grant's intentions that day the way she read those of the animals she tended around the ranch. When he'd grabbed her, she'd felt rage, fear and a lust for revenge that nothing could slake. She'd always been good at sensing the impulses of living things—trouble was, she didn't always trust her gut. Didn't always follow it. Got tangled up when the words people said didn't match their actions. She had a tendency to believe words too much. To want to believe them.

That's where she'd gone wrong with Grant. And Sean Pittston, too.

It still made her angry she'd fallen for Sean, when every instinct she'd had shot off warning rockets.

She'd sensed pain in him when they'd met at the Dancing Boot; some unhealed wound from long ago, and Jo had ached to help him, the way she helped her animals when they got sick or hurt. That impulse kept her with him far too long. For a month or two, she'd had a boyfriend to bring along to her nights out at the Boot. That had felt good.

But ignoring her instincts about his dangerous side had felt bad.

And the results had been disastrous.

"What do you mean by skittish?" she made herself ask Lena. She knew her sisters worried about her and she didn't want them to. They would be shocked to know she'd weighed the pros and cons and decided taking the man's life was worth it if she saved so many others.

They'd expected her to fall apart after it was over, and they kept tiptoeing around her like she might do just that at any moment. Jo didn't think she was going to fall apart. Instead, she was reevaluating her life. And her ideas about men.

Twice she'd stopped listening to her gut in order to keep a man's interest. Twice she'd paid much too high a price for her lapse in judgment. If she was so prone to errors around men, maybe it was time to stop being around them—

At all.

That meant no more boyfriends. Not now, not ever. She'd focus on the ranch. On helping with the cattle, tending the horses and other animals, breeding her dogs. Animals didn't pretend. They didn't say one thing and mean another. They didn't let you down.

"Brian keeps looking at his phone," Lena said, drawing her out of her thoughts. "He's jumpy as anything. When one of the Mathesons bumped into him earlier, he about leaped out of his skin."

"That doesn't sound like Brian at all." Jo stopped scraping. "Do you think he's afraid we'll be attacked again?" She didn't want to think about that.

Lena's expression shifted. "Of course not. We're perfectly safe now." But she crossed to the window to look out, as if to verify that.

"Bullshit."

Lena turned to her. "Since when do you talk like that?"

Jo bristled. She wasn't a child—and Lena was in no position to judge her for the way she spoke. Especially not when she'd just told a blatant lie.

That was another thing that drove Jo crazy. People lied—constantly.

Animals didn't.

"Since those drug dealers started messing with us. If Brian knows something, he'd better tell us," she said to Lena.

"Exactly how I feel. I'm going to ply him with alcohol and see if I can make him talk."

A smile tugged at Jo's lips despite her bleak thoughts. She had a feeling it would take a lot of alcohol to get the man to divulge anything, and she doubted Cass would put up with Lena's attempts. Cass would be staying sober because she was pregnant, although she wasn't showing yet. Lena slipped out the back door, her long dress swishing.

Jo turned back to her work with a glance at the kitchen clock. Still far too early for the reception to end. Could she hide out in here until the guests finally left?

When a knock sounded at the front door, Jo groaned, rinsed her hands, dried them on a tea towel and went to answer it. People needed to go home, not keep arriving, she thought dispiritedly. That would give her the chance to go to bed and bury her head under her covers, like she did every night, to try to forget about her mistakes.

Never again, she promised herself for the hundredth time that day. She'd learned her lesson: animals were to be trusted. People weren't—especially men. She was done with them.

Forever.

From now on she meant to be independent. That meant no one got to boss her around anymore; not her sisters and not any man. She was never going to second guess herself again. She didn't need entanglements, anyway. They just brought pain. She would stand on her own—live on her own.

Jo pulled the front door open, took in the stranger on the other side and sucked in a surprised breath. He was tall, muscular, with a sharp gaze that seemed to take in everything about her at once. He was dressed for the wedding in clean dark jeans, a crisp white shirt, a dark blazer and a black cowboy hat. He was handsome—oh, so handsome—but there was something haunted about him.

This was a man who'd seen war, she realized.

Which meant the General had sent him.

He reached out a hand, and she shook it automatically, immediately sensing conviction in him. Here was someone who believed in truth—and commitment. But there were other things at play within him. Sadness. Conflict. The pain that came from not being able to be true to one's sense of what was right and wrong.

Jo's heart squeezed in reaction to the hurt in the man, balanced by his need for honorable action. As always, she wanted to heal the wounds she sensed, but that was what got her into trouble every time. She wasn't going to make that mistake again.

"Howdy." His Southern drawl was thick as molasses, and his voice threaded through her, waking places she'd sworn to herself were asleep for good. "Name's Hunter. Hunter Powell. You must be Jo."

The longer they touched, the more his emotions threaded into her consciousness. His conviction in doing what was right emanated off him in waves of honest, true commitment, and the feel of it in a man was so new to Jo it was intoxicating.

"I'm not marrying you," she blurted. Best to get it out there right now, before the heady mixture of Hunter's emotions got the better of her. He still held her hand. Jo tried to tug it back, and he finally let go. The General had sent Brian, and Cass had married him. He'd sent Connor, and Sadie stood out back right now in her wedding dress, cutting her cake. There was no way—no way—she'd fall for this trap.

A slow grin spread over Hunter's face, tangling Jo's emotions into a breathless knot.

"We'll see about that."

As HUNTER STEPPED inside the large white clapboard house, and watched a white cat skedaddle up the stairs, he felt like he'd come home. Not because of the look of the place. It wasn't small and spare like his mother's cottage—nor was it a large, rambling post-and-beam monstrosity like Heartfelt Acres. Two Willows was a Victorian, with spacious, high-ceilinged rooms and a homey, lived-in air. It was that sense of history in its very walls that reminded him of the Franks' home. He'd learned to ride a horse, harvest hay, feed cows and do a million other chores at Heartfelt Acres, just like generations of Franks had done before him. He itched to get busy and start pitching in with the work here, but first he needed to be sure of his welcome.

Jo backed away from him as he set his bag in the front hall and looked around.

"I've got something—for your sister. From the General," he said.

Jo swallowed, still eyeing him like he might be harboring the plague, and Hunter knew he needed to bridge the gap between them. "It's good to meet you." In his experience, most women couldn't ignore a pleasantry like that.

Jo's good manners kicked in and she nodded. "Good to meet you, too." A spark of interest kicked to life inside him when her gaze flicked over him. Hunter wondered what she thought about what she saw.

When she found him watching her back, she quickly turned away, her cheeks flushed, and satisfaction settled within him. He'd seen interest in her eyes. That was a start.

She led him wordlessly through the house, and he took in the neat interior. The kitchen was a large room that overlooked the backyard. Jo moved toward the back door, but Hunter stopped at the table. The Franks' dinner table was a lot like this one. Hunter couldn't help but run his fingers over the table's smooth surface. So many memories—

His fingers slid into a rough gouge.

The Franks' table didn't have scars like these, though.

He turned to Jo.

"Bullets. From the shoot-out," she explained, as if she guessed he'd have heard all about that.

Hunter nodded and pulled his hand away. He had heard all about the shoot-out that had nearly taken Cass's and Lena's lives. Thank God Brian had been there to help, or who knew what would have happened? He took in the freshly painted walls and remembered the renovations Connor had talked about to patch the place up. This wasn't Heartfelt Acres. This was Two Willows. He'd have to work to fit in here.

Jo still watched him, wary as a doe and just as apt to flee if given the chance. "I mean it, I won't—"

"Marry me, I got it," Hunter finished for her. "I'll point out I haven't asked you."

"Still. Just making my position clear."

Hunter had spotted the wedding festivities through the kitchen windows. "Mind if I go pay my respects to the bride?" It was probably best not to let her dig in her heels too deep about marriage before they got the chance to know each other.

Hunter liked her resoluteness, though. Jo was a

woman who stood her ground. He valued that in people. Hated it when people cut ties and ran.

With a sigh, Jo waved him on. She followed him outside to where Connor stood with Sadie, who was dressed in a beautiful white wedding gown. Brian and his wife, Cass, stood nearby, as did Jo's other sisters, Lena and Alice, whom Hunter recognized from their photographs back at USSOCOM. Next to Cass stood a redhead Jo introduced as Wyoming Smith, Cass's best friend.

"Hunter—you made it." Brian came and clapped him on the back.

"Good to see you again."

"How was the trip?" Connor asked.

"Uneventful." Hunter ignored the silent communication shooting between sisters. A look here, a raised eyebrow there. Were the women alarmed at yet another man sent into their midst by the General?

"Your father sent me," he said to Jo's sisters. "I'm supposed to—"

Hell. What was he supposed to do?

The Reed women waited expectantly for him to finish his sentence. Five sets of sharp, clear eyes waiting to judge him if he lied. Six, counting Cass's friend, who was watching the whole exchange avidly.

"—to make Jo happy. She gets whatever she wants," he finished lamely. That's what the General had said, though, hadn't he?

"Are you supposed to build something? Like Connor did for me?" Sadie asked.

Hunter knew Connor had built his bride a walled garden—a legacy project, he'd called it. Sadie's mother had built the greenhouse and, more importantly, planted the large hedge maze on the property. Connor had come ostensibly to help Sadie add a new feature to Two Willows.

Of course he'd really come to marry Sadie, the way the General had sent Hunter to marry Jo.

"Something like that." Hunter thought fast. What would the youngest daughter of a dictatorial General want most? "Something of her own. Jo gets to pick."

A throwaway line, but the right thing to say if Jo's expression was any indication. Her eyes widened. Her lips parted in shock. "I get to pick?" she repeated.

"Of course." Too late Hunter realized how open he'd left that to interpretation. What if she—

"I want a house," she said quickly. "My own house."

Cass's mouth dropped open. "What's wrong with Two Willows?"

Hunter knew that Cass took primary responsibility for the running of the home. From everything Brian had told him, she was a sweet woman who cared for her sisters very much, but even though Hunter was an only child, practically living with the Franks had taught him much about birth order. Marlon was third in the family, which meant he'd bucked authority at every turn but was quick to order around his younger siblings. Cass was the oldest Reed daughter. She was married and the first of her sisters to get pregnant.

He bet she tried to rule the roost—even if she did it

kindly.

He turned his attention back to Jo, the youngest of the Reeds, who was quivering like an arrow nocked to a bowstring.

"A house," she repeated. "Just for me."

"I can do that." Hunter had no idea if he could. His time with the Navy had made him handy, of course. Taught him all kinds of skills. But fall was drawing in, soon to be followed by a Montana winter. "Might have to wait until spring," he added uncomfortably.

"That won't work," Connor said sharply.

All the Reed women turned to Connor at his pronouncement, and Hunter could have kicked himself. Of course it couldn't work; he needed to persuade Jo to marry him fast. Waiting for spring was out of the question.

"Why wouldn't that work?" Cass asked Connor.

Hunter saved him. "Because Jo doesn't want to wait that long."

"You're right; I don't. And I don't see why I would have to."

"Hard to build in a Montana winter," Lena pointed out. "What do you need a house for, anyway?"

Jo ignored her and kept her gaze on Hunter, and he knew if he failed this test he might as well go right back to Florida. His mind raced. How could he follow through?

"A small house?" Brian ventured.

"I don't want a small house. I want a real house," Jo said emphatically.

"A trial house." Hunter met her gaze and held it. "I can build it in a month. You can test it out over the winter. If you like it, I'll build you a bigger one in the spring."

"She doesn't need a house. You don't need a house," Cass told Jo.

"You wouldn't know how to keep it up on your own," Sadie put in.

"Yes, I would," Jo said, obviously stung by her sisters' interference.

Lena snorted. "The General's doing it again—he's shoving another man down our throats. This one will end up staying here, too. Just you wait."

"No, he won't," Jo said. "When he's done with my trial house, he can go. I'll build myself a new one in the spring."

Hunter's jaw tightened but he made himself speak evenly. "Then you'd better work with me, to see how it's done." And he'd have to research fast to learn how to do it himself.

Her reaction was so slight he thought he'd imagined it. Her features hardened.

Hunter got the message.

Game on.

HE THOUGHT HE could trick her with a house, did he? And not even a real one—a trial house, whatever that meant. Some kind of little box without a kitchen or a bathroom, she supposed. If he expected her to traipse back and forth to the big house every time she was hungry or needed to pee, he could think again.

It would be a real house, or it wouldn't be anything.

Still, unease trickled through her veins as Jo sized up the man again. The General had sent him, which meant he wasn't to be trusted. He was a worthy adversary. Sharp. Hardened by his work and what he'd seen. She'd felt echoes of that when she shook his hand. But then she was always sensing something when she touched people, which was why she tended not to touch folks she didn't know well. She knew she often came off as standoffish.

But Hunter seemed determined to get past that—to her. And as much as she'd sworn she wouldn't let another man do that, she had to admit he intrigued her. There'd been something about him when they'd touched. Something… interesting.

Jo sifted through her intuitions. She thought of the puppies she'd given away to their new owners only yesterday. Thoroughbred McNab pups that would work on ranches all around the county with avid eagerness and utter loyalty. If only you could find humans like that—

Jo nearly stumbled.

Loyalty.

She raised her gaze to Hunter again. Men were never loyal.

But she'd felt—

"Jo, can you help me inside for a minute?" Lena said. Without a word of explanation, she took Jo's arm and hustled her toward the house. When Hunter looked like he'd follow, Lena put up a hand. "Just Jo."

Jo wouldn't have been surprised if Hunter had followed regardless; he looked like the kind of man who pursued what he wanted.

What did he want from her?

She doubted it was marriage—despite their exchange at the front door. He was… old, for one thing. Over thirty for sure. He wouldn't want her.

And she didn't want him.

No more men. Period.

Even if he was… interesting.

"What are you doing?" Lena burst out the minute they were inside. "Can't you see what's happening? The General sent him to marry you—just like he sent Brian and Connor. We can't let him get away with this."

"Hunter isn't going to marry me."

Lena stared at her. "*He* isn't going to marry *you*? Don't you mean *you* aren't going to marry *him*? Or is it already too late? Have you fallen for him? Like—love at first sight?" She looked like she was frightened the condition might be catching.

"Don't be ridiculous!" Jo automatically reached for a dirty dish.

Lena pulled it from her hands and slapped it down on the table. "The General wants control, and we're practically handing it to him on a silver platter."

Jo tried to keep her cool. She knew what Lena was angry about—that just when it finally seemed like she might get her chance to run the ranch, the General had sent first Brian and then Connor.

And both of them were staying for good.

"Brian and Connor have been letting you take charge," Jo pointed out.

"For now. But just wait until the first time we disagree. Then we'll see how it goes." Lena paced from one end of the room to the other. Picked up a dirty ladle, looked at it and slammed it down again. "Why? Why won't he leave us alone?"

"I don't know." She was beginning to worry about Lena. If the General pushed her to the limit, what would she do? Leave?

"He had better not send anyone for me," Lena spat. "If he does, that man won't make it out of here alive."

"You don't really think…" Jo trailed off. Despite what she'd said to Hunter, she couldn't say it to her sister.

"That Hunter's here for you? Hell, yeah—that's exactly what I think."

"But why would the General pick him? Hunter's… old," Jo said.

Lena's lips suddenly twitched. "I dare you to say that to him."

"But really—" Jo held up her hands. "What was the General thinking?"

"I don't know." Lena shook her head. "I mean, Hunter's maybe thirty-three, thirty-four. That's not that old, Jo."

"Isn't it?" Jo asked doubtfully.

Lena's smile quirked again, but then she groaned and covered her face with her hands. "Why is our family so weird?"

It was Jo's turn to smile. Lena in a bridesmaid gown was a funny sight no matter how you sliced it. Lena in a bridesmaid gown losing her mind was even funnier. "Can you blame me for wanting my own house?"

"I can't blame you, but I think you're nuts. Cass won't do all the hard work for you if you move out."

They shared a conspiratorial grin. Since they both focused on outdoor work, tending to the cattle, horses and other critters on the ranch, they'd long had an understanding that they were the only sane ones in the family.

"You'll have to do laundry. Cook. Sweep, for God's sake."

"I do chores now," Jo pointed out. She began to stack the dirty dishes by the sink again. Lena automatically moved to help. They might be in charge of the animals, but they knew their way around a house, too. Cass often corralled all of them when things needed a thorough cleaning.

"Not every day." Lena shook her head again and handed Jo the dirty ladle. "If I were you, I'd send Hunter packing. The whole thing is a trap."

"I don't need you or anyone else to tell me what to do." She was sick of that.

"If you smartened up, we wouldn't have to tell you anything."

Before she could answer Lena, the back door opened, and Hunter leaned in. "Don't suppose you'd dance with me, Jo?"

His thick, Southern drawl wrapped around her like a cotton blanket.

Lena glared at her. "Say no," she mouthed.

"I'd love to." Jo made a face at Lena as soon as Hunter's back was turned, then followed him out the door.

Chapter Two

WHEN THEY REACHED the makeshift dance floor, and he turned to take Jo in his arms, Hunter found her watching him. His chest tightened in an unfamiliar way when he took in the curve of her cheek and the arch of her brow. Jo was so untouched. So fresh in the face of the world's ugliness. Her gaze met his and she held it, fearless. She reminded him of the fierce Greek goddess Artemis. Poised. Powerful. Dangerous.

And oh, so beautiful at the same time.

She could be a match for him, Hunter thought. As improbable as it seemed, this young woman—this young *warrior*—could be exactly the woman he could share his life with. Strange how a series of events kicked off by his best friend's marriage falling apart had led him here.

Holding Jo lightly with one hand at her hip and the other clasping hers, he moved her around with the other couples. She was light on her feet. Graceful. Womanly in an altogether unstudied way.

"You're worried about your friend," Jo said suddenly.

Hunter nearly stumbled. How the hell had she known that?

"And you're… interested… in me," she added with a private little smile that hinted at depths unplumbed. Jo had a sense of humor. A wicked one, he'd bet.

"I am interested in you, but what man wouldn't be interested in a pretty woman? And I am worried about my friend, but I don't know how you figured that out."

"It isn't important. Caring is a good thing." She pronounced it like a wise edict, and it was, Hunter mused. If more people took the time to think about people other than themselves, it might spare a lot of trouble in the world.

"I thought Alice was the one who was supposed to see the future."

Jo stiffened in his arms. "She is. I don't see the future."

He kept swaying. "You guessed about my friend. Out of nowhere."

He could almost feel her trying to form a lie. When her shoulders slumped, he guessed she'd decided to tell the truth. He was curious to hear what she'd say.

"I just… feel what people feel in the present."

Hunter hesitated, losing the beat for a moment, as he took that in. She couldn't be for real. Could she? He'd been joking about Alice.

"Everyone?" That sounded awful. And wouldn't the military love to know about a trick like that? Had the General ever thought about his daughters' abilities that way? He filed the question away for later. He felt sure Jo must be talking about hunches, not something truly quantifiable. He wasn't sure if he believed it Alice's visions either, although Brian and Connor seemed to.

"No. Usually, it only happens if I touch someone." She smiled that wry little smile again. "And now you know more about me than anyone else does."

"Really? Your sisters don't know you can sense things?" He tried to keep his voice neutral, as if they were discussing something like the weather or a football game. Something actually real.

She shook her head. "I don't like to talk about it. It's… hard."

"I can imagine." He kept dancing, wondering if Jo believed her own words.

"You don't believe me."

Hunter swallowed. "That's an easy guess. You're talking about something that defies logic."

"Mother."

He frowned. Why had she said that? Unbidden, thoughts came into his mind. Love, confusion. Pain. That old desire to understand the woman who'd given birth to him.

"You're feeling sad that you and your mother aren't closer. Hurt that she's kept secrets. Love mixed with confusion over the past."

Hunter backed right out of her arms. They stood still in the middle of the swirling crowd, until Jo approached him again. Reluctantly, he took her hand, placed another at her waist and started dancing again.

"How'd you do that?"

She shrugged.

"If you haven't told anyone else, why tell me?"

She looked thoughtful a moment. "You can keep a secret, can't you?"

HE NODDED. HE supposed he could. Without thinking, he tugged her closer.

With a sigh, Jo leaned her head against his shoulder.

Every nerve in his body came alert. It had been too long since he'd held a woman. Suddenly he couldn't hold a thought in his head.

"Down, boy," Jo said.

"Jesus." Hunter pulled back. "That's not fair."

Jo laughed, a bright, cheerful sound he immediately wanted to hear again. "Don't worry; I'm taking it as a compliment." But she kept a distance between them.

This was going to be even more difficult than he'd thought.

HUNTER WAS REALLY something, Jo admitted to herself. She was more aware of his nearness than she should be. The pressure of his hand at her hip, the way he guided her around the floor and the width of his shoulders under her fingers all tugged at her senses. His crisp shirt had tickled her cheek when she'd rested her head against his chest, and the faint, clean scent of his aftershave made her want to breathe him in.

Jo searched for something innocuous to say to bring them back to solid ground. He was right; it wasn't fair that she could read the desire in him, but it was a heady sensation to know a man like him could be aroused by someone like her. It made her want to give him a chance. After all, she was perfectly safe at the moment. This was her house, her friends, and she was the one who could sense his feelings. Besides, she'd send him packing soon. Right after he'd built her a house.

"What do you think of Chance Creek? Have you been here before?" she asked.

"No. Never been to Montana. I'm from Alabama."

"That explains the accent."

He nodded. "I'm actually toning it down."

"Are you?" She realized she was smiling, and that gave her a turn. She was enjoying herself far too much. Wasn't he supposed to be the enemy? Hadn't she just sworn she'd never fall for another man?

Somehow she was having a hard time remembering her promise.

"You bet." He swayed with her. "You have a lot of sisters."

She laughed. "I've noticed, believe me."

"Must be kind of nice having a close family, though."

"I guess so."

Hunter pulled back. "You guess so? That doesn't sound like a ringing endorsement."

"I'm the youngest," she explained. "That means I have four sisters who think they can boss me around. And now two of them have husbands. Brian and Connor are nice enough, but what do you bet they start acting all 'father-knows-best,' too."

"I don't think they will."

"I do. That's why I need my own place."

"Understandable."

She tilted her head up. "Why are you really here?"

She thought he'd feed her a line, but he surprised her again. "I need a clean slate," he admitted. "Had some trouble in my last assignment. Your father's given me a chance to show him I can do something right."

Jo digested this. "So you'll build me a house?"

"A trial house."

"With running water, a full kitchen and a bathroom. And a washer and dryer." If she had to run in and out of Two Willows, she might as well stay in her current room.

"With all of those things," he assured her smoothly, although she swore he'd hesitated about that last bit. "What do you say? Will you let me stay long enough to do that?"

Jo surveyed him. This felt like a trap, but if she kept her head, she could get a place of her own and still get rid of him when he was done.

Suddenly, a blur of black and white fur bounded through the swaying couples and jumped up eagerly to put his paws on her long dress.

"Max! Sorry, he's still learning how to behave," Jo told Hunter when the puppy leaped up on him next.

Instead of backing off and fussing about paw prints on his good jeans, Hunter crouched right down and let Max sniff him, laughing when the McNab licked his face. "He's friendly."

"He is. He's Connor's dog; he's supposed to stay indoors in one of the bedrooms during the wedding."

"You don't want to stay indoors, do you?" Hunter asked the puppy. "You want to have some fun like everyone else."

He stood up when Connor came to fetch the happy puppy away. "Sorry about that, Jo."

"No worries." She bent down to give Max a quick cuddle. "It's all right, boy. I'll come play with you later."

"Look at his tail," Hunter said.

She had to smile. Max's tail was wagging a mile a minute, as if he hoped the display of excitement would change his owner's mind about shutting him back inside.

"That's a good dog," Hunter said.

Jo's heart warmed. She couldn't help it; she was a sucker for people who liked dogs.

"Okay," she said, wondering if she was making a big mistake. "You can stay."

DOGS. THE WAY to Jo's heart was through dogs. Or maybe all animals. Hunter wasn't sure. He was sure that he wanted to find the way to her heart, though. In the short time he'd known her, she'd surprised him more than most women did in months. Her open smile was a revelation. The way she lavished love and attention on Max made him want to be the recipient of similar overtures from her.

Happy. She was happy. And he ached to feel that way, too.

Hunter realized for the first time how unremittingly grim his life had been for months now. Worrying about Marlon. Worrying about his own future. Wishing he could tell everyone he hadn't let them down—

But knowing if he did he'd let down the friend who'd once saved his life.

He'd been too long in an untenable position, but now things were looking up, because he was attracted to the woman he was supposed to marry.

That had to be good, right?

He was a long way from knowing if they were compatible, though. Or if his attraction could turn to something more—or if she was at all attracted to him.

He caught her looking at him from under her lashes. Yeah, she was attracted to him. At least a little.

He was glad he'd taken the time to clean up a bit before he'd arrived for the wedding. He felt good in his skin, and those surreptitious glances she kept sending his way assured him his confidence was working on her. In truth, he'd worried that she'd take one look at him and slam the door in his face when he washed up on her front stoop. There was that age difference, for one thing.

Dancing with her now, he didn't feel that difference as acutely as he'd feared he might. He was simply a man, and she was a woman, and God knew exactly what he'd been doing when he invented slow dancing. Jo fit in his arms so comfortably they might have been partners for years. He wondered if that would ever be the case. Would they look back together on this night years in the future and think about their first dance together? How would Jo remember it?

Would they tell the story to their grandkids?

If they did, he wanted that story to be good.

"Jo Reed." He bent down to move his lips close to her ear. "I intend to get to know you real well."

Jo stiffened, just for a moment. Then she tilted her head back and laughed. "In the Biblical sense, no less!" she exclaimed.

Hunter dropped his hands and stepped back so fast he nearly trod on another couple. He'd forgotten she could read him like that, and she was right—he'd been thinking about…

Hunter stepped forward, tugged her into his arms again and swirled her away. "You're incorrigible."

"And you're brazen. You don't even know me."

"Oh, yeah? I know something." Time to give her a dose of her own medicine. "You were thinking biblically yourself just a minute ago."

The flash of shock that crossed her features gave her away, and the bright red flush that followed confirmed his wild guess. She tried to pull out of his arms, but he tightened his hold on her.

"Settle down. So we're both human, so what? It doesn't mean either one of us is going to jump the other one. Right?"

He thought she might lose her cool, but instead Jo laughed again. "Right. You're safe from me."

"I don't think so." Hunter ducked, and Jo's fist bounced off his ear, but her jab hadn't been serious.

He liked this—goofing around with Jo. Having fun—for once.

"The question is, am I safe from you?" she retorted, but she was smiling.

"The answer is no. Not in the slightest."

And he kissed her.

HER LIPS WERE still tingling from that kiss when Jo met up with Cass in the kitchen several hours later. Sadie and Connor had left for their honeymoon to India. They'd spend a night in Billings and fly out first thing in the morning. Their guests had drifted away until it was only family left.

And Hunter.

After dancing with him several more times, Jo's nerves were tuned far too tightly to let her rest—even if he hadn't kissed her again. Once was enough. It was a nice kiss. A thorough kiss. One that promised far more to come if she was interested.

And she was interested, she admitted to herself.

But she'd have to think about that later, because they'd said good night after she'd shown him up to the guest room, and then she'd come back down to clean up, knowing she wouldn't sleep for hours.

Unfortunately, cleaning up meant facing Cass.

And Cass didn't look at all happy.

Jo knew the set of her sister's shoulders too well to doubt what Cass was feeling. She headed toward the back door, thinking to go outside and fetch in more of the dishes from the buffet dinner.

"Has it really been that bad?"

Cass's question stopped her short. Jo knew exactly what she meant. "Of course not—I appreciate everything you've done since Mom died," she began.

Cass cut her off. "But you want out. You want your own place." The quaver in her sister's voice nearly undid Jo.

"I just need some space."

"Why? Because I'm too overbearing? Because you think I'm a bitch?"

"Cass!" That wasn't it at all, except sometimes... sometimes Cass did interfere far too much.

"I know it's true. You hate me for trying to parent you, but who else was there to do it? Do you think it was fun for me all those years? Watching out for everyone? Trying to keep this place together? Trying to be Mom?" She laid a hand on her flat stomach, and Jo knew she had to be thinking of her unborn child. Was she worried about being a real parent?

They'd all disliked the women the General had sent as surrogate mothers to watch over them, and they'd united in their efforts to run them off the ranch. That had left Cass to take up the slack. Which maybe hadn't been fair.

"I don't hate you. Not at all, but I don't need a mom anymore—"

Cass wiped her hands on a kitchen towel and stalked out of the room without another word.

Jo didn't follow.

She knew she'd hurt her sister, but she was twenty-one and it was far past time for her to stand on her own two feet, no matter what Cass thought. That didn't have to diminish what Cass had done in the past. Or what she'd do in the future. Cass was about to be a mother in her own right; that's what she should focus on.

Jo sighed and was about to head outside when her sister stalked back into the room.

"Here's the thing; you do need a mom. You need people around you. You've been through too much to be living on your own. You can't go through two attacks and a... a..."

"Killing," Jo supplied.

Cass went pale. "Jo, that's not what happened—"

"Yes, it is," Jo said matter-of-factly. "I killed a man. A man who was trying to kill you. I don't feel bad for that."

"Yes, you do!"

Jo stared at her. This was the problem in a nutshell. Cass felt so close to her she genuinely couldn't tell the difference between their feelings. It was Cass who felt bad about it—Cass who was traumatized. Not her.

Not anymore.

"You know what I mean," Cass said, a little more quietly. "Yes, it was the right thing to do—that doesn't mean it didn't affect you."

"You're right; it did affect me. It was terrifying. I was in shock afterward, and I needed to process it, which is why I went to the counselor."

"And why you'll keep going," Cass interjected.

"Maybe. Maybe not. But I'm more at peace with it

than you think," Jo told her. "You can't use what happened as an excuse to control me anymore." It was a low blow, but she stood her ground.

Cass's expression crumpled. "Is that what you think? I try to control you?"

"Don't you?" Jo challenged her. They needed to clear the air. "I want my own place. And Hunter's going to build it for me. If you don't like that, too bad." She swallowed, knowing she was about to go too far. Knowing she had to if she was ever going to stop being the baby of the family. "You aren't my mother, Cass. So get out of my way."

WHEN HUNTER ROSE early the following morning, he found Jo in the kitchen, trying to sneak out without being heard. The white cat, Tabitha, was eating from her food dish in the corner. Jo raised a finger to her lips, and Hunter followed her out onto the back porch and shut the door behind him.

"What's wrong?"

"I don't want to wake Cass. She'll be up soon, anyway. We kind of had a fight last night." Jo leaned against the porch railing. In jeans, a T-shirt and battered boots, she was dressed for work this morning. She wasn't wearing makeup and she looked softer today. More real, somehow. The sun glinted on her auburn hair, picking out strands of gold in it. Hunter wanted to reach out and touch it, curl a lock around his finger and give it a playful tug, but she looked too serious for that to be appropriate.

They hadn't kissed again after the first time. He'd wanted to when they'd said good night, and he had a feeling she'd hoped he'd try, but he'd held back, wanting to do things right.

"What about?"

"The house. She can't understand why I want to move out." Jo surveyed the gardens, carefully not meeting his eye.

"She's having a hard time backing off, huh?" He'd seen that with the Franks as they'd grown up. The older ones never seemed to understand that the younger ones were adults, too.

"That's one way of putting it."

"Give her time; she'll come around."

"I don't need to be bossed around anymore."

"You can't prove to someone you deserve respect by running away, you know," he countered, then wished he'd kept his mouth shut. Jo wasn't some new recruit in the Navy. She was the woman he was supposed to marry someday.

Jo's expression hardened. "Fuck you." She clattered down the steps and strode away from him in a flash, her ponytail swinging, and he knew beyond a shadow of a doubt she was hearing his words echo in her mind and cursing him again—because now she was running from *him*.

Hell.

Not a good start.

Hunter considered going after her, but the door opened behind him and Cass came out. She took in Jo's receding shape and sighed. "She's pissed at me."

"She's pissed at me, too."

Cass handed him a glass of orange juice and crossed her arms over her chest. "She's right, though; I do treat her like a baby. I just don't know when she grew up. I swear to God she was fourteen the other day."

"You're like a mother to her." He took a sip of the juice. Freshly squeezed. Nice.

"Which isn't fair to either of us, because I'm not Mom." She rested a hand on her belly briefly. Caught herself and moved it, blushing a little. "Not *her* mom, anyway."

Hunter tried to consider his next words more carefully than he had his prior ones. "Maybe it's time to back off and let her choose her own way, then."

Cass turned on him. "She's been put in harm's way twice in the last two months. She was nearly killed—we all were! So pardon me if I don't want her living—and sleeping—in a house out there all by herself when for all we know someone else could come after us!"

Hunter nodded. She was right; this wasn't the best time for Jo to be living on her own.

But she wouldn't be. Not if he could help it.

"No—don't even say anything." Cass held up a hand when he began to answer. "I don't want to hear your plans. You just listen to me. You put Jo in danger, and I will make your life a living hell. I will skin you alive and roast you over hot coals. I'll—"

"I got it—I got it." Hunter set the glass on the railing and backed away. "I'm not here to hurt Jo. I promise." He made it down the steps and angled toward the barns.

"Prove it," she yelled after him.

So HUNTER THOUGHT she was a baby, too. Resentment burned Jo's throat at the automatic way he'd fallen into advising her, just like everyone else on this ranch, as if she couldn't reason things through for herself. Maybe she was the youngest. Maybe she'd made a few mistakes. That didn't mean she wasn't ready to lead her life her own way. How was she to learn if she didn't try?

Max padded into the barn on silent paws, and shadowed her as she moved through her morning chores, going through the equipment, taking stock, making repairs and keeping a list of things they might want to replace before winter. The dog was probably missing his owner already while Connor was on his honeymoon.

She didn't acknowledge Hunter when he joined her, too, but he stuck close, moving to help her after a bit when he'd figured out what she was up to. Together they got the work done more quickly, but Jo refused to even look at him, let alone say a word.

She would have preferred to go riding, her favorite way to shake off a bad mood. They kept a stable of horses at Two Willows, and Bright Star, a roan mare, was her favorite. She loved to ride into the wilder areas of the ranch and pretend she was all alone—an old-fashioned explorer on the trail before the whole continent had been mapped and paved with roads. Too often people confounded her, but Bright Star never did. The mare could sense Jo's moods as easily as Jo could sense hers. Together they moved through the landscape until Two Willows's beauty worked its magic on them.

She couldn't go riding until her chores were done, though. Safety first, Jo thought wryly. Not that things seemed very safe around the ranch these days.

To his credit, Hunter kept his mouth shut and followed her lead, and Jo couldn't help but notice the way his muscles bunched and flexed under his shirt as he moved, the way his competent hands got each job done with a minimum of fuss but a maximum of masculine attractiveness.

She knew he wasn't doing that on purpose; it was just the way he was. Strong, competent—

Hot.

She was glad he couldn't really read her reactions to him. That would be embarrassing.

He'd done a good job of guessing at them last night, though. She remembered the easy way they'd moved together on the dance floor, and couldn't help regretting that things had already become complicated. Hunter was an interesting man; far more interesting than anyone else she'd met.

The way he watched her made her aware of the differences between them. She'd always prided herself on being competent—and strong, too. Next to Hunter, she felt petite, which she was but didn't acknowledge very often. She felt aware of her own curves; probably because Hunter seemed aware of them.

He didn't say a word she could fault him for, however. Didn't make a move that crossed a line. Just worked hard—

And appreciated her. Silently.

It felt good to be appreciated, she admitted to herself.

By the time her phone buzzed in her pocket she was vibrating with awareness. Somehow his quiet, confident movements had touched something inside her that left her—wanting. Wanting what, she wasn't sure. Something carnal, she supposed. She was as much of an animal as all the other critters on the ranch. Stick a male and a female together for long enough, and watch what happened.

She pulled her attention back to the work at hand, stuck a hand in her pocket and pulled out her phone. "Hello?"

"Jo? It's Megan. I'm back in town. Got time to grab lunch with me today?"

"Hell, yeah." Megan Lawrence was her best friend, the one woman who got her all the way. She'd seen right through Sean from the start and had made her feelings clear. Megan had never met Grant, unfortunately, being out of town most of the time he'd been around. Maybe if she'd been in Chance Creek, things wouldn't have gotten out of hand.

What would she think of Hunter? Jo squashed the errant thought. She didn't care what Megan thought, because even if she did appreciate him appreciating her, his stay here was only temporary. She couldn't let him make her forget her resolutions. She'd put up with him until her house was built, then send him packing.

Megan's invitation couldn't have come at a better time. She needed to get away from Two Willows, from Cass—and from this man who was getting under her skin. She agreed to meet her friend in town, and hung up to find Hunter frowning at her.

"You're leaving?"

"For a while."

"I just got here," he pointed out.

"It's not like I invited you to Two Willows." She'd meant the retort as a joke, but Hunter's frown made her think he'd taken it seriously.

"I didn't come here to put you out," he began.

"I was kidding." Why was she apologizing to him? She'd spoken the truth; it was the General who had arranged to throw him in her path. After Cass's and Sadie's marriages, she couldn't pretend not to know what he was doing. The General wanted control of the ranch and he was using the men he sent to accomplish that.

Which made Hunter the enemy, she reminded herself. She was supposed to keep her distance, not babysit his feelings.

"I've got a job to do here," he said. "Build you a house. The best one I can manage. Try to convince you to let me build you an even better one come spring. I'm not going to push you into doing anything you don't want to do."

If he stayed here at Two Willows all winter, she'd be lost, Jo realized. He represented a risk even in the short term. She shouldn't be interested in men at all after the past few months, but her heart didn't care about *should*.

It cared about Hunter. Already. Even though she'd known him less than twenty-four hours.

"Whatever you came here for, you're wasting your time," she snapped, suddenly sick of trying to figure it all out. "Meanwhile, I've got work to do. And when I'm finished, I'm going to town."

Two hours later, after finishing her chores and going back to the house for a quick clean-up, she sat across a booth from Megan at the Burger Shack, having left Hunter to fend for himself back at the ranch. By the time she got to the restaurant, she was ready to stop thinking about her own troubles and listen to some gossip.

"What's new?" she asked as she unwrapped her burger and took a big bite.

"Not much. Except I've got this client from hell. He doesn't know what he wants. He's looking at property all over the place with no rhyme or reason, so Sharon's dumped him on me. Ten to one he'll turn out to be a looky-loo who doesn't buy a thing. But I've still got to traipse all over town showing him everything." Megan's usually sleek updo had frayed around the edges, leading to tendrils that softened her careful, businesslike look. Jo knew Sharon was a senior member of the real estate company Megan worked for. She had a way of palming off bad prospects on Megan.

"I'm going to get a house soon. A small one." Too late, Jo wondered if she should spill that news.

"A house? Can I be your realtor?" Megan brightened.

"I'm building one, actually. With help." She set her burger down and concentrated on her fries. "The General sent a man to help me build something, and I told him that's what I want. Since it's late in the year, we'll build a small, temporary house for now, and next year I'll start a real one."

"Wait, your dad sent you a man?" Megan nibbled on a fry. "That sounds interesting. He wouldn't be the tall drink of water you were dancing with last night at Sadie's wedding, would he?"

"How do you know about that?"

Megan gave her a look. "It's a small town, and I went to Linda's Diner for breakfast. I heard it from three different people."

Jo stifled a groan.

"The General's been sending you and your sisters a lot of men lately, come to think of it. Cass and Sadie each got one. And if I'm not mistaken, they married theirs." Megan pretended not to be sure.

Jo rolled her eyes. Megan had been at Cass's wedding. "He did and they did, but that doesn't mean anything."

"What's he like up close?"

"Hot." Jo's shoulders slumped in defeat. "Megan, he's…" She fanned herself. "I don't know—trouble."

Megan laughed. "That sounds about right, given the way you look now."

"But I'm not supposed to be interested in men."

Megan grew serious. "Hey, you've had a run of bad luck, but that doesn't mean—"

Jo snorted. "Run of bad luck? The last two men I've dated have tried to kill my family. That's more than a run of bad luck!"

"Okay, settle down and eat." They both did so in silence for a minute. "Is it possible the General has sent a man he thinks won't try to kill you?" Megan kept a straight face only for a few seconds before she dissolved into laughter again. "I'm sorry; that's awful. I can't believe I just made a joke."

"I can," Jo said, biting back her own smile. "The worst thing is, it's actually funny—and actually true, too. And it's not fair; the last person I want to be beholden to is the General."

Megan sobered. "You and your sisters aren't kids anymore, Jo. You shouldn't treat your father as an enemy. He's just a guy doing his best, don't you think?"

"His best hasn't measured up very well." Jo didn't want to talk about the General. She had no sympathy left for him. He'd walked out on them when they'd needed him most—when she'd needed him to make sense of the world after her mother died. She might have been able to forgive him for that lapse, but not for all the surrogates he'd expected them to accept in lieu of their mother. Or the men who'd come to run the cattle operation and ran roughshod over her and Lena. That was unforgivable.

"Maybe he's trying to fix that."

"Maybe." This was too sensitive a topic to debate

with anyone—even Megan.

"Tell me more about the house. Have you designed it yet?" Megan seemed to sense she wanted to talk about something else.

"No," Jo admitted, willing to meet her friend halfway. "Not sure I know where to start."

"I do. With house plans. Look." Megan pulled out her phone and showed Jo where to find sites full of plans for various houses. "Figure out the square feet you want, and then search for that. You'll find a million photos and drawings. Then customize something for yourself. You want to be able to show this… Hunter… exactly what you want. You can look up building codes, too—to be sure you're doing it all right."

"That's a good idea." Jo's fingers itched to take the phone and start on the project right away. Of course she should design her own home. She knew exactly what she wanted.

"And then there's the floor coverings, the paint, the tile in the bathroom, the backsplash in the kitchen…" Megan began to flip through sites to show Jo the possibilities. "Subway tile has been big, but there are also all these glass tile choices that are pretty amazing. And look at this—"

The more she talked, the more Jo's heart sank. "I don't know a thing about interior design."

"Don't you watch house shows on cable TV?" Megan asked her. "Come on, every woman who hires me as a realtor knows about subway tiles."

"I don't really watch TV."

Megan rolled her eyes. "Hurry up and eat. We'll make a quick stop at Renfrew's and start looking at a few things. You need help. The one thing I've learned about renovations and building projects is you'd better be decisive, or someone else will."

Jo's thoughts immediately flashed to Hunter. He was definitely the decisive kind. So was Cass. Megan was right; she had to make up her own mind or she'd get railroaded.

Having plans and decisions to make was a good thing. It would keep her mind off the events of the past couple of months—

And keep her from falling for Hunter.

Chapter Three

"HOW WAS LUNCH?" Hunter asked when Jo entered the kitchen again later that afternoon. He'd been helping Lena but had come back to the house for a drink, and—if he was honest—in the hopes of finding Jo home. He'd given her space for several hours. Now it was time to mend some fences.

"It was fine."

She was still keeping her distance—and she didn't want to look him in the eye. Was that because she was angry? Or because she didn't want him to read what was on her mind? He thought she was curious about him.

Was she hoping for another kiss?

Thinking about the way she felt in his arms had kept him up half the night. He could use another kiss right about now.

"Hey, look—I shouldn't have said what I said earlier." The apology felt awkward. Hunter realized he didn't make them too often. His wasn't in the line of work for pleasantries. You made decisions, you carried them out, you moved on.

"No, you were right; I was running from a confrontation." Jo hesitated near the door. "Thing is, I don't like confrontations much—not with family."

"Most people don't. But the more you hold your ground and face arguments, the more people will listen to you."

"No one listens to me around here."

Hunter thought about the respect he'd heard in Connor's voice about the way she'd handled Grant's attack. "Is that true?" he asked.

Jo, who had just crossed the room to pull a glass from a cupboard, stopped. "Of course it's true. You heard Cass bossing me around yesterday."

"I heard her expressing an opinion. You had a different one. That's how people communicate."

"She wasn't *expressing an opinion*." Jo finger-quoted the phrase. "She was telling me what to do."

"But she's not your mother. You don't have to listen to her, right? So is the problem that she's bossing you around? Or is the problem that you're letting her?"

"Why don't you butt out of it?"

Jo was getting angry, and he sounded far more like a dad than a potential boyfriend, which wouldn't accomplish anything. Hunter decided to change the topic. "Let's talk about the house. We need to get a move on to get it done before the weather changes." It was early September. He figured by mid-October it would cool off considerably.

"You'd better believe it." She pulled the glass from the cabinet and filled it with water. Tabitha wound around her ankles, and she reached down to pet the cat absently.

"Any thoughts about what you want?" It was like walking on eggshells. If she was in his unit, he'd tell her to get over herself and get her mind on the job. He couldn't do that with Jo. Was he ready for this? he wondered, not for the first time. He was a man who'd spent far too much time with other men, in difficult situations, doing jobs that were far from glamorous. Would he be able to settle down and make Jo a good husband?

"What size house can you get done?" Jo stood up again and Tabitha wandered off.

At least that was a direct question. One he could answer. He gladly shook off his dark thoughts. "Here's the thing. If you want to build a house, the first thing you'll run up against is the permitting process. That takes time, and we don't have time. There's a way to get around that, though." He'd looked into home building briefly the night before, spotted the problem immediately and had searched for an answer.

"How?"

"Build small—and in our case, build mobile."

"What does that mean?"

"It means we buy a metal trailer—not the house kind; just a frame with wheels, the kind you use to haul things around. We build your little house on top of the trailer. Park it anywhere you like. If you want to move it to a new location later, we just hitch it up and move it again."

"That's going to be small."

"Maybe not as small as you think. Think of it like an Airstream; big enough to be comfortable, as long as you keep the weight down. I've got a lot of ideas."

"So do I," she rushed to say.

"I found someone advertising a frame like that online," he told her. He pulled out his phone and found the ad. "Take a look at this. Here are the dimensions."

"One hundred and eighty square feet," she mused.

Hunter couldn't help noting the dusting of freckles over her fair skin. Sweet. Like she was.

He cleared his throat, suddenly uncomfortable. "How about we go outside and find where to put this thing?"

MAYBE HUNTER HAD learned his lesson. He was sure treating her better than he had earlier. He was listening to her. She liked that.

Jo followed him outside, noting again his tall stature and the wide spread of his shoulders. His body had felt awfully good pressed against hers last night when they were dancing, and she'd found herself thinking about being close to him in an entirely different way.

That was natural, she told herself. He was a man, she was a woman. Of course they'd think about each other. That didn't mean she'd let him get past her guard.

"One thing to consider when you're talking about location is where you have utilities already in place," Hunter said. "I get that you want to be on your own, but if you build too far away, it'll be a big spend to hook up your house to new water lines and so on. We should keep it reasonable. It's only a temporary house, after all."

"I'm okay being close," Jo hurried to say. His reasoning made sense. Besides, as much as she wanted to have her own place, last night, lying in bed, she'd begun to picture sleeping alone—away from everyone else. She'd never been afraid of that kind of thing before, but she was a realist. Her family's problems weren't over—that was clear. It was obvious the first men who'd tried to grab their land hadn't been working alone. They'd been hired by someone who wanted a property big enough to hide a drug-running and manufacturing operation. Why that person hadn't simply bought a property of their own, Jo couldn't say, but it was clear that first failure had angered him. In revenge, he'd sent Grant Kimball and his friend, Ron Cooper, to extort enough money from her family to recoup his losses from the first debacle.

Now Grant was dead, and Ron had been extradited back to Tennessee, where he had outstanding warrants. Whoever was behind the trouble probably was based there. "They must be trying to establish a pipeline," Cab had told them. "To open up a new territory. They've lost men and money now, and it feels to me that whoever is at the head of this is taking it personally. You all have to watch out."

Jo pictured Grant again, charging into the kitchen, a pistol in his hand. The way she'd played drugged by Sadie's sedative tea. Waited for her chance—and nearly panicked when he'd tossed her over his shoulder to carry her off.

The way she'd grabbed the knife from the counter and plunged it into his back.

It hadn't stopped him—had only bought her and the others time to hide in the carriage house in Alice's studio.

She'd hoped he'd leave then. But he'd kept coming.

No matter what they did.

Kept coming up the stairs. Attacking them. Waving the gun at them.

Until they'd all scrambled to fight over it on the landing, and she'd taken it from him just as he'd thrown Sadie down the stairs.

So she'd shot him.

She'd shot him—and she'd do it again.

"Jo? Jo? You paying attention?"

"Of course I'm paying attention," she snapped. "I want the house here." She stopped only a few dozen paces from the main house along the track toward the outbuildings. "Right here."

"Here?" Hunter looked from the main house to the empty grass before them. "I thought—" He broke off, shook his head. "Here's just fine, I guess."

"It won't be hard to get utilities here, right?" she demanded. She knew he thought she was being cowardly. She wasn't; she was being sensible. Why did everyone think she was such a ninny? Sure, it would be nice to park her tiny house in the woods or on a peak with a beautiful view, but neither of those options were practical with a pack of killers out to get them, and she was nothing if not practical.

"No. Shouldn't be hard at all. I think it's a great location. And you know what? You can do some landscaping to make it stand apart. We could even put up a little picket fence."

She looked at him askance. Was he making fun of her?

He must have sensed her question. "Think about it. You could ham it up. Take this tiny little house and make a tiny little yard, a little garden. Like it was—"

"A child's house?" She balled her hands into fists. He *was* making fun of her.

"That's not what I meant at all. Like—a cottage. A witch's cottage. Something out of a fairy tale. Damn it—" He waved a hand. "I can see it in my head. I don't know how to describe it."

Jo could see it in her head, too. She knew she shouldn't, but she reached out and touched his wrist, needing to be sure their shared vision really was shared. She'd know if he was mocking her. She'd also know if he was picturing something special.

His skin was warm, his wrist wide, muscled and strong. She sensed in him a need to please her. A desire to create something perfect—something beautiful. Something magic—like he thought she was.

Jo swallowed hard, suddenly off balance. "You mean, make it look like it's meant to be there," she said in a quieter tone, dropping her hand to her side. "Like it's always been there."

"Exactly. Maybe a picket fence is all wrong."

She understood what he meant to say; they could gear the landscaping around the house to its own size to make it look like it was all intentional and like it belonged.

"That's a good idea," she said grudgingly.

"Thanks."

Max loped up to them from the direction of the house, and Hunter bent down to give the young dog a good rubbing. "Aren't you handsome?" he asked. Max licked his nose in answer. "I'm jealous of Connor," Hunter said. "Are you going to breed more puppies soon, Jo? Could I have one?"

"It'll be about six months before I breed his mother again." She wrapped her arms across her chest, suddenly uncertain about everything. Who was this man her father had sent? Was he truly as different from the others as he seemed to be?

"Guess I'll have to be patient. I can still be your uncle, can't I, Max?"

The dog wriggled under Hunter's attention, tail wagging furiously.

Jo couldn't help herself; she bent down and touched Hunter's wrist again, needing to check that his words matched what was in his heart. She'd learned the hard way—twice—how important that was. This time she felt warmth, care and happiness emanating from him, and her heart softened. The waiting list for her dogs was a mile long, but she didn't think she'd tell Hunter that.

She'd make sure he got a puppy from the next litter.

"I'LL THINK ABOUT your ideas," Jo said and continued into the house.

Hunter stayed to play with Max until his phone vibrated in his pocket, then he stood up, pulled it out, nodded in satisfaction when he saw the caller's name and lifted the phone to his ear.

"Hey, Marlon." He watched Jo slip into the kitchen.

"I'm still here. Still behaving myself."

The two sentences were as terse as every communication with Marlon had been lately.

"Glad to hear it." Hunter knew it was costing his friend to do the mature thing in the situation he found himself in. He wanted out of the Navy badly. His marriage was disintegrating, and Hunter figured it was hell for Marlon to cool his heels waiting for his time to be up. Only another month and a half and he'd be home free. It was Hunter's job to make sure he didn't bolt a day sooner.

Marlon grunted, and Hunter knew he was about to hang up. "Heard anything from the home front?" he hurried to ask.

"Yeah. May's lawyers got in touch yesterday."

Hunter's heart fell. His friend was in a world of pain and he wished he could help, but there was little to do except encourage Marlon to safeguard his future. He wished he could shake May, but was it really anyone's fault when a marriage didn't pan out? Marlon and May had gotten hitched too young and the passion they'd felt back then hadn't survived the struggle of starting out and raising kids. Marlon's son was twelve. His daughter nine. It was killing Marlon that his family was falling apart.

"What'd they say?"

"The paperwork is coming. I should sign it. Not make things harder than they have to be."

"I'm really sorry to hear that."

"Sorry doesn't help, does it? I need to see her. Talk to her. She's going to have me on a schedule! A schedule to see my own freaking kids!"

"Settle down. You need to do this right." Hunter paced first one way, then the other on the dirt track.

"You shouldn't have stopped me when I tried to—"

"Marlon!" Hunter stood stock still. "You serious about that?" His friend had nearly taken a drastic step some months back. Hunter had left everything behind to help him.

Marlon sighed. "No. I'm not serious. This is just… fucked up. She's taking my kids, Hunter."

"She's not taking them," Hunter reasoned. "She's trying to make the best of a bad deal, don't you think?"

"No. I don't think. I don't think she's thinking at all. Why won't she fight for us? What about counseling? Isn't that supposed to fix everything?"

Hunter began to pace again, not bringing up the fact it was Marlon who'd refused to go to counseling last year when May had asked him to. One of their issues, Hunter thought, was that May had refused to do the typical Navy-wife thing. She wouldn't live on base. Wouldn't move to be close to Marlon. Instead, she'd stayed in the town in which they'd all grown up, which meant Marlon wasn't home nearly as often as he could have been. And when things began to go badly, he didn't have the face time he needed with his wife. He was currently stationed at Coronado, far from Alabama.

"I don't know, buddy. Hang in there, okay?"

"Yeah, I'll hang in there like the chump I am. Hope you're satisfied." Marlon hung up.

He was far from satisfied, Hunter thought as he continued toward the house. Marlon's mood wasn't good, and a few months ago, when May had first brought up the divorce, it had been even worse. He was worried for his friend. He knew the man had built his life around his family. Without it to anchor him, he was drifting in a bad direction.

As he approached the back porch, he spotted Brian sitting on the wicker love seat, holding a bottle of beer. "You want one?" Brian offered. When Hunter nodded, he got up and went inside, coming back moments later with an open bottle in his hand. He gave it to Hunter, who took a long drag.

"Tough day?" Brian asked.

"Tough five minutes. The rest went okay."

"Jo giving you trouble?"

"No. A friend from back home. He's having a bad time. Don't know if he can hold it together."

"That's too bad. How about you? Are you going to hold it together? What do you think your chances are with Jo?"

"I don't know." Hunter thought about the way she'd touched his wrist—twice. It had been such an unexpected gesture, it had left him off-kilter. "Maybe better than I'd guessed."

"Glad to hear it." Brian clinked bottles with him. "What surprised me when I came here was how compatible with Cass I turned out to be. I mean, what were the chances? I decided the General got lucky, but then Connor came and fell hard for Sadie. And we know how that turned out. Two for two—a hell of a coincidence. Now you're here."

"Now I'm here," Hunter agreed.

"If things work out for you and Jo, it's going to be downright uncanny."

"Uncanny seems to be the word for this place from what you and Connor have said."

"Have you witnessed anything strange yet?" Brian asked him. He shifted in his seat and lifted the bottle of beer to take a swig.

"Not yet," Hunter lied. He'd keep Jo's secret.

"Brace yourself. It'll happen sooner or later."

THE FOLLOWING DAY, after a morning spent working with Hunter, who true to form had talked little but whose presence kept her all too aware of him, Jo slipped away and headed into town again on her own to the feed store, more to have some time to herself to consider the predicament she was in than because they needed anything. She wound her way through the store, breathing in the familiar musty scents of the animal kibble, and checked out the price of the supplemental feed they'd need for the horses when the weather got worse. Next she moved on to the aisles where dog food was stored, although she didn't need any of that, either.

She was staring at the large bags of dog food, and trying to figure out her attraction to Hunter, which defied all reason, when a man she didn't know pointed to the premium brand she usually bought and said, "Seems overpriced, doesn't it?" He was heavy and swarthy, with a florid face that hinted at too much alcohol and not nearly enough exercise.

"Sometimes it's worth it to pay for quality, don't you think?" Jo answered automatically, still buried in her thoughts.

"The cheaper version gets the job done."

Jo bit back a sharp retort and edged away before she put her disdain into words. Her dogs were her business—and her passion. She wasn't going to feed them cut-rate kibble.

The man stuck close as she moved down the aisle. He was about Hunter's age, she estimated. Thirty-four, thirty-five. Somehow the extra flesh on his bones didn't make him look any younger, or gentler-looking, though. She found herself pulling away. Wanting to move on.

"You got dogs?"

She stopped herself from rolling her eyes at this conversational salvo. "Yes." She turned her empty cart toward the front of the store, wishing the man would leave her alone. Instead, he followed her down the aisle.

"I could use some advice."

"Buy the good food," she said. "That's a start."

"About training. What if I want a guard dog? What

breed is best?"

"What do you want to guard?"

He pulled back, then smiled an oily smile that made Jo pick up her pace. "Smarter than you look, aren't you?"

She bristled. She looked smart.

"I mean, you're young," he went on. "No one would blame you for being a little dumb."

Who the hell was this guy? She grabbed a random chew toy from the end of a rack, wanting to bring something home to amuse Max while Connor was away but wanting to get out of the store as soon as possible. She reached the till and pushed her cart as close to the next customer in line as she dared.

"You didn't answer my question," the man said.

"You didn't answer mine either." She was relieved when the customer ahead of her finished his transaction and she was able to push her cart forward. "Hi, Penny. How are you today?" she asked the middle-aged woman at the till.

"Fine. You?" Penny scanned the bar code on the chew toy.

"Maybe I'll see you around," the man told Jo. "We can talk more then."

"Maybe." Jo kept her gaze on Penny. She hoped she never saw the guy again. One thing she'd learned early; you could tell a lot about people based on how they treated their pets. This man was the opposite of Hunter. She could tell without touching him he didn't give a damn about dogs. Which meant he wouldn't give a damn about her, either.

She remembered Hunter's words. That she had to make her own decisions—set her own boundaries. Maybe it was time to set some boundaries right now. "Actually, I doubt it," she said loudly.

The man stiffened. "Doubt what?"

"That you and I will talk. I don't want to meet you again and even if I do, I don't want to have another conversation."

Several customers nearby watched their exchange with interest, something the man seemed all too aware of. He didn't answer, but a muscle in his jaw leaped, and Jo had a feeling she'd just made an enemy.

She didn't care. Anyone so careless about animals was already an enemy.

"Just trying to be friendly," the man said, but the glint in his eye wasn't friendly at all.

"GOING SOMEWHERE?" HUNTER asked when he caught up with Jo in the stables later that afternoon. He'd seen her truck pull in and expected her to come to the house where he had ducked in for a word with Lena, but she'd strode right on past toward the outbuildings, with a set to her shoulders that didn't look happy. Now she was efficiently saddling up a pretty mare.

"Been too long since I took a ride."

"Can I come along?"

He expected her to say no. Something had riled her, but he wasn't clear what. She turned on him, but bit back what she'd been about to say. After a moment, she nodded. "Yeah, sure. You can ride Button. He's pretty laid back."

Did she think he couldn't handle anything more than laid back? Hunter didn't ask that out loud. The gelding looked like a perfectly fine mount despite his name, and he wanted to go on this ride.

Fifteen minutes later they were on their way. It was a crisp, clear fall day with the hint of smoke on the wind. The kind of day that got your blood up and your heart racing with the desire for action and movement. It didn't take long for the fresh air to clear the cobwebs from his head and make his worries leach away. Obsessing about Marlon's state of mind wasn't going to help anything, he decided. All he could do was keep encouraging his friend to make the best of a bad situation.

He tried to let go of his need to control Marlon's emotions, and concentrate on nothing more than the fresh breeze, the beautiful scenery and the even more beautiful woman riding ahead of him.

Jo led the way along a winding track and Hunter was content to follow, interested to see where she went when her heart was troubled. In his experience people were drawn to places that resonated with their moods— places they'd found solace before. In time, they reached an overlook and Jo dismounted, leaving her mare to crop the spare grasses dotting in between the broken rocky ground. Hunter joined her where she stood looking down over the outspread ranch.

"Beautiful up here," he said.

She nodded.

"Did something upset you in town?" He wasn't sure if she would answer, and she took her time, thinking over her words.

"It's funny," she said quietly. "Casual cruelty—thoughtless cruelty—bothers me far more than outright anger or violence. When someone gets mad enough to attack, they have a reason, and you can try to understand it, even if you don't agree. Casual cruelty—the kind someone perpetrates just because they can—makes me feel like clawing off my own skin."

Hunter put an arm around her waist, not to belittle what she'd said at all, or even to steady her, because Jo was steady, but to show her he was there, and he agreed. He'd seen how destructive humans could be to one another. It was bad enough when men rained that destruction down on their foes. He'd witnessed more deaths than he cared to count on the battlefield, and he'd crouched in a quiet dawn himself, waited for an enemy to rise and step out of his house at first light so he could take him out. Those deaths weren't pleasant, and he lived with his fair share of demons, but what stuck with him—what kept him up some nights—were the small, callous acts he'd witnessed while waiting for his chance to pull the trigger. A man kicking a mongrel dog. A gravestone pushed over and smashed. A crying child slapped to shut it up.

"Was someone cruel to you?" The thought of it made him want to punish the offender, a hot flash of anger making his fingers clench.

"No. Not to me. Not to anyone. The intent was there, though. Those are the people I hate; the ones full of casual cruelty. The ones just waiting for their chance."

He pulled her into an embrace, not letting himself think about it or anticipate her pushing him away. He wrapped his arms around her as if he could protect her from everything evil in the world.

He wished he could.

Jo stood tensely inside the cage of his arms, but just when he thought she'd break free, she relaxed instead. Leaned against him for a moment, her head on his chest, like she had the night they'd danced. He lifted a hand to stroke her hair.

He didn't say a word, and neither did she. As soon as her muscles tensed, he backed away. He never wanted to push her to do something she didn't want to do.

"Time to go back," she said, but Hunter noticed she moved more easily now; her anger gone.

He'd done that. He and the ride.

A sense of accomplishment carried him all the way home.

"YOU'RE LETTING HIM get too close," Lena said when she cornered Jo in the barn that night. "I saw you two go off for a ride. That's how it starts, you know. Soon enough he'll try to ride *you*."

"Shut up." Jo kept working on the ax she was sharpening. It was long past time to make sure their stock of wood was sufficient to get them through the winter. She had no doubt as soon as they heard her, Brian or Hunter would try to take over the job. The ax had to be sharp enough to ward them off.

"It's not funny," Lena said, mistaking her smile. "You know he's trying to make his stay here permanent."

"He hasn't said so."

"He will. The way he looks at you, he'll be waving a ring in your face any day now."

Jo stopped working. "How does he look at me?"

Lena made her face exaggeratedly moony. "Like this."

"I doubt it's like that." Jo got back to work.

"Maybe not that bad, but close." Lena grew serious. "You said he was too old for you, remember?"

"He is."

"You said you wanted to be independent."

"I do."

"So why is he still here?"

Jo wasn't sure how to answer that. When she asked herself why she hadn't bucked him off yet, she kept coming back to his kindness—and that sense of loyalty she always felt when she touched him. The way he treated Max told her he was a good man. The way he treated her made her feel... cared for. Not in a motherly way like Cass cared for her—but in a masculine, cherishing way she'd always hoped a husband would feel for his wife.

Besides, he was building her a house.

Neither Sean nor Grant had a touch of loyalty in them, she thought, growing serious again. She hadn't thought to consider that when she'd first been with them. That didn't let her off the hook for making such bad choices, however. She'd felt the warning signals every time she'd touched them—

She'd simply chosen to ignore them.

At the time she'd been restless. Wanting something she'd never had. Wanting to belong, to feel attractive to a man. So she'd taken their words at face value and ignored what her touches revealed about them. How ironic that the minute she turned her back on her longings, Hunter had appeared.

"Just… think long and hard before you let him too close," Lena said. "For all our sakes." She left the barn before Jo could ask her what that meant.

She didn't need to ask, though, did she? She knew what Lena feared—

If Jo finally picked a good man, the General would strengthen his control over the ranch.

If she picked a man like the previous two—

They could all wind up dead.

Chapter Four

"I'M STILL HERE," the voice on the other end of the phone connection said three days later.

"Glad to hear it."

"Well, I'm not glad," Marlon snapped. "I need to make May see sense. I can't just let her destroy my family."

"You have to do things right. Wait for the court case. Tell the judge what you want." Hunter bit back a sigh. He was going over old ground.

"I want my family back!"

"You can't force May to love you." Hunter hadn't meant to be so abrupt—not when Marlon's mood was so precarious.

"Why did she stop? Tell me that. What did I do wrong?"

Hunter scrubbed his face with his hand. "Nothing. People change, sometimes. May wants something different, that's all. You have to pull yourself together."

"Right." Marlon's answer was gruff. "Like that's so easy. She won't even listen to me. She won't take my calls. Won't answer my texts. I don't know what's happening back there! What if she's poisoning my kids against me?"

This was getting worse by the day. "When's the next time she's bringing them to see you?"

"She says they don't want to see me. She says they don't like me yelling at her."

Hunter stopped pacing. He was alone in his room, which was a good thing with the direction this phone call was taking. "When did you yell at her?" That didn't sound good at all.

"I didn't—" Marlon broke off. "Maybe I raised my voice. I was upset, okay? The last time I flew home she made me pick them up at the grocery store instead of at the house. She called it neutral territory. She treated me like I'm some kind of sex offender. I'm their dad—and that's my house!" His voice cracked, and Hunter's gut tightened. Marlon was pushed to his limit, and he was afraid of what might happen next. That week five months ago—the week that had landed him in trouble in the first place—wasn't an experience he wanted to repeat.

"What did I tell you about getting it together?" Hunter demanded. "You're a grown man. If you want to be your children's father, you need to start acting like one. Stop yelling at your wife. Stop scaring your kids. You're sad; I get that. They're sad, too. This isn't a picnic for anyone, so grow a pair and act like an adult. You got it?"

Marlon was quiet so long Hunter was afraid he'd hung up.

"Can't you go and talk to her? Fly down and fly back—just see what she's doing? Make her see reason."

Hunter's heart sank. For one thing, he doubted it would do any good. May was done with her marriage to Marlon. She'd moved on and only wanted to sort out the details. Marlon wasn't ready for that, but he had to be, or he'd find himself holding the short end of the stick as far as visitations with his kids were concerned. For another, Hunter had a mission here, and he doubted the General would like it if he left.

"I can't go anywhere until after I marry Jo. You know that."

"When's that going to be?"

"I don't know; I just got here."

Marlon cut the call before Hunter could say another word, and Hunter sat back in the hard wooden chair at the desk in his guest bedroom, fighting a sickening feeling that everything he'd sacrificed so much to fix was about to blow up in his face.

Keep calm, he texted to Marlon. *Don't do anything you'll regret.*

He got no answer, but then he hadn't expected one. He sometimes felt like he was dragging his friend through the days—or rather, tethering him to the world so he didn't simply disappear. The dissolution of his family had unmanned Marlon in a way Hunter hadn't thought possible. He'd barely made it to his friend's side the day May had told Marlon she wanted a divorce, and if he'd let his team down chasing his friend around the country, he'd told himself ever since that he'd probably saved a life. Their daily phone calls were his guarantee that Marlon was still alive—still trying. He'd thought they were over the worst of it, but maybe the worst of it was just starting.

He glanced at his laptop screen. At least one thing was going right, he told himself with a sigh. The plans he'd designed for Jo's house were done.

In between helping Jo, Lena and Brian with the chores around the ranch these past few days, doing his best to make himself indispensable, he'd spent every spare moment scouring house plans on the internet, downloading a drafting program and teaching himself to use it. He'd studied local housing codes, a variety of small home blogs and so many house images his vision had blurred, before beginning to create his own tailored plans for Jo's little house.

Now it was perfect. Everything had its place and he was proud of all the space-saving tricks he'd managed to use. Everything would be at Jo's fingertips when she moved in. More than that, it would be a handsome, snug home for someone starting out in life.

He hoped it would catch her fancy with its ingenious storage spaces and built-in furniture. He'd tried to make the small house seem airy—quite a trick, if he did say so himself.

He hoped that maybe—just maybe—if she admired his work, she might admire him, too.

Hunter hadn't kissed Jo again, although he'd wanted to, because he could tell that she was pondering the connection between them and what she wanted to do about it. Another man might have pushed things, hoping to capitalize on his earlier success, but that wasn't Hunter's way. He knew what was at stake: his future, and that of the other men from USSOCOM— and the future of Jo and her sisters, too. After all, the General had threatened to sell the ranch if they didn't all marry.

That didn't mean he would railroad her. Jo deserved to make her own choice, so all he could do was show her his real self and hope she chose him after knowing him. Working together would reveal a lot about their temperaments, he'd decided—and whether or not their temperaments mixed.

Despite the way she'd kept her distance, Hunter thought he'd detected interest from Jo once or twice in the past few days. She often watched him when she thought he wasn't looking, and that revved him up. He wondered what she was thinking when her gaze ran over him speculatively. Sometimes he thought she was appreciating his athletic body.

Other times he feared something far different was running through her mind.

Was he old in her eyes? He used to take a certain pride in his world-weariness, feeling like it conveyed experience on the battlefield and helped him command respect.

Respect wasn't what he wanted from Jo, however, and he was afraid he kept inadvertently advertising their age difference in ways she wouldn't find compelling. He watched her as much as she watched him, trying to find the places they could connect. All he'd come up with so far was she liked his work ethic.

So he kept working.

She liked his affinity for Max, too, so whenever the puppy came near, he made sure to give it attention. Which he would have done regardless. He liked dogs.

Jo hadn't said a word about Grant—about shooting the man, after stabbing him, and Hunter wondered about that. He remembered the first time he took down an enemy target. It wasn't something you got over easily, and he'd been trained to the task. Jo didn't seem fazed, but was that a smokescreen?

She wasn't uncaring. Watching her around all the various animals on the ranch taught him she was highly intuitive about all kinds of living things. And she genuinely loved her dogs, her horses—and her sisters. She was guarded around him and he couldn't blame her for that, but she wasn't hardened in any way.

Which made him wonder what was going on in her head.

When Brian had told him the story of what Jo had done, Hunter wondered why none of the General's daughters had entered the service. Seemed to him that more than one of them had shown remarkable grace under pressure. When he mentioned that to Brian, however, the other man said the General had actively dissuaded them from joining.

The Reeds had a complicated relationship with one another.

And Jo… he wasn't sure what to make of her. The

situation had to have affected her. Pulling a trigger on a man was one thing. Difficult enough, but it kept you at a distance from your adversary.

Stabbing a man—

Hunter wondered if other potential suitors would be afraid of Jo if they knew what she'd done. He wasn't afraid of her. He understood that kind of loyalty. Jo had fought for her own life, but more importantly she'd fought for her sisters. She'd used cunning, trickery and strength.

She was something.

And he was going to build her a house. He was itching to start. As soon as he did, he'd get to work by her side day in, day out for weeks, and you got to know a person that way—good and bad.

What would they feel for each other when the house was done?

He couldn't wait to find out.

JO BENT OVER the card table she'd dragged from the basement to her room several days ago, where she'd spread a large piece of drawing paper, worn thin in places from the number of times she'd erased lines. First she'd penciled a light grid to keep her measurements as accurate as possible. Then she'd spent hours scouring home design sites online to get ideas. She'd experimented with a number of different layouts before finding the one she liked best. She kept the samples she and Megan had collected from Renfrew's nearby to get ideas about the interior.

Now it was done. More than done; it was wonderful, and Hunter would be impressed at what she'd managed to design. She'd made sure to check the county website and stay within all the code requirements, and she'd looked online to find out basic rules like the sizes of doors and windows, the location of plugs, efficient ways to keep the plumbing all in one area and more.

She'd been surprised at how interesting the process was—and how much she enjoyed it. She'd never thought of herself as particularly creative, but surveying the results of her work, she was pleased.

A knock at her door brought her to her feet. She crossed the room and opened it, and couldn't help but smile at Hunter, who stood in the hall. "Perfect timing. Come on in, I've got something to show you."

"I've got something to show you." He swept past her, set the paper she'd been drawing on aside without a glance and plunked down the open laptop in his hand. "Look at this."

"But—"

Jo glanced at the screen he indicated. Were those… building plans?

"Here's your house. Take a look—I thought of everything. You won't believe it." He sat in the chair she'd just vacated, looked around for another one, didn't find it and waved her over. "Here—take my seat." He stood up again and pushed her gently down into it before she could tell him that actually, the seat was hers. "See? Here's your living room and kitchen. It's an open-concept plan. Here's the bathroom." He was off and running, explaining everything in a tone that told her he was as excited about his ideas as she was about hers.

But he hadn't even asked about her ideas. And now he was presenting his as if they were a done deal.

"Here's the washer/dryer. I found one machine that acts as both; it's really popular in Europe. And look at this. Your shower—"

"I don't want a shower. I want a tub." She had to say something—he wasn't letting her get a word in edgewise, and Jo was beginning to get the feeling she always had when people tried to run her life. Like she was suffocating—trapped. She didn't want to feel that way anymore. She'd finally begun to shake free of Cass's mothering. She didn't need a man to step in and tell her what to do.

"—is fitted right here, which… wait, what? A tub?"

That stopped him. Hunter straightened. Scratched his head. "I don't think there's room."

"There is in my plans." She reached for the paper he'd placed on the bed.

"Your plans?"

"Yes, my plans." She moved his laptop aside and spread out the paper. "See? I've got an open concept, too, but my kitchen is over here, and here's the bathroom—and it's plenty big enough for a tub like this."

"Jo, a tub isn't practical—"

"I want a tub."

"But I'll have to change everything around." Hunter pulled his laptop close again and frowned at the plans displayed on screen.

"No, you don't, because my plans already have a tub."

"That's just a bunch of scribbles on a page. You don't have measurements or—"

Jo stood up, scraping her chair over the wooden floor. "It's not just a bunch of scribbles. Maybe I don't have some fancy computer program, but that doesn't mean I didn't think it through. I did—and I measured everything down to the inch. It all fits and it all works and it's all up to code."

"Come on—"

She picked up the laptop. Shoved it into his hands. Went to the door and flung it open. "Get out."

"Jo."

"Out! The General didn't send you to come and tell me what to do. He sent you to keep me happy. You said so yourself. Well, guess what? I'm not happy!"

She pointed to the hall. A moment later he pushed past her, strode away and slammed shut the door to the guest room.

Men, Jo thought, closing her door and crossing to her desk to straighten her crumpled plans. They treated you like you were invisible. Like you didn't have a voice—or a brain. Well, she didn't need Hunter.

She'd build her own damn house.

Chapter Five

"IT'S ME," MARLON said curtly when Hunter answered his phone four days later. "I'm fine. Later."

"Hey—wait a minute!" Hunter paced the small guest bedroom, his phone jammed against his ear. "Tell me how you're doing." Marlon's bitter tone grated on him, and so did the way he was acting—like he was doing Hunter a big favor by calling.

"What the hell do you care?"

"You know I care." He was the one who'd done the favor—one that would cost him for the rest of his life if he didn't convince Jo to marry him. Seeing as how Jo hadn't said a word to him since their argument, that didn't seem likely.

"I'm doing the same as yesterday. And the day before. And the day before that. How am I supposed to be doing? My life is over—"

"No, it's not." Hunter had learned to put an end to this line of talk, fast, when Marlon got going on it. "You want to leave that legacy to your kids? You want them carrying the burden of your suicide the rest of their lives?" That was harsh, but at one time Marlon had thought about taking that path, and Hunter had risked his career to stop him. Marlon was past that, and he needed to stay there.

Silence greeted his blunt question. "Hell, no," Marlon said finally. "Of course I don't. I just don't know what to do. I left twenty messages yesterday—"

"Jesus." It was the worst thing Marlon could have done. As far as Hunter could see, May wanted an amicable divorce. She wanted to share custody over the kids, but if Marlon kept pushing her, she might change her mind.

"She finally called and said she'd sic the cops on me if I didn't stop," Marlon said bitterly. "Can you believe that?"

Hunter's patience was wearing thin. "I put my career on the line—"

"I never asked you to!"

Marlon hung up. Hunter debated calling May, but what could he say to her she didn't already know? He knew what she'd tell him; that Marlon was a big boy and had to fight his own battles. Did she realize how far Marlon had crashed when she'd asked for the divorce?

Should he tell her?

He didn't think it was his place. Marlon would never forgive him; he knew that much. He always said Hunter interfered too much. That he thought he had far too many of the answers, even when no one was asking him questions.

All Hunter knew was Marlon might not be alive if he hadn't followed Marlon the night May announced she wanted a divorce.

Hunter shoved his phone in his pocket and headed downstairs to grab some breakfast, still mulling the matter over. When he caught sight of Jo in the kitchen, he took in the stiffness of her posture and realized she was still angry with him, too—even after four days. Would she agree with Marlon that he was too bossy—too interfering?

Probably. He had bossed Jo around, and she'd hated it as much as Marlon did. Hunter had taken pride in all the research he'd done about building her house, but he supposed the world wouldn't end if he did things Jo's way—as long as certain specifications were met to keep it all to code. The layout she'd created might not be as efficient. She hadn't even noticed the way he'd built in so much storage.

But it was her house.

Time to remember that and keep his big mouth shut. He'd keep his mouth shut when it came to May, too. Let Marlon work things out with her. He just hoped his friend didn't let his emotions ruin his future.

"Morning," he said as he crossed the kitchen.

"Morning," she said stiffly.

"Look, I think we should talk—"

Jo jumped, held a finger up to stop him, pulled her phone from the pocket of her jeans and lifted it to her ear.

"Lena? What's wrong?" She listened a moment, then stiffened. "Bright Star? Got it. Be right there."

"What's going on?" Hunter demanded as she tried

to push past him.

Jo hesitated, and he could see her weigh her options. She still didn't want to speak to him, but evidently the information was too important to keep to herself.

"Something must have spooked the horses last night. One of them got tangled in the barbed wire fence. My mare, Bright Star. Lena needs help getting her out."

"I'm coming, too."

She didn't answer but she didn't stop him from following, either, although she didn't speak another word to him on the way down the dirt track to the pasture behind the stables. As they approached, Hunter took in the mare tangled in the pasture's barbed wire fence and immediately saw Lena's predicament. Bright Star was in pain, and if Lena had tried to free the horse herself, the mare could easily have lashed out with her hooves and done Lena an injury.

"I'll try to calm her down," Jo said. "You help Lena."

He was about to say of course he was going to help Lena, but he realized he and Jo weren't in a competition to run this operation. They were on the same side. Jo moved around to approach Bright Star from where the mare could see her, murmuring comforting noises as she approached. The mare huffed and nickered, but she didn't rear, and Hunter let out a breath when Jo was able to stroke Bright Star's throat.

"That's a good girl. We're going to get you out of this."

Lena moved closer to where the mare's right leg was

tangled in the barbed wire. Hunter approached, too, and as Jo kept whispering to the animal, he kept her leg steady while Lena snipped away the wire with wire cutters.

"I've got the vet coming to look her over," Lena said in a low voice. "We'll have to repair this fence, too. I called Brian…"

"I see him now. He and I can take care of that."

Jo was still murmuring to the mare. Hunter stood up, but when he caught sight of a strange, pebbled roughness to the animal's flank, he bent closer. "Lena, come take a look at this." He kept his voice calm, not wanting to spook the horse. As Brian reached their little group, he waved him over, too.

"Buckshot." Lena balled her hands into fists. "Someone did this deliberately."

Jo ducked around the horse, still making calming noises, and her eyes widened when she took in the damage.

"The vet's coming," Lena told her.

"Who would do this?" There were tears in Jo's eyes, and Hunter's heart contracted in sympathy. At the same time, he fought the urge to track down the perpetrators of this heinous act and deal out some rough country justice on their asses.

"Who else? Those men who want our ranch," Lena said.

"We don't know that for sure," Brian cautioned.

"Are you kidding me? Playing dumb won't change anything; they're coming at us again."

"Maybe. Maybe not, but we'll definitely keep watch for them," Brian said. Hunter could see his calm tone was riling Lena. She opened her mouth to issue a furious retort, but Jo stepped in.

"We'd better stable the horses at night, at least for the time being," she said practically, all traces of the tears shining in her eyes a moment ago gone. She was hardening her heart.

Holding in her pain.

Hunter wondered what other hurts she was keeping to herself.

"That's a good idea," Lena said. She looked over Hunter's shoulder. "The vet's here."

They all watched as a battered truck pulled up and a woman got out.

"Good morning, Lena. Morning, Jo. Heard you got an injured critter. What's the problem? My brother will be out when he can, but he's got a case on the other side of town. I told him I'd check in with you."

"Thanks for coming, Bella. You know Brian, I think, but this is Hunter Powell. Hunter, Bella Morti-mer. She's one of our local vets."

"My brother deals with livestock. My specialty is pets, but we help each other when necessary," Bella explained, putting out her hand.

Hunter shook it. "Good to meet you." He stepped back to let Lena and Jo tell Bella what had happened.

"We'd better fix that fence," Brian said to him. "I'll get what we need."

"Sure thing." He filed away his questions for Jo later, watching her deal with the vet and her mare with respect. Jo felt things deeply, but she kept her head when the chips were down. She could sum up a situation in a moment and create a plan to deal with it a moment later. Maybe he had been overbearing about the house plans. If she approached everything with this kind of thoroughness—and from what he'd seen, she did—then she didn't need him to tell her what to do.

The military had lost out if the General had really discouraged his daughters from joining up, he thought.

Hunter joined Brian at the fence, doubly determined to win Jo's heart.

WHEN WOULD THIS end?

As Lena answered Bella's questions, Jo fought against a rising panic as she thought about the shoot-out at the ranch, Grant's attempted kidnapping of her and the way she'd had to fight him.

She needed this to be over. Wanted to feel safe at Two Willows.

Wanted life to get back to normal.

She couldn't say for sure what the buckshot meant. Had some stupid teenagers tried to scare her horse for a lark? Or was something more sinister happening?

"She'll heal up just fine," Bella was saying when Jo forced herself to focus again. "We'll wait for my brother to get here, though. I'm not used to treating an animal this big. He'll get the pellets out and clean the wounds—and treat the cuts on her leg, as well. Nothing looks too bad. Bright Star will be back to herself in no time."

Jo touched Bright Star again and willed the horse to know how much she loved her—and how hard they were working to get her fixed up. The mare was already more comfortable now that the barbed wire wasn't tangled around her leg.

"What about the rest of the horses? Anyone else get hit?" Bella asked.

"I don't think so, but we haven't checked yet," Jo told her. While she waited with Bright Star, Lena and Bella did their best to examine the other horses, but none seemed worse for wear. Brian and Hunter got the barbed wire fence restrung. She was glad she wouldn't have to tackle the job when she was done with Bright Star.

"You all have been having some trouble here at Two Willows, haven't you?" Bella was asking when another truck pulled in.

Jo closed her eyes, fighting off defeat. Two Willows had gained a reputation—and not a good one. It was so unfair, and ultimately it could damage their ability to do business as a ranch.

"We're taking care of it," Hunter assured Bella from where he was working on the fence. Jo noticed Bella's curious glance travel between her and Hunter. If she thought there was a connection between them, she could think again. The Navy SEAL was attractive, and she'd enjoyed spending time with him at first, but he'd shown his true colors with the house plans.

Even if he was being awfully helpful today.

"Hey, sis. Hey, Jo, Lena…" Bella's brother approached, a rangy man whose dusty clothes made it obvious he'd already done a peck of work that day.

Bella and Jo made the introductions and showed him the damage to Bright Star's leg and flank. The horse seemed to know this was when things would get serious. She sidestepped a little, and Jo moved in to calm her again as Craig made his inspection.

"We'll need to bring her in to the clinic to do this right," Craig said a few minutes later. "If you can bring her over now, I'll get right to work and we can have her back home this afternoon."

"Okay." Jo was relieved that Bright Star was on her way to health again. It would be a long day, but she felt better already knowing her mare would be home in her stall tonight. "I'll be sleeping in the stables for the foreseeable future," she warned Lena.

"Me, too," Hunter said quickly.

"Sounds cozy." Lena rolled her eyes.

IN HIS ROOM that evening, prepping for a night out in the stables, Hunter thought about the plans Jo had drawn by hand and wished he'd looked at them more carefully. He wondered if they were still on her table. Out in the hall, he saw her door was partially open. When he nudged it, he saw all was spic and span in her room—bed made, no clothing on the floor. The card table still sat in the middle of the room, however, and on it was the large sheet of paper she'd used to make her drawing. Jo herself was downstairs talking to her sisters. He figured he had a few minutes before she'd make her way upstairs.

He bent over the drawing, hoping there were one or two places where their vision might match. Hoping her numbers weren't too far off, either—he knew she'd take it as a personal affront if he told her he needed to change the plans.

After a moment or two, Hunter pulled out the folding chair, sat down and propped his elbows on the table.

Wrong again.

Jo had been as diligent about researching the rules as he had. Her drawing wasn't as sophisticated as his computer-generated one was, but her doorways were sized correctly, as were her windows. She had the proper number and spacing of outlets per room, and had situated the various plumbed fixtures in a way that their lines could be tied efficiently together.

He hadn't even bothered to look at what she'd done before he'd hopped to twenty conclusions about the quality of her work.

Hunter heaved a sigh. There were still one or two ideas he'd like to discuss with her, but overall he had to admit her plan was as good as his was. Different—but not in a bad way.

This was her house, after all.

What about the next one, though? Would they grow close enough over the intervening months to share it? Would they fight over details until they found common ground—and make up for any rancor between them in bed?

He couldn't pretend it was the first time he'd thought about the possibility. Jo had intrigued him right from the start.

Did he intrigue her?

He glanced at the window. Time to go round up Jo and head to the stables. He'd bring up the house later tonight—when it got dark, maybe. See if they could agree on those one or two places he thought there might be problems.

But first he'd better tell her how impressed he was.

And maybe angle for another kiss.

BY THE TIME darkness fell, Jo was exhausted. It had been a long and emotionally wrenching day. Bright Star was like a member of her family, and the mare's fear and confusion at being taken to the clinic and treated had entered Jo every time she'd laid a hand on the horse to calm her.

Brian and Lena had joined Hunter in a circuit of the pasture where the cattle herd was enclosed for the night, looking for any signs of trouble, before they headed up to the house. They'd already corralled all the horses safely in their stalls in the stable. Jo and Hunter now sat on the large stone doorsill, their sleeping gear piled inside.

"I'll be back around eleven to do another patrol," Brian said. "But I don't expect trouble tonight."

"I'll come, too," Lena said. "Cass and Alice offered to lend a hand, but I told them we didn't really need them."

"I don't want Cass any part of this. Not when she's pregnant," Brian said. Lena exchanged a look with Jo that said she wouldn't want a husband making decisions for her like that.

Jo knew what she meant. Alone with Hunter after they left, she searched for something to say, aware he was as apt as Brian to think he had all the answers. Her desire to spend the night in the stables with Bright Star was born of a genuine anxiety about her favorite horse. She hadn't suggested it as a ruse to get Hunter alone, but she worried he might think so.

Of course, he was the one who'd angled to join her. Demanded to join her, more like it. If anyone should feel sheepish, it was him.

He didn't look sheepish.

He looked pleased.

And her body reacted to that in a way that dismayed her. "Bet you've spent a lot of nights in the open air," she said to distract herself. Did he think she'd put out just because they were alone together? If so, he was wrong. Maybe he'd proved he could get under her skin, but that was before he'd called her house plans scribbles. He couldn't charm her now.

He nodded. "This is pretty cushy."

"I can imagine." She wondered about Hunter's past. What he'd faced before he came here. As much as his attitude toward her had pissed her off, she had to respect who he was. She knew what it took to be a Navy SEAL and could only imagine what he'd been through as a sniper. This wasn't a man who shirked duty, obviously. He was just bossy.

Although he'd been less so today. Instead, he'd acted like he respected her. He'd made sure to keep nearby in case she needed him, but there'd been none of the take-charge gruffness of the night he'd dismissed her plans as worthless.

Maybe he'd had time to regret that.

"You going to be okay down here?" he asked, not like he thought she was weak, but like he cared about the answer.

"Yes." She thought she would be. Especially since he'd be here, although she wouldn't tell him that. In the past she wouldn't have thought twice about sleeping in the stable, or out under the stars, but that was before she'd been attacked. "Don't see how it's any different than sleeping in the house," she added with as much bravado as she could. She didn't like feeling scared, and she liked it even less that Hunter's presence made her feel better. She'd learned long ago that when you depended on a man, bad things happened.

"No bed," Hunter pointed out.

"I'll manage." Jo worked up the courage to ask something she'd been wondering about. "Are you armed?"

He nodded again. "You?"

"Yes." Now that it was dark, she was glad she was.

"You know how to shoot—obviously."

"The General made sure we all know. After he left, he had the overseers he sent keep us up to snuff." She was proud of her ability to fire weapons of all kinds.

Like her sisters, she practiced regularly, although not nearly as often as Lena did.

"Good man."

She couldn't help the sound that escaped her. The General was a lot of things, but *good* wasn't one of them.

Hunter chuckled. "What is it between you all and the General? Back at USSOCOM he's pretty respected, you know that?"

"He's a…" She'd been about to say coward, but of course he wasn't really. "He left us alone, when he shouldn't have," she finally said. "Can you imagine taking off after your wife's funeral—not even going to the reception—and sending strangers to watch five children who'd just lost their mother?"

They'd all been devastated back then, and Jo didn't want to overstate her feelings, but sometimes she thought that was what had sent her life astray. When she was little, she'd followed the General around like he was a hero. He had been to her. She'd been his little soldier.

Then he'd simply stopped coming home at all.

"I've got a theory about that, actually. Don't know if you want to hear it."

"Shoot." She'd listen, even though she wasn't sure she wanted to know what this SEAL thought about her father. It galled her that he probably knew the General better than she did. He'd certainly spent far more time with him these past few months than she had.

"PTSD. From losing his wife, not from any incident in the service, although I imagine there's some of that, too. From everything I gathered back there at USSO-

COM, she means as much to him today as she ever did."

Jo digested this. "What makes you think so?"

"The photographs, for one thing. Amelia's everywhere. So are you."

She looked up at that. "Me?" She could barely credit it. Why would a man who couldn't even visit his children keep photographs of them? In her imagination he simply erased them all from his mind whenever he wasn't forced to deal with them.

"All of you. Everywhere you look in his office the man's got photos of his family. You could have knocked me over with a feather when I found out he was estranged from you. I'd have never guessed."

That was hard to fathom. "We lost her, too. Doesn't he understand that?"

"I'm sure he does, and maybe that's the worst of it. Men like him will move heaven and hell to solve a problem. But if they can't solve it—"

"They don't know what to do," she finished for him. "That's supposed to excuse him for staying away for eleven years?"

"No. It's not. Bungling the funeral is one thing. Abandoning you—for good? That's a whole other issue." Hunter shifted position. "Problem is with men, sometimes we set ourselves on a course and don't know how to change it, even if we want to."

In her head she heard the logic of Hunter's statements, but her heart refused to forgive the General. She'd been the closest to him of all her sisters, but that had meant nothing to him when he'd gone away.

"Thank you," she said finally.

"For what."

"For being honest. For treating me like... an equal. Like just any other man you might share an evening with."

He nodded gravely. "I have a lot of respect for the way you protected your family. I'd be honored to have you by my side if trouble broke out."

Pride swelled her heart, although she tried to squash it. She might not like it that the General sent him, but Hunter was a warrior and she respected him.

"But if you think I see you as any *man* I might share an evening with," Hunter went on in his honey-smooth Southern drawl. "Well, Jo Reed, you're mighty mistaken."

Chapter Six

H UNTER KEPT HIMSELF from smiling at the telltale
signs of Jo's surprise—and interest—at what he'd
said. Sitting so close together, the night cooling down as
the shadows deepened, he noticed the flicker of her
eyelids and the straightening of her shoulders.

She turned to him, and he met her mouth with his
own, sliding his lips over hers softly at first, then
cupping her head with his hand and bringing her closer
for a real kiss when she didn't protest.

Jo tasted… good. Toothpaste fresh—minty and
sharp with a tang that was hers alone. He wanted much
more than this, but as his fingers tangled together the
collar of her jacket and strands of her hair, she chuckled
beneath him.

He pulled back. Cocked his head.

"You're pulling my hair."

"Sorry." He let go immediately.

"Don't be. It's just so… normal… in the middle of
something so…" She searched for a word.

"Amazing?" he supplied.

"Yeah," she said simply, and Hunter couldn't help

himself. He pulled her close and kissed her all over again. "You're pretty good at that," she told him when he next drew away.

The simple compliment warmed him in a way few statements ever had. He was good at kissing? That was gratifying to know. "You're pretty good yourself."

Jo shrugged.

Hunter knew he could push things along, but this opportunity for togetherness was too good to squander. He could get laid—which would be nice—or he could build a foundation for a life with Jo. As hard as it was to ignore the ache of his desire for her, he decided to exercise a little restraint. For now.

"Should we set up for the night? It's getting late." He braced himself for a quip from her about how eager he was to get her alone, but Jo just shrugged again, rose to her feet and moved indoors.

The stables were pungent, but Hunter was no novice to the smell of horses. Plenty of fresh air came in from the open front door, and besides, he'd dealt with far worse quarters lots of times. They'd carried down some camping equipment Jo had rustled up from the cellar of the main house, and Hunter got to work pumping up two air mattresses that would make the night far more comfortable. When he was done, they unrolled their sleeping bags.

Hunter wasn't sure what Jo expected, but he stripped down to his boxer briefs, placing his pistol nearby, ready to hand. Normally he slept in the buff, but out here, he was the first line of defense. If those kids—

or anyone else—came back to bother the horses again, he'd have his boxer briefs on in case the night called for swift action.

After pulling off his boots, stripping off his pants and yanking his shirt up and over his head, he found Jo watching him unabashedly. She stripped down, too, after placing her own firearm on the floor nearby. First her boots and jeans. Then she unhooked her bra and, with a few complicated motions, extricated it from under her T-shirt. Hunter waited, hoping against hope for more, but she bent to crawl into her sleeping bag, still wearing her panties and shirt. He stifled a groan, knowing he'd never sleep tonight, but reminding himself that patience was a virtue. Someday soon, he promised himself, he'd make love to Jo over and over again until he'd taken his fill—and left her so satisfied she never wanted another man.

For now, however, he needed to learn more about her, and let her discover more about him.

"I haven't done something like this since I was a kid," he began.

"Sleeping in a stable?"

"Sleeping out on a ranch in general."

"Did you grow up on one?"

He settled into his own sleeping bag and linked his fingers behind his head. They'd brought pillows with them. His Navy SEAL teammates would laugh if they could see him. "I grew up beside one, but I might as well have lived there." He explained about Marlon and the rest of the Franks. "Sue-Ann was like a second mother to me. I ate at their table every night I could get away with it. The Franks were like my siblings."

"So you grew up with a bigger family than I did."

He thought about that. "In a way. But I still had to go home most nights."

"What was that like?"

"Quiet, mostly. Mom kept to herself, so our life was pretty dull. She read a lot. Wrote her poetry. Watched some TV. She liked police procedurals." He smiled at the memory.

"She was a poet?"

"Yes. Even won a prize or two." He'd never quite gotten her poetry himself, but he was proud of her for it.

"I'll have to look her up. What about your dad?"

"He wasn't in the picture. Not really."

Jo's touch brought him back to the present. "That hurt a lot," she whispered. "Not having a father."

He realized missing a father was something Jo understood in a way few people did. Once, it had hurt him really badly—so badly he'd considered…

"I'm okay now," he assured her.

But she was still touching him, and her fingers tightened around his wrist. "Don't—" Pain laced her voice. "If it ever gets hard again, don't—"

Hunter pulled away from her. "I won't," he said sharply. He knew exactly what she meant, although he had no idea how she could know he'd once thought of ending his life. "I was young. I had no idea how hard life could get—or how you have to stick with it for the times when it's sheer heaven."

He lifted a hand to touch her chin to soften the moment, and when she allowed him to, he leaned in and kissed her. Jo met his desire with her own, and he soon forgot what they were talking about, lost in the feel of her.

IT WAS A long time before they stopped kissing and started talking again. Jo wondered what had happened to her determination to keep him at arm's length. She wasn't sure how the SEAL had gotten under her defenses again. All she knew was she liked it when he touched her.

She didn't know what the morning would bring. Didn't want to think about the future. For once she wanted to keep to the moment. To simply be here alone in the dark with Hunter.

"I need to apologize to you." His voice came from the gloom.

"What for?" Had any man ever apologized to her? Not that she could think of.

"For assuming your plans wouldn't be as well thought out as mine. I took a look at them, and you did a really good job. I'm impressed."

She didn't know what to say to that.

"And I'm sorry I ever doubted you. That wasn't fair."

"Thank you." She'd watched the General all her life and had seen just how hard it was for most men to admit they made mistakes. Hunter was different than most men, she supposed.

She reached out impulsively and touched his arm, needing to be sure his feelings matched his thoughts. He didn't move, but she saw him watching her, his eyes shining in the darkness.

"Why do you do that?" he asked curiously.

"Just to see what's going on with you."

"I just told you what was going on with me."

"Words and feelings are two different things."

He nodded. "I want to kiss you again. Just a kiss," he assured her when she hesitated.

She wasn't naive enough to believe that, but she found herself inching closer, glad when he closed the gap between them and pressed his mouth to hers again. He was warm, soft but soon demanding more from her. Jo gave in willingly, wanting what he was offering, wanting to give him what he asked for.

Her whole body shimmered with desire, that sweet ache deep inside her telling her that soon—soon—she'd be with Hunter, whether or not it was wise.

She wanted him. Wanted to be close to him. And touching him, she knew he wanted her just as much. In fact, something was deepening inside him. His desire was turning into something more—something she'd never felt from a man. A combination of heat, want and—

She was afraid to put it into words.

He pulled back. "Jo Reed, where have you been all my life?"

HE WAS FALLING in love. This wasn't lust. Nor was it simply a case of being without female company for too long. Hunter had never talked to women he dated about his father—or lack of one. He'd rarely talked about his childhood with anyone, as a matter of fact—not even Marlon after the awful night he'd learned the truth about his father.

Jo stiffened. "What is it?"

He realized she was touching him. Had she felt his distress at the memory?

"Nothing."

"It's not nothing. Whatever it is goes to the heart of it all."

He wasn't sure what she meant by that, but she was right; it wasn't nothing. That night had been the worst of his life—worse than anything he'd been through since, and that was saying a lot.

"My mother never wanted to talk about my dad," he forced himself to say, thinking at first he could sum it up in a few lines and brush the ancient pain back under the rug where it belonged. He was grateful for the dark. Grateful Jo couldn't see how much it all still affected him.

Of course, she could feel it.

He pushed that thought down and kept going. "She put me off whenever I asked about him. So I didn't ask about him, no matter what happened at school or on the playing field."

"Playing field?"

"Football. I was a wide receiver. Marlon was quarterback. We were pretty good, but not good enough to get recruited. Still, it was fun." He thought back to the football games. Friday nights full of testosterone and partying. Sometimes he'd felt like he was like all the other players—when they won. When he was in the thick of a throng of high fives and celebrations.

"I didn't have a dad growing up. Didn't even know who he was. You can imagine how other kids were when they wanted to get a rise out of me," he said. "I tried to shrug it off. Act like I didn't care. Of course I did."

"It all blew up?"

"Prom. Junior year. I went with Karen Henderson. Marlon took Marie Jones. Karen was supposed to go with this two-bit thug named James Mitchell. I knew that. I asked her anyway, and she said yes."

"What happened?" Jo's voice came out of the darkness. She was still touching him, and Hunter liked the soft pressure of her fingers on his arm.

"James showed up, drunk and ready for a fight. He called me every name in the book to draw me out, and when he called me bastard, he got the brawl he was looking for. Then he said something else. A name. No one had said that to me before, though looking back I'm sure a lot of people had guessed. He probably heard it from his folks."

"What name?"

"Judge Drake Stone. The man whose courtroom my mother worked in at her first stenographer job—before she was transferred to Finley. I got kicked out of the dance for knocking James unconscious, but I didn't care. I had a name. I had a connection. I drove straight to the man's house two towns over and confronted him."

"What did he say?" Jo pushed up on one elbow.

"He didn't deny it, although he brought me out on the porch to have his say. Said it had to be clear to me I couldn't enter his house. He said he'd done all he could for me. He had a family already, and he had to stick to it. I told him getting my mother pregnant wasn't doing much. He wished me well and said good night."

Jo waited as if she knew there had to be more.

"I meant to go home. Instead I found myself at the Franks'. In Marlon's father's office, where the gun safe was. I knew Marlon's parents were out of town." Marlon was the only one who knew this part of the story. Hunter couldn't believe he was telling Jo. "I also knew where Mr. Frank kept the key. I got it. Opened the safe. Took out a pistol and fetched the ammunition from his desk drawer."

He hadn't known whether to kill his father or himself.

"Marlon caught up to me. He'd heard what happened and left Marie behind." He didn't want to put the rest into words. "He saved a life that night." To this day he wasn't sure whose.

"What did your mother do when she heard?" Jo whispered.

"Talked to me. Finally. Not much, but a little. Told me she'd lost her head over Stone. Told me she'd never regretted what happened, even though she wished I'd had a traditional family. When I got my anger under control and asked her why she'd never found another man, she said… she said she got stuck."

Jo was silent for a moment. "Do you know what she meant by that?"

"No. Except once burned, twice shy, I guess."

"Or…" Jo bit her lip. "Is it possible she still loves him?"

"Loves him? She hates him. She has to for what he did."

"Maybe. We don't truly know what happened between them."

"He didn't even acknowledge me." Hunter couldn't believe what he was hearing. Didn't she understand how much it had hurt to have his father—the man who should have loved him more than anyone else—turn his back and shut his door on him?

"Not to the world," she agreed quietly. "But he did acknowledge you when you confronted him. He didn't lie about what he'd done. He owned up to being your father. I'm not saying that's good enough," she went on when Hunter would have pulled away. "I'm saying he did what he thought he could do. He had a wife already, right? Did he have kids?"

"Yeah. They were a few years older than me. Both of them off at college by the time I figured it out. I've never run into them."

"I wonder if they know about you."

He'd never really thought about that. He had a

brother and sister out there somewhere. A half-brother and sister.

It was unfathomable.

"Have you ever talked to him since you grew up?"

"Hell, no. I don't want to talk to him. He made his choice. He could have come after me at any time, and he didn't. I don't want him in my life."

"That's understandable." She squeezed his wrist. "Besides, you're your own man now. You're making your own way in the world. The past is the past."

He wished that was true. "Not for Marlon."

He hadn't meant to say that out loud, but Jo's quiet nature invited confidences.

"In what way?"

Did he really want to talk about it? Somehow, here in the stable, out on their own, he felt like he could talk about anything.

"He was supposed to propose to Marie that night. Instead, he spent it with me." Kept him from pulling a trigger and ending a life. Most likely his own. He'd never felt such grief before or since, and he'd never wanted to step out of his body and leave it all behind so strongly. Marlon had walked him through those coal-black hours, talked to him, plied him with coffee, wrenched the gun from his hand, locked it back in its cabinet and pocketed the key. It was weeks before Hunter woke up to the damage he'd done to his friend. "Marie spent that night with James Mitchell, and they were married three months later, before she began to show."

"Oh, no."

Hunter was thankful Jo didn't brush it all off as teenage angst. She was raised in a small town, too, and he assumed she'd seen a number of weddings among her school-age friends. He'd been surprised to find that some of his city counterparts in the Navy scoffed at the idea of marrying young.

"They're still together. Four kids." He took a deep breath and to his surprise he realized he felt lighter than he had in a long time. That story had pressed on him. He'd never felt comfortable with his mother's choices. He still wasn't sure why she'd done what she had. And he still felt responsible for ruining Marlon's life. May was Marlon's rebound relationship, and they'd rushed right into marriage, both of them searching for something to make them whole. It was no surprise it hadn't turned out well.

"When did you join the Navy?"

"The very next day. I refused to stay in that town one more night. Marlon drove me to a recruiting office the next afternoon and signed up with me. I didn't realize he'd already heard about Marie and James. We told each other we were done with Finley. We wanted to see the world. I shacked up at a hotel until it was time to go. Refused to return home. Marlon did all the running around for me and didn't say a word about his planned proposal or the way I'd ruined it until we were on our way."

"You blame yourself for what happened between him and Marie?"

"Of course I do."

"Hunter." Jo seemed to be considering her words. "Do you really think a seventeen-year-old who slept with another man at the very first opportunity would have made Marlon a good wife?"

"She was angry—"

"Because her date's best friend went through the biggest crisis of his life?"

"She misunderstood. By the time he could explain to her, what's done was done."

Jo sat up. "In other words, Marlon was the one who refused to get back together with her. If that's true, he must not have loved her very much."

"She'd been unfaithful to him. She was pregnant."

"Exactly my point. Look, either she wasn't that into him, or he wasn't that into her. Otherwise they'd be together no matter what happened that night."

Hunter sat up, too, finding he couldn't pinpoint the problem with her logic. "I... guess."

"I think sometimes we carry the burdens from our pasts for too long. Maybe it's time to set yours down and make a fresh start."

He wished he could.

HE WAS SO loyal. Hunter's concern for his mother—and for Marlon—had poured out of him when he'd explained his past to her. He took their troubles on as his own. Jo couldn't doubt that part of his personality anymore. It was far too intrinsic to who he was.

She had to admit, too, she found that loyalty far sexier than just about any other part of him. Except for his body. His inquisitive mind. His sense of humor—

No wonder her resolve to keep her distance had crumbled. Unlike any man she'd ever met before, he was truthful about his feelings and his motivations. He hadn't sugar-coated what he'd done in his past, and he didn't hide what he wanted from her now. They had clashed when he tried to call the shots, but she'd begun to understand that wasn't anything personal. He wasn't trying to rule her. He was just doing what he thought of as his job.

"Maybe it's time for you to let go of the past, too," Hunter said.

"In what way?"

"You're holding all this anger against your father. Maybe it's time to give him another chance."

She supposed she deserved this for the lecture she'd given him. "I would have been glad to—for years. But he's taken too long about coming home. And it's no fair that he wants it both ways."

"What do you mean?"

"He won't come here and help with the ranch or consult with us about it, or spend any time with us at all, but he wants to make all the rules and keep control over everything. How is that acceptable?"

"I don't know. I guess it isn't," Hunter admitted. "But I know holding onto anger isn't healthy."

"So have you stopped being angry with your father?" she challenged him.

Hunter chuckled. "Wish I could say that I had."

"Don't expect me to be better than you." If he

thought women were more forgiving he didn't know much about women.

"Maybe we can work on it together." He took her hand and Jo let him, liking the contact between them.

"In what way?"

"We could lean on each other a little more. Be each other's family. Let go of any leftover need for our fathers."

"Do you still feel like you need yours?" She wouldn't have put it like that. She'd learned not to need hers, because needing the General didn't do any good. He wouldn't be there to help, even if you did.

"No, I guess not. Not in the sense that he might come and help me in some way. I guess I miss— something, though."

"Approval?" That's what she wanted. Or maybe assurance was a better word.

"Yeah, something like that. Some kind of gold star to show I'm not fucking it all up too badly." He chuckled.

Jo smiled. "I approve of you," she said. It was true. Hunter was a good man. "You're not fucking it all up— too badly."

"Thanks. I think. I approve of you, too. You're doing a real good job here on the ranch."

"Thank you." Her heart warmed toward him. He would know far better than the General. Something eased within her, and Jo found that her mood had lifted, despite the trouble that had them sleeping out here. Maybe it was time to let go of the past and focus more on the present.

More on Hunter.

As she lay back down and tugged him down, too, Jo thought about something else she'd sensed: his decision to take things slowly with her.

She couldn't lie to herself; if he tried to take things further, she would join in willingly. She ached to know what it would feel like to be with him. Knowing he was willing to take the time to get to know her made him even harder to resist. He was so close to her in his sleeping bag, their bodies barely a foot apart. She could simply lean over and kiss him, but she held back from starting anything too heavy. If he was willing to take it slow, so was she.

Instead, Jo squeezed his hand in the dark. As Hunter's strong fingers closed around hers, she sensed his worry about Marlon, and his regret. His confusion about his mother.

But all of that was overshadowed by the unmistakable lust he was projecting her way.

Chapter Seven

TWO DAYS LATER, Hunter watched in satisfaction as a truck pulled in behind the house right on time.

"There's your trailer," he told Jo, who was slicing an apple.

"That looks really small," Jo said with a frown. She finished cutting up the pieces of fruit and tucked them into a container for later, joining him at the window.

"It is really small. It's supposed to be temporary, remember?"

She nodded, but she didn't look particularly impressed. He hoped that would change when they built her house.

He and Jo had discussed her plans at length these past few nights and he'd been confident enough to place an order for materials this morning. He'd been right; alone out in the stables, it was easier for them to talk about the places where their plans had diverged and come to common ground. Jo had told him about the materials she wanted to use inside, and Hunter had to admit he hadn't thought much about them, except the wooden built-ins, so he was easy to lead on those.

It surprised him how good it felt to think about building a home to please her. Generally, he was a man who liked to do things his own way, because he thought things through far more carefully than most people did, but Jo thought things through, too. And when she spoke about the little house, she lit up.

He liked that.

Outside, they greeted Norton Dale, who'd brought the trailer. He was all too happy to unload it. "Got it for my nephew when I was in Colorado," Norton said when he got out of his truck and hitched up his jeans under a substantial beer belly. "He was all hot to build a little cabin in back of his folks' place, then he met a girl and next thing we knew he hightailed it to Virginia."

"Kids," Hunter said, as if he knew anything about it.

"Hope you folks make better use of it than we did."

"We will," Hunter assured him. He paced around the trailer and made sure it was in good shape. "Looks pristine."

"Like I said, just got it and the kid took off!"

Jo looked to be biting back a smile, and Hunter was glad to see that flash of humor. He thought Jo was far too serious for the most part. Building a house might be just what the doctor ordered. There hadn't been a repeat of trouble these past few nights, and he was beginning to think that the incident with Bright Star was caused by kids on a joy ride rather than a restart of the difficulties with the drug dealers from Tennessee.

Alone together in the stables each night, they'd talked for hours, swapping stories of their childhoods and their hopes and dreams for the future. Several times they'd held hands. Once or twice they'd kissed. He was having a hard time keeping his libido in check.

Hunter didn't haggle over the price with Norton. He paid in full, glad to put his hands on a trailer so quickly that fit the bill for what they wanted.

"Now what?" Jo asked as they watched Norton—much happier now he had a fistful of dollars—drive away.

"Now we level the ground, move the trailer into place and brace it. As soon as those materials get delivered we'll get started."

The process of picking a site, leveling the ground, moving the trailer into place and making sure it couldn't roll took longer than Hunter had anticipated, but he didn't mind. It gave him time to work with Jo and see how she reacted to adversity and pressure. Jo was so excited about her house she wasn't thrown at all by the setbacks.

As for him, he found it easier to work with Jo than with most men he had worked with in the past. She was quicker to see what he was after. Quicker to jump in to help—or to figure out the problem for herself.

Once they'd leveled the ground, tugged the trailer into place and braced it, Hunter wanted to make sure the frame was level, too, but before he could even issue the order, Jo had already knelt in the dirt to put the level on the metal frame of the trailer.

"Looks good here." She glanced up. "What?"

"Could have used you on a few missions. It's like

you can read my mind."

"Maybe I can." She stood up, still holding on to the level.

"I thought that was Alice's trick. You're supposed to read emotions."

Jo shrugged and moved to another position, placing the level on the frame again. "It's good here, too."

"What am I thinking right now?" Hunter knew he was playing with fire, but he couldn't help it. Jo was so damn cute in her slim jeans, fitted T-shirt and the baseball cap she wore to keep the sun out of her eyes.

She eyed him again, moved closer to him and touched his wrist, but instead of speaking she simply shook her head. "I'm not going to repeat what you're thinking."

When she went to move away again, Hunter caught her, cupped her chin in both hands, tilted it up. Brushed his lips over hers once, twice.

"What was that for?" she asked when he reluctantly pulled away.

"Because I wanted to."

"Why don't you have a girlfriend back home?" Jo moved away and tested another portion of the frame. "Level, here."

"Never found the right woman." But thinking of home made him think of Marlon.

Who hadn't called today, Hunter realized with a start. He pulled his phone from his pocket and checked. Nope. No calls at all.

"Something wrong?" Jo asked, looking a little

miffed that his attention had wandered.

"Yeah—no. Hold on a sec." Their agreement was that Marlon would initiate the calls, and he had never failed to check in by their agreed-upon time, but he was late, so Hunter would do the dialing. Hunter's pulse kicked up and he paced while he waited for the call to go through. His friend knew what Hunter had given up to cover for him. There was no way Marlon would go against his word.

Even if he'd made it clear he resented the intrusions into his life.

He got no answer. Hunter cut the call, then tried it again. "Get back to me as soon as you get this message," he told his friend when voice mail kicked on.

"Marlon hasn't called," he answered Jo's inquisitive look. "I was supposed to hear from him today."

"And you're worried?"

"He's going through a hard time—a real hard time. His marriage is falling apart. But that's no excuse. You've had a hard time, too, and you don't let your emotions cloud your judgment."

Jo frowned. "Hard time?" She set the level on the frame again, only inches from the last place she'd tested.

"That gunfight you were in—"

"God, not you, too." She raised her hands in defeat. "I'm not made of spun glass, okay? I'm fine."

"It's not like you kill someone every day, though." He was provoking her, but he thought she might need to talk about it. Besides, he needed to think about something other than Marlon. He wanted to keep calling until he got an answer, but his friend had made it clear how much he resented Hunter's interference in his life. So he wouldn't interfere—for now. He'd give Marlon a little time. Meanwhile, he'd focus on Jo. Was she holding in her fear and sorrow? That wasn't good.

"A man who tried to kidnap me, kill my dogs, kill my sisters!" She lifted her hands again. "Jesus, if someone came after you and pointed a gun to your head, what would you do?"

"Kill him."

"And would you need rest and counseling?"

"I—"

"No, because you're a man, and men make tough decisions, but we women are supposed to roll over and die the minute things get hard—"

"I'm on your side, here," Hunter protested.

"Really? Here's the thing: I knew it was the right thing to do. When I was doing it," she added. "I didn't have to think about it. And afterward, I wasn't afraid I'd made a mistake. But everyone's acting like that's how I should feel. Honestly? That's driving me crazy. I can't manufacture something that isn't real."

He understood what she was saying; sometimes reactions took over and events played out the way they were meant to whether you thought about them or not.

"There are moments like that in any skirmish," he told her. "Moments where there's only one way out." He'd experienced too many of those and wished Jo hadn't experienced any, but there he was, thinking she was more fragile than him again.

"It's like I could see it—what I'd do, what he'd do—" Her gaze grew distant, and he knew she'd traveled back to that day. He traveled back to the tough times, too, when he wasn't careful to block those kinds of thoughts.

"The moment steps out of time," he agreed. "And the path becomes clear. I've experienced that."

"Really?"

"Really." He held her gaze, wanting her to know he was there with her, and would continue to be so. That was something the men he'd served with had always done for each other: witnessed the memories—good and bad.

"Does it make me a monster that I don't have any regrets?" Jo asked softly.

"That makes you a warrior."

Her lips parted. He saw relief and something else in her eyes. Hunter waited, knowing there was something else she needed to say.

"Kiss me."

JO HELD HER breath. She'd just given the hardened fighter standing in front of her an order.

Would he obey?

Hunter took a step closer. Slid a hand to the base of her neck. Bent down and kissed her thoroughly. When he pulled back, she followed him, wanting more, and he must have understood.

Jo melted against him as he swept her close in his arms, and she closed her eyes, the better to feel the soft pressure of his mouth on hers again. But even as she did his kiss grew more insistent. She'd been holding back for days—and nights. Spending time with him, working with him, talking to him. Sleeping in the stables with him—no one else to witness what they did.

With each passing day, the ache in her had increased. She craved his touch.

Craved him.

No one had ever understood her the way he just made it clear he did. No one had validated her feelings so completely as he had with those five small words: that makes you a warrior.

He hadn't tried to brush away what she'd done, or diminish it, or pretend it hadn't happened. He'd stood witness to her feelings and had lifted her up instead of tearing her down.

Jo had no idea how much she'd needed that kind of validation. Nor had she realized how strong her instinct was to find the kind of man who could see her that way.

It was as if some small part of her that still believed in love was fighting for its life. Every time she told herself it was crazy to trust another man, Hunter did something that knocked her socks off.

Now she had to choose. Back off from men permanently—or take a chance.

If she was wise, she'd back off, Jo cautioned herself. Hadn't she seen what men were capable of?

Jo guessed she was still too young for wisdom to have taken hold in her.

As she opened her mouth to allow Hunter's tongue

in, a hunger caught fire inside her—a need to get him even closer. A desire to throw her worries to the wind and submit herself to fate one more time.

Not here, though. Not in plain view of the house.

Where?

She pulled back and her gaze swept their surroundings, taking in Sadie's garden, which was too exposed; her greenhouse, which felt like trespassing; Alice's carriage house studio—

Certainly not there.

The maze.

She hadn't taken Hunter to see the maze yet. And he'd been here nearly two weeks. Had anyone else lasted so long on the property without a tour of it?

She grabbed his hand, determined to rectify the oversight. "Come on."

He allowed her to tug him toward the maze. Together they crossed Sadie's garden to its entrance, and then they were inside its tall green walls.

"I've never been in one of these," Hunter said.

"Shut up and kiss me again." Jo bit her lip. Had she really just said that?

Hunter looked about as surprised as she felt. Then he laughed, pulled her close and obliged. "Like that?"

"Just like that." She was so grateful he was playing along. Loved the feel of his strong arms around her. The hard planes of his body turned her on, made her want to touch him. Taste him.

Glancing up she caught an expression on his face that made her breath catch. It wasn't lust, although she felt that thrumming through every fiber of his body.

It was… fondness.

She supposed it should have irked her. Wouldn't desperation or longing be better?

Maybe.

But fondness… that meant more to her. Any man could desire any woman for a moment or two. Fondness took more. It took the kind of caring that developed over time.

Her body warmed underneath his gaze. The sailor hadn't been at Two Willows long, but she understood how he felt. She was growing fond of him, too.

Flush with desire, she tugged away from him and led him through the green passages of the maze, stopping now and then to demand another kiss, grateful to be hidden by the twenty-foot-high hedges that bordered the paths.

Each time he complied with a look on his face that said he'd do plenty more—whenever he chose. But he was letting her call the shots for now and that felt good.

Really good.

Jo stopped before they reached the center. "Kiss me, and…" She wanted him badly, but still she hesitated. This was her last chance to exercise caution.

"And…?" Hunter prompted, gathering her close again. Jo felt the sincerity emanating from him. She wasn't fooling herself this time. Hunter wanted her, but more than that—he cared for her.

"And… touch me."

It was like stepping into the abyss. Solid ground no

longer held her up. She'd taken flight, but whether her wings would work or she'd crash into the chasm below was anyone's guess.

Hunter's eyes darkened with desire and Jo's body tingled all over in anticipation. Would he…?

Yes.

As he kissed her, he slid both hands higher and palmed both her breasts. Jo closed her eyes, pleasure heating her until she thought she would swoon.

She didn't object when he tugged her shirt up and over her head, nor when he bent to kiss the soft skin bordered by her lacy bra. She shivered as his lips traced the edge of it, and she didn't even notice him undo the bra's clasp until he pulled it away and left her bare from the waist up.

No fair, Jo thought, and yanked on the hem of his shirt until he took over the task, pulled it over his head and cast it off with hers. His wide, muscled chest was a sight to behold. Manly in the best of ways. This time when he cupped her breasts, she moaned aloud. His hands felt so good on her skin.

But first they needed to reach the center of the maze.

She led him, reveling in the feel of the autumn breeze on her bare flesh. This whole experience felt utterly decadent.

When they reached the center, Hunter slowed to a stop, taking in the enormous standing stone.

"It's something to see, isn't it?" Jo asked him.

"It sure is." He let his gaze rest on her long enough

to let her know he included her in that statement.

She knew the stone was impressive, though. She'd seen it a thousand times and it still drew her. No one knew who'd stood it here, or how they'd gotten it from Silver Falls where the granite was quarried. Jo moved closer and leaned against it, smiling her best come-hither smile at Hunter. He followed, leaned down and kissed her shoulder.

"You're beautiful, you know that?"

HUNTER WASN'T LYING; Jo was beautiful. And she was offering herself to him in a way he'd only dreamed about. How many times had he pictured what it would be like to undress her? He'd come here worrying Jo was too young for him, but she'd proved herself his match at every turn. Now he wanted to meet her as equals—

Naked.

"Are you sure you want this?" he couldn't help but ask, though. Some protective impulse was still alive and well within him. He wasn't sure if he was protecting her or himself. He'd never been the kind for hit-and-run relationships, and that was the last thing he wanted with Jo. He needed this to be long-term, for his own sake.

And forever for everyone else's.

He wasn't drawn to her because of a need to clear his name, however—or a desire to own a stake in a ranch as wonderful as Two Willows.

He was drawn to her because he saw so much he understood in her. He knew that went two ways. Most women could never relate to what he'd been through, not once, but over and over again in his time as a Navy SEAL. It was one thing to kill a man in the heat of battle. It was another thing altogether to be tasked with the job in the carefully controlled way a sniper set out to do it.

Hunter could never pretend to himself that luck or accident played any part in the lives he'd taken.

He'd set up the shots.

He'd pulled the trigger.

Because he'd known if he hadn't, others would die.

When he allowed himself to think of a partnership with a woman, he'd always felt it would require compartmentalizing his life. With Jo that wasn't necessary. Her father was a General. She was raised knowing more about the service than most civilians.

And she'd shot a man to protect her family.

She could be his wife. Bending to kiss her again, Hunter allowed himself to think all the way through that.

She could be his—forever. And he could be hers without keeping his military life from her. Without holding back.

In a flash Hunter realized why loving a woman had seemed so out of reach for so long. He hadn't wanted to contaminate a woman with the death he'd known. He hadn't wanted the cruel world he worked in to leach into an innocent woman's life.

And he hadn't been sure he was up to the task of keeping part of himself separate and at the same time being open enough to allow a woman to love him.

That kind of marriage seemed doomed to fail.

But now he was with Jo. He didn't have to hide anything from her.

Couldn't hide anything from her. And he wanted her.

Now.

Here.

Jo laced her hand in one of his, half turned and placed it flat against the flank of the rock. She caught Hunter's gaze and held it.

Torn from his thoughts, Hunter wasn't sure what she was doing until she asked in a clear, loud voice, "Can I trust Hunter Powell?"

He turned his head to see if someone else was there, but he already knew she was asking the stone. Brian had told him all about this custom in his early days at Two Willows.

Why else would she bring him here except to test him?

The stone always answered, apparently.

Sooner or later.

And it never lied.

When Jo let go of his hand, Hunter kept it there a moment, feeling the warmth the stone had absorbed from the sun. He wasn't afraid of the question she'd asked because he had no intention of being untrustworthy. The stone itself intrigued him. He wondered how old it was.

"When—?"

Jo clapped a hand to her mouth and pointed up.

Hunter shaded his eyes and spotted what she was looking at.

Two large birds few overhead on silent wings, so majestic—and so unexpected—it took him a moment to recognize what he was seeing.

"Swans?"

Jo nodded, blinking rapidly.

"I don't—"

"Symbols of fidelity." Her voice was strange. High. She was fighting tears, Hunter realized. "My mother's favorites," Jo went on. "They're really rare in this part of the state; they usually stay closer to the southwest. It's a message." She turned to him, her eyes shining. "They're beautiful, aren't they?"

"Yes." But it had to be a coincidence, and he didn't want to take advantage of—he really shouldn't—even if he wanted—

"Make love to me," Jo said.

Hunter struggled against his baser instincts. Almost mastered them.

Lost the battle.

He couldn't hide what he felt from her. Didn't want to. Couldn't fool himself into thinking that Jo didn't know exactly what she was asking of him. She had thought this through and she wanted him.

God, did he want her.

"Hell, yeah."

JO HAD HAD sex before—and regretted it.

Not so much the first time—a fumbling experience

at sixteen in Mitch Hearny's family's barn that left them both too shy to mention it again. Maybe not the times she'd been with Todd Rankin either. She figured now their rather short, offhand relationship was par for the course for two seventeen-year-olds who were too busy working on their families' ranches to spend enough time together to make it something more.

But the men she'd been with this last year were unworthy of her, and she wished she could take back the time she'd wasted on them.

All she could do was chalk it up to experience—and make better choices.

She had a feeling Hunter had meant to say no when he'd said yes. He was older than her and he obviously felt he was supposed to keep a clear head.

Which made it doubly delicious that he'd clearly lost his head where she was concerned.

She did this to him. Made him want her. Badly enough to throw caution to the wind.

When she reached out to undo his belt, he didn't stop her. He outright groaned when she undid the button of his jeans, her fingers brushing his skin. Soon enough his fingers were working at the fastenings of her jeans and it became a race to each undress the other—an exercise that left them laughing and tangled in a heap since neither of them had taken off their boots before they shucked down each other's pants.

After a fair amount of wiggling and kicking, she got her boots, jeans and panties off. Hunter arranged them in a kind of mat for her to lie on, adding his own to the mix.

"Naked as jaybirds," she said aloud.

"That we are." He sounded fairly pleased.

"We could do something about that."

"We could." But for a moment they both lay on their backs and watched the sky. Was he looking for more swans?

She was.

She didn't need the confirmation, though. She wanted to be with Hunter, no matter what the circumstances. Maybe it was reckless to give love another chance after what she'd experienced, but it didn't feel reckless. Hunter was special.

He was true. Loyal. And he cared what happened to her.

When he rolled over on top of her, she welcomed him with a satisfied sound.

He was hard and ready, and when he nudged her legs apart to rest his own between them, Jo's whole body heated in anticipation. He bent down, took one nipple into his mouth and drew a lazy circle around it with his tongue.

Jo moaned.

As he nuzzled and teased her breasts, making good use of both his hands and his tongue, Jo relaxed and let him take charge—for now. He was good at what he was doing, and he coaxed such good feelings from inside her as he moved.

Soon she was so ready she couldn't wait for him a moment longer.

"Please, Hunter—"

He lifted himself on his elbows. "Please, what?"

Was he going to make her say it again?

He was—the bastard.

"Make love to me."

"Now?"

"Right now."

"Like this?"

He nudged her with the tip of his hardness and Jo sighed, an almost guttural sound.

"Wait a minute. Better not take any chances."

She murmured a protest as he moved to grab his jeans, but when he sheathed on a condom, she realized he was thinking far more carefully than she was.

"Hurry up," she urged him.

"Hold your horses." But he was smiling a very knowing, very happy smile, and she could wait—

"Oh," she breathed, when he nudged up against her again and this time pushed inside.

He was big. Bigger than she'd had before, and oh, what a difference that made.

Jo found herself digging her fingers into the soft dirt, clutching at the ground as Hunter filled her full. When he pulled out and pushed in again, she let her eyes close and gave herself up to the sensations overpowering her.

This is what it was meant to feel like with a man.

This is what she'd been missing.

She never wanted to be without it again.

"Jo—" Hunter's husky whisper told her it felt as good to him as it did to her. His pace picked up and she moaned again.

God, he felt good. His pace was perfect. He was thick and full inside her, pushing her to higher heights, urging her to a rousing crescendo of ecstasy she didn't know how she'd contain. Somehow it was right that their first time was happening underneath the wide open sky. It made this true.

And that's exactly how it felt.

Hunter worked inside her until he'd built a delicious friction that threatened to overwhelm her. His muscled hips thrust him in and out of her and all she could do was hang on.

When she went over the edge she couldn't hold back her cries. Hunter came with her, grunting as he moved, coaxing every ounce of pleasure from her until she fell back, exhausted.

He collapsed on top of her and they breathed together until Hunter chuckled, the movement making him pulse inside her again.

"What's so funny?"

"Nothing. It's just—good."

She knew exactly what he meant. "I think you've spoiled me for other men," she confessed.

He came alert, pushing up to look her in the eye. "No other men."

She wasn't sure if he was asking or telling her. Maybe a little of both. It was clear he wanted her assurance. It should have been aggravating, but it was kind of sexy.

"No other men," she promised him.

And meant it.

Chapter Eight

THE NEXT DAY, Hunter wondered if he was doing the right thing dialing the Franks' number. He and Jo had slept in the stables again and had made love twice, but now it was daylight. Time to get to work. Once they'd all pitched in with morning chores, he and Jo had returned to their building site to go over their plans, but he'd found it hard to concentrate as the time for Marlon's daily call ticked past again.

Hunter was worried. Marlon wouldn't rotate overseas again this close to the end of his enlistment. That meant he should have access to his phone. And should be able to answer calls, too.

Which meant Marlon was avoiding him.

Hunter needed to know he was still in San Diego. If he'd run again…

Hunter didn't even want to think about it.

It was nearly lunchtime, and the others had gone ahead into the house, but he knew it was a good time to catch Sue-Ann, so he'd lingered on the back porch to make the call.

"Frank residence," Sue-Ann said, picking up. She

didn't sound her usual, chirpy self. Hunter straightened.

"Sue-Ann?"

"Glad we're back on familiar terms," she said dryly.

"Have you heard from Marlon?"

She paused. "No. I was hoping you were him, actually. Not that I'm sorry to hear from you—you know that."

"I haven't heard from him in a couple of days. It's got me worried."

"Well…" Sue-Ann seemed to be picking her words. "You know he loves you as much as any of us," she said gently. "But your behavior has been a little off-kilter recently. Maybe it's put a strain on things, and he needs a little break to sort things out. I'm sure he'll come around."

Hunter stifled a curse. She had no idea how recent events were going to put a strain on things if he didn't hear from her son. He'd stepped into this mess so that Marlon could be free of it.

"Could you call him? Just make sure he's all right. For me?"

"Sure, I can do that. I'll call back in a few minutes."

Hunter paced the back deck until his phone buzzed again—far too quickly for Sue-Ann to have had a real conversation with Marlon. Tabitha appeared out from under the wicker couch, jumped up on the railing, stared at him for a moment and jumped down again. The cat seemed to sense he wasn't in a good mood.

"He's not picking up. I tried several times." She sounded worried, too. "Hunter, he's been strange lately.

For the last few months." She sighed. "Longer than that. Tell me truthfully: Did he know all along you were struggling with your time in the service? Did he at least try to help?"

Too many questions that were impossible to answer without implicating Marlon. Sue-Ann didn't know yet that May was filing for divorce. Marlon had insisted on it. He'd hoped to patch things up with his wife before anyone knew. Hunter understood why; he wasn't the only one who'd had a quiet conversation with his friend before his wedding years ago. Marlon had still been in love with Marie when he'd rushed into his marriage. May had been running from her own troubles. Neither of them were making good choices, and no one was surprised when they grew apart.

"He knew." Best to keep it short if he didn't want to break his promises to his friend. Marlon had made him swear not to get anyone else involved. "I've got to go."

"Keep calling me, Hunter," she said. "I need to know you're okay, too—that you're getting the help you need. Are you seeing someone? Are you going to be able to wrap up your career with the Navy right?"

He bit back a laugh. He was seeing someone and he hoped his alliance with Jo would help end his career on a positive note, but not in the way Sue-Ann meant. "Yeah." He cut the call short with a curt goodbye before they went down that rabbit hole.

This was a mess. Where was Marlon? Had he made a run for it again?

He wracked his brain for someone else to call, but

he had few connections left in the Navy. He'd burned all his bridges to save his friend. So if Marlon was busy burning them again, he'd—

What?

Try to get his old life back?

Was that what he wanted?

He turned to survey the trailer, braced and ready for Jo's little house.

No. That wasn't what he wanted at all.

"I WONDER WHAT Sadie's doing in India right now," Alice mused as she and Jo did the dishes after lunch. Cass had needed to run to town to do some shopping, so they'd stepped in to help. Jo didn't mind; her chores were under control and they were still waiting for the supplies to be delivered before she and Hunter could start on her house. She took a clean dish from the rack and dried it absently, trying to picture her sister in a foreign land with her new husband.

"I bet she's eating some fantastic meals."

"At midnight?" Alice glanced at the clock.

"Either that or—" Jo broke off, embarrassed. She'd been about to allude to hot sex between Sadie and Connor, but she and Alice didn't usually banter about things like that.

"Or she's getting it on with that husband of hers," Alice finished for her, unperturbed. She glanced at Jo. "She's allowed to have sex with him—just like you're allowed to go for it with Hunter."

"Alice!" Scandalized, Jo made sure they were alone.

"How did you—?"

"I didn't. Until now." Alice laughed. "I suspected, though. You're glowing! What else could be going on?"

"You must think I'm an idiot—after Sean, and then Grant—"

"I think you finally might have met your match. And I think every princess has to kiss some frogs to find her true love."

"My *match*? Do you… really think so? Is that one of your hunches?" Jo was used to living with Alice's premonitions and she knew that some of them were stronger than others.

Alice frowned as she plunged her hands into the soapy water and found a last dish to scrub. "Don't say anything, especially not to Cass. But my hunches… something's… muddying them up." She rinsed the dish and put it in the rack, then drained the sink.

"What do you mean?"

Her sister shook her head. "The only other time something like this happened was right before Mom died." Alice scrubbed the sink clean and moved to wipe down the counters.

Jo set the plate she'd been drying on the counter with a thump as Tabitha wound around her feet. "You think someone's going to die?"

"No! No," Alice said again, more softly. "I think something's going to happen that affects me too directly for me to see. Does that make sense? Mom's death was so overwhelming—to me, personally—I couldn't look right at it until it was too late."

"So what's going to happen?" Jo set aside the towel and bent down to stroke Tabitha, who'd been lying low lately with Max hanging around all the time. Luckily, the puppy seemed to be dividing his allegiance between Brian and Hunter while Connor was gone, so he was often outside of the house.

"That's just it; I don't know."

Jo didn't like it. Alice's hunches were erratic at the best of times, but once in a while they were helpful. Given the ongoing trouble they'd had, they needed every advantage they could get. She stood up again, and Tabitha stalked off to investigate her food dish.

"Well, I hope it's good, whatever it is."

"I hope so, too." Alice stopped. Closed her eyes for a moment. Opened them and glanced her way, a smile tugging at her lips. "I'm getting some kind of message for you. Something about giving and taking orders? Don't worry about it so much? I don't know what that means—it's edging in sideways around whatever's blocking my vision." She rinsed the cloth she'd used to wipe all the horizontal surfaces and hung it to dry. Wiping her hands on a towel, she crossed the kitchen, tugged a chair close to the counter, used it to step up and from there leverage herself onto the top of the refrigerator. It had always been her favorite place. The kitchen's high ceiling left her plenty of room to sit cross-legged up there. She pulled out a sketch-pad and pencil from a stack of supplies she kept handy, leaned back against the wall and began to draw.

Jo hoped she wasn't blushing. She'd been giving orders in the maze yesterday, and Hunter had followed them. But then he'd issued one of his own.

No other men, he'd said. She'd thought, *of course no other men*. Hunter was all she could think about.

What else would he demand, though?

Last night when they were together again in the stables, Jo had begun to think they had a real future together. But if they did get serious, would he think he could call the shots like he'd initially tried to when it came to the house plans? Would she always have to struggle to find her voice like she had all her life, first with her sisters, then with Sean and Grant?

Would she end up right back where she'd started?

When her phone buzzed in her pocket, she reached for it gratefully. A distraction was just what she needed.

"Who's that?" Alice asked.

"Megan." She accepted the call.

"Good, I got you! Want to go to Silver Falls with me?" Megan asked cheerfully.

"What for?"

"I've got to air out a house up there before a showing. It's old, and no one's lived in it for a couple of years. You know how those places up on the ridge get. So it'll smell bad, but at least it gives us a chance to hang out."

"I'm in." Why not? It would give her an excuse to leave the ranch, which she needed. She could clear her head and figure out what she wanted from this relationship with Hunter.

Before she got home, she'd decide how to proceed.

WHEN HUNTER NEXT checked in at the house, Jo was gone. Alice, sitting cross-legged on top of the fridge with a sketch pad in her lap, told him she'd run into town. He was disappointed; he'd hoped to spend more time with her, maybe wander through the maze again. Last night had been amazing, and if he was honest, he couldn't wait to get alone with her again.

Restless, and still worried about Marlon, who definitely was ignoring him, he decided to head to town, too, to gather the supplies that wouldn't be included in the lumber delivery the following day. He'd long since exchanged his rental for a second-hand truck Brian had helped him find in town.

He liked the winding drive into Chance Creek—long enough to let a man get his thoughts together, but not so long that it became tedious. The landscape suited him. Productive, but wild—kind of the way he thought of himself, although he figured if someone asked Marlon to describe him, his friend would probably choose words like overbearing, annoying and oppressive.

He wished the man would just call. He got it; Marlon didn't want him riding him all the time. But wasn't he entitled to, after what he'd given up?

"You've got a martyr complex, you know that?" Marlon had asked a few weeks back.

The phrase got under his skin and rubbed at him. He'd never meant to be a martyr—never meant to be anything but a Navy SEAL. Marlon was the one who'd made all the choices that got him here.

Right where he wanted to be, as it turned out.

He kept turning over the conundrum in his mind but got nowhere with it, so he was glad when he reached town and pulled in at the hardware store.

He was choosing screws from a set of big, open bins near the back of the store when a man walked up, grabbed a small paper bag from the rack and began to measure out some of his own.

"You're Hunter Powell, right?" the man asked.

"That's right." Hunter tipped his hat back. "You've got the jump on me. Can't say I recognize you."

"Steel Cooper. I know Connor."

Hunter nodded. "Good to meet you, then."

They kept at their work, but Hunter had a feeling the other man had more to say.

When Steel hefted the paper sack and rolled up the top, he turned to Hunter and lowered his voice. "Trouble's back in town. Just letting you know."

"What's that mean?" Hunter matched his tone. He'd worked with enough informants over his career that he knew when someone stepped up to offer intelligence they were taking a risk. That meant they judged the information important enough to warrant it.

"I want my family kept out of it. Just keep an eye out, that's all I'm saying." He walked off before Hunter could ask any more questions. He'd save them for Brian—and Connor, when they could reach him.

Not that he'd learned anything new. He thought about Bright Star, still convalescing in her stall. As far as he was concerned, trouble had already arrived.

"WHAT DO YOU think? Would you buy it?" Megan asked when she'd unlocked the door to the dilapidated house and let Jo inside. They'd driven far into the hills of Silver Falls to reach it, into an area that Jo had heard plenty about but never visited.

"I don't think so." Jo was intrigued by the cabin's age, but even her untrained eye could see the necessary repairs were beyond her. She wrinkled her nose at the smell of decay. At some point this house had been loved, but not for a long, long time. "Did your buyer want to see it?"

"I told you; he wants to see everything." Today, Megan's blond hair was pulled up into a no-nonsense bun on top of her head. "You don't have to do anything. Just keep me company."

"I'll help." Jo grabbed the broom Megan had carried in. "I'll sweep, you clean."

"I don't know how much we can do for the place." Megan eyed the cobwebs in the corners where the walls met the ceiling. "I'm fine with sprucing up a house a bit to get a sale, but this one needs to be renovated top to bottom."

"We'll tackle the worst of it. It'll make a difference," Jo assured her as cheerfully as she could. She wanted to help her friend get a sale.

A half hour later, she wasn't as sure as she'd been before, however. She'd swept her way through most of the rooms, but all it did was expose how dingy the floors were. Everything needed a good scrub, and that was more than they had time for. She found herself itching to go to town, gather supplies and do the house justice; first her mother and then Cass had kept her home spic and span all her life. She couldn't abide a mess like this.

"Why hasn't the house's owner fixed this place up?" she complained to Megan when they met in the kitchen again.

"The owner is dead. Her children have given up on it. I'm only fighting so hard for this commission because things have been pretty slow lately. I'm too new to get the good listings. I'm going to be hustling for years at this rate."

"Sorry to hear that," Jo told her. She was pretty sure Megan would create a business for herself in real estate in time, though. She was a people person and an extremely hard worker. Jo knew Megan still lived at home and longed to be able to move out, but her practical nature was another of her strong points. She'd declared her intention of staying put until she'd saved up for a down payment on a house of her own.

A sharp knock on the door startled them both.

"Who's that?" Jo asked.

"I'm not sure." Megan moved to a living room window and peeked out. "Oh, my God—it's my client. What's he doing here?" She looked down at herself in horror and lifted a hand to her hair.

"I'll let him in. You go clean up," Jo said. She waved Megan into the rear of the house where there was a bathroom, and approached the door, curious to see the person who was running her friend ragged.

When she opened the door and recognized the man on the front stoop, her heart sank. He was the one from the feed store who'd been so forward—and so annoying. His impatient expression morphed into an oily smile that brought her hackles up.

"We meet again after all," he said. Jo found herself taking a step back. Every instinct told her not to trust this man, and she was done questioning her instincts. She was glad Megan was here, too.

"I guess so." She straightened, aware that she'd already betrayed her dislike, but not caring.

"Where's Ms. Lawrence?" He entered the house without an invitation.

"She'll… be here in a minute." Jo realized too late she should have blocked his entry. But that was ridiculous—he simply wanted to see the house, right? Still, she didn't like it when he crossed into the living room as if he already owned it.

"Megan? Megan—we have company," she called, wanting to give her friend a head's up he was inside. Megan came around the corner and nearly walked into him.

"Mr. Ramsey. What are you doing here? I thought we were meeting tomorrow for the showing."

"Came by to look the place over from the outside. Saw your car. No sense putting something off until tomorrow when you can do it today."

He seemed pleased with this nugget of wisdom, and Jo was beginning to think he wasn't too bright. That didn't make him less dangerous, though. He was a

Southerner, she thought, but not from the deep South like Hunter was. His drawl was light, not honey-thick. It had a twang to it.

"I'm not quite ready to show the place. My partner and I were just spiffing it up a little—"

"Didn't know you had a partner." Mr. Ramsey looked Jo up and down, and she felt like he'd seen right through Megan's ruse.

"I'm just helping out—" Jo began.

"You looking for a job?" Mr. Ramsey stepped closer to Jo than she found comfortable. She took a step back. Cursed herself for doing it. Ramsey was the type of man who only understood one thing.

Strength.

"No—I'm busy enough—"

"Doing what?"

"I—uh—live on a ranch. I've got plenty to do there."

"A ranch, huh?" He looked her over again. "Married?"

Jesus, had he really asked that question? "Uh—no." She gave Megan a pleading stare. This was too much. But she didn't want to ruin things for her friend. Megan needed a sale.

"We'll have dinner, then."

"Hell, no! I mean, I have a boyfriend." Jo couldn't believe the nerve of the man. Did he really think he could order her to have dinner with him?

Did that kind of line actually work on women?

She sure as heck hoped not.

"Boyfriend." He said it like he didn't believe her. "Who?"

Anger and confusion warred within her. She didn't have to answer his questions, she told herself, but his boldness made it hard not to. She had a feeling if she tried to resist they'd spend the rest of the afternoon arguing about it. "His name is Hunter Powell. Not that you'd know him."

He didn't answer, but she was sure he'd filed the name away. Jo didn't like him one bit. Ramsey swept his gaze over his surroundings and frowned.

"This isn't the place."

"You haven't even looked upstairs." Megan reached toward the staircase as if to point the way.

"It isn't the place," Ramsey repeated. "I need a ranch."

Chapter Nine

"**Y**OU'RE BUILDING WHAT?" the General asked.

"A house—a temporary house. For Jo." Hunter heard the man's swift intake of breath and knew an explosion was coming. He tried to head it off. "Remember what we talked about? That I should build something for Jo the way Connor did for Sadie? Well, I'm doing it, and I need to know what my budget is."

"I didn't mean a house!"

Hunter supposed he should have made this call when he first arrived, but the truth was he'd gotten so caught up in designing the house with Jo he hadn't thought to check in with her father. Which was dumb; even a tiny house cost money. Quite a bit, in fact, when it was plumbed and wired and completed the way Jo wanted it to be.

"Look, it's not as bad as you think. I'm building it on a trailer; the women can move it wherever they want. It'll be a guest cottage."

"That's supposed to make me feel better? That someone can hitch up my daughter's house and take off with her while she sleeps? No way. I'm not paying for that. If you haven't noticed, people keep taking pot shots at my girls. I don't need Jo living in some kind of portable shed. Considering she's supposed to be your wife, I'd think you'd have thought about that."

"Considering she's supposed to be my wife, maybe I'm planning to sleep there with her," Hunter retorted.

Which might have been a mistake.

"If you plan to sleep there, too, then you pay for it!" The General cut the call.

Hell.

He should have seen that coming.

Hunter scrubbed his face with his hand, the stubble of his beard scraping against his palm. The General was right, though. If he planned to sleep in it, he *should* pay for it. Only problem was, Jo didn't just want a temporary house, she wanted a real one, too, and he'd already promised her he'd build it come spring. He'd saved up a fair amount of cash over the years, but not enough to do both without taking out loans.

He most likely wouldn't get a loan for a tiny house built on a trailer. He'd have to pay cash for that, and leverage the remainder of his savings for the bigger house. This wasn't practical at all. The sensible thing would be to wait until spring and build a single house.

Sensible didn't come into it, though, he supposed.

Jo needed this bridge from living with her sisters to living with a husband, and although he damn well did intend to sleep with her in the tiny house, he also intended to give her the space to make it her own. Everyone needed a chance at independence, even for a few months. He had to give her hers, even if it made for an awkward winter.

Building two houses would leave him strapped for cash. He wasn't sure how things would work once his position here was permanent. How would they split the income from the ranch? Would they split it at all? Should he be looking for work in town or on another spread?

Too many questions.

He decided to make a call to USSOCOM, needing to talk to someone who understood the position he was in.

Logan answered. "You dumb fuck; you went AWOL?"

His broadside caught Hunter by surprise. "What?"

"Heard it from a friend. What the hell were you running from?"

Jesus. What was he supposed to say? "It's not what you think—"

"Oh, fuck me. When someone starts with that line, it's *exactly* what you think. You going to run again? We've all got a lot on the line here."

"I'm definitely not going to run again." Not unless Marlon did something truly stupid.

"Never thought I'd be working with a deserter."

"Yeah? What did *you* do to get canned?"

Logan's silence told him everything he needed to know. All of them had messed up big time to end up under the General's control.

"I didn't cut and run when things got tough. That's

for sure." Logan ended the call.

Hunter sat back. This wasn't good. Last spring, when May had announced to Marlon she wanted a divorce, Marlon had gone off the deep end. May had called Hunter next, screaming she thought Marlon might do himself harm. Hunter, stationed with Marlon at Coronado, would never forget his midnight dash to Marlon's quarters and the sinking feeling when he found his friend gone. It was obvious what he meant to do. Hunter followed him to the airport, and stopped him from getting on a plane, but couldn't get him to return to base. Instead they'd compromised on a nearby motel. The next few days were rough. May stuck to her guns even when Marlon called and begged her to change her mind. As time ticked past and Marlon realized she was serious, he'd flipped back and forth between anger and despair, taking his grief to a place so dark, Hunter feared he would lose his friend. Hunter had watched him around the clock, listened to his ravings, bore witness to his tears, talked him back from the brink.

Finally... finally, Marlon had calmed down, pulled himself together and agreed to return to base.

Too late.

They were both AWOL, but Hunter knew his friend wouldn't make it through a court martial. He knew Marlon needed his job if he was going to lose his family. He'd embraced the SEALs and given them as much as he'd tried to give to May. If he lost both at the same time—

Hunter didn't want to think what might happen.

So he took the fall himself.

He told the Navy he was the one with the family crisis. He cast Marlon as his savior—the friend who'd come and persuaded him to go back. The Navy bought his story. Decided Marlon deserved a break for going after his friend. Marlon went back to their unit.

Hunter ended up at USSOCOM.

And now here.

He couldn't tell Logan what had really happened, though. If people knew what Marlon had done, the information would make its way back to the General. People thought women gossiped, but no one beat the military when it came to passing on news.

Marlon hadn't meant to desert his team. He was a stand-up guy who'd been pushed too far. He deserved a second chance.

Except Marlon wasn't calling him.

Which meant maybe he wasn't such a stand-up guy after all.

WHEN JO LET herself into the sheriff's station, she wasn't sure with whom to speak. The closest desk was empty. Everyone else seemed busy.

Maybe this was a mistake. After all, nothing had happened—

"Jo? Are you looking for me?"

Cab Johnson strode toward her from the back of the station. Well over six feet tall, broad as a barrel, he was an intimidating man when he wanted to be. He was honest to a fault, though, and had always taken an interest in the safety of the women at Two Willows—to such an extent she had a gut feeling he might be in contact with the General. Which made her relationship with the man complicated. She was far more used to avoiding the law than turning to it. During their teenage years, after their mother died, when she and her sisters had run off the overseers and guardians the General appointed, they'd avoided other people, especially Cab's father—who'd held the position of sheriff before him. It was hard for her to count Cab as completely on their side.

She nodded. "Yes, do you have a minute?"

"Sure thing." He ushered her into his office, waved her into a seat and took his own behind a wide desk. The room was nondescript, the furniture ancient and battered. Jo sat down and tried to gather her words.

"Something... strange... just happened."

"Where?"

She gave him the address for the house she and Megan had gone to prepare for the showing. "It's up on the ridge in Silver Falls."

Cab nodded. "I know where it is."

"Megan Lawrence and I went to give it a bit of a cleaning. She was supposed to show it to a potential buyer tomorrow and the place was a mess. She asked if I'd help out."

"What happened?"

She liked the way he cut to the chase; no beating around the bush for Cab. "The potential buyer showed up early. He was... weird."

Cab leaned forward. "Want to elaborate?"

"He was trying to intimidate us. Me. His name's Ramsey."

"First or last?"

"Last. I don't know his first name." She hadn't thought to ask Megan, either. "I'd met him once before—in the feed store. I didn't like the way he acted then, either."

"Why do you think he wanted to intimidate you?"

"I don't know. But… I didn't like it. He… asked me on a date." When a smile flitted over Cab's face, Jo felt her cheeks grow warm. "I'm not being silly!"

"I'm sorry." He actually looked contrite. "Jo, you're a beautiful young woman. And I'm not saying that to discount your hunch. If you felt something was off, then something was off. But you're going to get attention. You know that, right?"

Jo swallowed. No, she didn't know that. Compared to Alice—or even Cass—she wasn't beautiful at all. Cute, maybe. That was about the extent of it.

"Maybe I am being silly." So much for her resolve to follow her gut. What did she know? She was a lousy judge of men.

"No. Definitely not." Cab tapped a finger on the table. "You know, this is the first time one of you Reed women has ever asked for help."

Jo reared back. "Great, so I'm dumb, and a big baby." She half rose from her seat. Cab waved her down.

"That doesn't make you a baby; it makes you an adult. You don't see yourself, Jo. You're a hell of a woman, and I don't say that lightly. You saved your sisters' lives. If the chips were down, I'd want you on my side in a heartbeat."

Jo didn't know why tears stung her eyes at his words. He'd said something nice. It should make her happy.

But it was so... strange... to hear praise from a man. Two men, in such a short time—Hunter had praised her, too.

Jo sat down again. "So what do I do? I don't know this guy, but if he's moving to town, I'm going to see him again. He barely spent a minute in the house before saying he didn't want it. He said he wanted a ranch. It felt... it felt like a threat."

"Tell you what; let's get you home. I'll follow you in my cruiser to keep watch."

"You think he'd follow me?"

"He might." He met Jo's gaze. She knew what he was thinking; these strangers could be involved in the drug ring that had attacked her family twice.

"Okay," she said. "Thank you."

"Thank you. For doing the right thing."

HUNTER WAS COMING up from the barns when Jo's truck pulled in, followed by a sheriff's cruiser. He increased his pace.

"Jo? Everything all right?"

"I'm fine." She waited for a large man in a sheriff's uniform to exit the cruiser, and together they came to meet Hunter. "Hunter, this is Cab Johnson, the county sheriff. Cab, this is Hunter Powell. The General sent him to give us a hand."

Cab looked him over. "Good to meet you." He stuck out a hand and gave Hunter a firm enough handshake to establish he felt he was in charge. That didn't bother Hunter. The man should feel responsible for his jurisdiction.

"Good to meet you, too. Did something happen?"

Jo filled him in about the house on the ridge and the man who'd arrived without warning.

"I didn't like the way he was acting, so I went and told Cab."

"And I told her I appreciate the head's up. People down here at Two Willows have a way of taking things into their own hands, which can be dangerous. I'm going to keep an eye out for that man," he told Jo, "and you call me if you see him, you hear me?"

"Will do, Sheriff."

"Did Jo tell you about Bright Star?" Hunter asked. When Cab shook his head no, Hunter told him all about the buckshot incident. "I'll keep my eyes open, too," Hunter finished. He didn't like the sound of that encounter at all. He hated the thought of a man playing games with his Jo.

"How about a lemonade, Cab?" Jo asked.

"Wouldn't mind one. Can't stay long, though."

"Come inside and I'll get it in a jiffy."

Hunter was about to follow them when his phone buzzed in his pocket. He hung back, although he wanted to get more of the story. "Powell here," he said when he'd accepted the call.

"It's Mark from the lumberyard. I've pulled together that order you placed earlier, but I'm coming up with a bigger number than I quoted you before and I wanted to check in and make sure it's okay. You can come in and pick it up any time." He named a sum for the supplies that made Hunter wince. Jo deserved her house, and he'd make sure she got it one way or the other, but he had to stick to a tight budget for this one or he wouldn't be able to afford the one he wanted to build her in the spring.

"What do you think?" Mark asked. "Want to go forward?"

"Yeah, I guess. With a couple of changes." He didn't have a choice. He'd have to substitute cheaper materials for some of the higher end finishes in the interior. "I'll pop into town in about an hour, okay?"

"Got it."

Was he being a fool? Hunter wondered. Maybe he'd bitten off far more than he could chew. If the expenses for this little house were coming in over budget, what would it be like when he built the bigger one? He hadn't looked into zoning or costs for the real house he meant to build in the spring.

What if he couldn't afford it?

He was still ruminating about the matter when Cab came out of the house again. "Everything all right?" the man asked when he reached Hunter.

"Yeah. Just thinking about money."

Cab guffawed. "That'll make anyone look constipated. Cheer up; there's a pretty girl inside that kitchen. I trust you know what you're doing around pretty girls?"

"I have an idea."

"Figured you would since the General sent you."

He was off before Hunter could ask him what he meant, but he supposed it didn't take a genius to see that when the General sent a man, that man married one of his daughters.

"Hunter?" Jo leaned out of the kitchen door. "Want some lemonade?" Her face was illuminated by the sunshine, and something stirred deep inside him—an urge to protect her.

To love her.

He slid his phone into his pocket and joined Jo inside.

IT WAS CLOSE to dinnertime when Hunter returned from town. Jo went to meet him happily; he was supposed to bring the materials for her house and she couldn't wait to get started on building it. It was September already, and at night there was definitely a nip in the air that hadn't been there just a couple of weeks earlier. By mid-October the rains would come—and then the snow. She wanted her home done and ready to house her through the long winter.

Hunter was quiet as they began to unload the truck, like he'd been earlier in the day before he'd left on the errand. She hoped he hadn't changed his mind about building the house—or about her, but when she asked him what was wrong, he just shook his head.

Jo focused on hauling lumber over near to where they'd braced the trailer, assuming he'd talk to her when he was ready. She worked with Hunter to carry the sheets of plywood he'd gotten, too.

"What's this?" she asked when she came to a roll of vinyl.

Hunter sighed. "That's your backsplash." He didn't quite meet her eyes as he leaned in to lift it out.

"My backsplash? What happened to the tile?" She didn't want a vinyl backsplash. She wanted something that would stand up to the test of time.

"It cost too much."

Jo frowned, not understanding. Her father had told him to come build her whatever she wanted. As far as she knew that meant she got to build it however she wanted, too. "What gives you the right to determine that?"

He didn't answer.

"Hunter? What gives you the right—?"

"Your father put me in charge, and I've got a budget. I can't go over it. So that's your backsplash. End of story."

Why was he snapping at her? It wasn't her fault she hadn't known they had a budget. And why should they? This ranch was worth a lot of money, and the cattle operation turned a tidy profit—or at least it had before the last overseer had screwed it up. She had worked this spread since she could walk, devoted countless hours to it. She and Lena were already building those profits back up, with Brian's help—and Connor's when he got back from his honeymoon. If she wanted a tiny house, she was owed a tiny house—with a tile backsplash.

"Fine. I'll buy my own tile." Not that she had a ton of discretionary cash; just the proceeds from her dog breeding enterprise, which she tried not to dip into. She didn't receive a salary, per se, just drew on the household income, like they all did for whatever they needed. Over the years that hadn't been much more than the clothing on her back, the cost of her first McNab breeding pair, her secondhand truck and some take-out food now and then. It pissed her off that she had to shell out for the backsplash now. She took the vinyl from his hands and set it aside.

Hunter picked it up again and put it with the other materials. "Look, it's already cut to size; we can't take it back. It would be a waste of money to buy tile."

He was calling her wasteful? He was the one who'd bought the vinyl without asking. The tiles she'd chosen had been almost elegant. An interesting counterpoint to the knotty-pine walls and rough-hewn contours of the little house.

She wanted them.

And Hunter hadn't even consulted her before changing the plan.

"I just said I'll buy them, so you don't need to worry about the cost." She picked up the vinyl.

"But that means the money I spent already will go to waste." He reached for it, and Jo had to keep herself from bludgeoning him with it. Instead, she set it carefully aside, determined to try to sell it to someone else. She turned to inform Hunter of her decision—

And stopped in her tracks when she noticed what else was in the truck.

"What is that?" Her voice slid up an octave and she fought for control. "What *is* that?"

"Laminate. For the floors."

"Where's my hardwood?" Fury had her fingers balled into fists. She didn't want laminate. She wanted a beautiful hardwood floor. It was a small house—hardly expensive at all.

"The budget—"

"To hell with the budget. And to hell with you." If he'd consulted her, they could have worked together to figure out what to trim and what to keep to match the number the General wanted to spend. Instead, he'd made his own choices.

The wrong choices.

"Jo—"

"Build it any way you want. I'm not going to live in it!" She strode past him into the house and slammed the door behind her.

Chapter Ten

H UNTER WASN'T SURE how he ended up in the maze, but as he paced its green corridors, searching for the way through to the heart of it, he decided it was a fitting place to be. He didn't know how to solve the problems facing him any more than he knew his way to the center. Jo had taken the lead when he'd been here before.

He should have given her the lead as far as her house was concerned.

The world seemed to grow quieter the farther he went in the maze. Hunter figured the thick evergreen walls muted the sounds of the ranch. It soothed him, too. Allowed him to think through the difficulties his situation presented him.

If he told Jo why he was stinting on the supplies, he'd have to admit he was the one paying for them and that her father didn't want to. That would increase the strain between the General and his daughter, and Hunter instinctively knew that wasn't a good outcome. Jo felt betrayed by her father on a level so deep Hunter didn't know if the relationship could be repaired. He knew how that felt. But he also knew she missed the General despite everything Jo had said. As the man who wanted to be her husband, it was up to him to help bridge the gap between them. He didn't want to pass the blame for the vinyl and laminate on to the General, even if he was to blame.

It would have helped if he could sell Jo on their future house, the one they'd splurge on and build together to her specifications. He truly hoped he could give her everything she wanted then, but if he went crazy on this temporary one, he wouldn't be able to afford the upgrades for the bigger one. It seemed important to him to show her what kind of husband he would make, too. He wanted to demonstrate common sense and the ability to do the right thing to provide for their future. If he wooed her with a flashy show now and couldn't keep it up later, how would that help?

When he reached the center of the maze, he sat down on the wooden bench positioned in front of the stone, far enough away to make it easy to contemplate. He wondered how the stone had gotten here. Who had gone through all the trouble to lift it into place?

Was it as special as everyone claimed it to be? Were the swans he and Jo had seen really some kind of cosmic message? Or just a coincidence?

Despite his best intentions—Hunter saw himself as a man of reason—he got up again, walked to it and placed his hands on the large stone's flank. Just like the last time, the rock was warm from the autumn sunshine, and Hunter let out a long, deep breath, some of his tension escaping with it.

"What should I do?"

He hadn't meant to ask the question aloud, and he drew away, feeling a little sheepish.

The stone didn't answer.

He didn't really expect it to.

Hunter supposed he couldn't hide in the maze all day, either. Time to go back and face the music—and try to explain himself to Jo without making her hate her father even more than she already did.

He set off through the green paths and nearly crashed into Lena when he rounded a corner. Both of them stepped back.

"Jesus, you scared me." Lena glowered up at him. "What are you doing here?"

"What does anyone do here?" Hunter countered. He meant he'd been walking and thinking, but Lena took his words another way.

"You asked the stone a question?" She didn't wait for an answer. "What did you ask?"

She folded her arms across her chest and he found himself answering, even though he hadn't meant to. "I wanted advice, I guess. Jo's pretty upset with me."

Lena rolled her eyes. "The General sent you, didn't he? Of course she's upset with you."

"It isn't that. I had to change a couple of things we'd planned for her little house. Because of budget constraints."

"Oh." Lena thought about that. "Jo spent a lot of time on those plans, you know. No wonder she's pissed.

Did you ask her to pitch in to cover the costs?"

"Not until after I'd bought cheap replacement materials."

"Why didn't you ask up front?" Lena seemed genuinely curious.

"She doesn't have a job."

"Jo makes money here and there. She raises McNabs. She takes care of other people's animals while they're gone. She's resourceful. Don't underestimate her."

Hunter scratched the back of his neck. Lena was right; he had underestimated Jo. He'd treated her like the kind of woman who'd be offended to spend money on her own house. "I didn't think of that. When I got here she seemed so—young."

Lena's expression darkened. "She might be young, but she's not dumb. Look what happened to Grant Kimball."

"Yeah, I wouldn't want to end up shot." Hell, that hadn't come out right.

But Lena laughed. Her smile faded as she went on, though. "It should have been me who pulled the trigger on Grant. I should have known what was happening. I should have—"

"Now you're the one underestimating Jo. She's going to be fine," Hunter told her.

"You really think so?"

For the first time she was asking his opinion, not treating him like an enemy, like she had since he'd arrived. If he was having difficulty with Jo, Logan was going to have a hell of a struggle with Lena. Hunter took his time with his answer. "I really do. She's strong—and confident about the decision she made."

"Maybe she's just as confident about the choices she made about her house," Lena pointed out.

He thought about that. Nodded. "You're probably right." Hell, he'd asked for advice and here he was getting it. Maybe there was something to that stone.

He did keep underestimating Jo. He made decisions for her as if she couldn't make them herself. He should have asked her before changing the backsplash and the flooring. He'd learned his lesson.

He hoped Jo was willing to give him another chance. Lena stepped aside and let him pass her before she continued on toward the center of the maze. Hunter wondered if she had a question for the stone, too. He'd nearly made it out when his phone buzzed. He braced for another confrontation with Marlon, but it was the General on the line.

"Who's been threatening my daughter?"

"You mean Jo, sir?" How the hell did the General know anything about that?

Cab.

Was the sheriff reporting back to the General? Spying on the goings-on at Two Willows?

"Of course I mean Jo. Who was giving her a hard time?"

"Someone named Ramsey. That's all I know so far. Says he's looking to buy a property in Chance Creek."

"I hope none of you idiots are fooled by that.

They're coming at Two Willows again. You keep your eyes peeled. And you keep my daughter in the house where she belongs. None of this tiny house bullshit."

"General. Sir. With all due respect, there aren't enough bedrooms in the main house for everyone."

"Sure there are. Five daughters. Five husbands. Unless you idiots don't know what you're doing with wives, that means five bedrooms, which there already are."

That was true; plus there was the master bedroom none of the girls touched. They kept it just the way their mother had left it, as far as he could tell. And the guest room, which they'd still need for guests.

"Think about it. Cass is already almost three months along. Soon enough there'll be grandkids, right? There aren't any extra bedrooms for them," Hunter said. "Sooner or later there will have to be more houses as the rest of us start families, too. Seems to me Cass and Brian should be the ones to stay in the current one. Cass loves it."

"Cass is… pregnant?"

Hunter stiffened. Didn't the General know that? Had he just spilled a secret he wasn't supposed to tell?

"Better ask Cass." He cut the call and nearly dropped the phone in his panic to get away from it.

Hell. Hell and damnation.

Now he'd really screwed things up.

"I'M GLAD YOU'RE here."

Jo was startled when Hunter spoke behind her later that evening. She was sitting at the kitchen table, looking over her personal accounts when he came in. She whirled around, ready to tell him off, but he put his hands up in a placating manner.

"I came to say I'm sorry."

"You did?" She was too surprised not to show it. The last thing she'd expected from the SEAL was an apology. Even if he had done so once before.

"Look, I'm used to calling the shots. Making decisions. There's not a lot of democracy in the military, so I got carried away. Do you want me to try to return the vinyl? If you're able to carry some of the cost, I think we can pull off purchasing the tile instead."

She thought about that. "I'd like that. The tile I chose previously is beautiful. I think it's a touch that's going to make the house charming." She knew that must seem silly to a man used to taking things as they came, but she wanted this house to be special. It would be hers and hers alone—at least for the winter. She'd always shared most things with her sisters before.

"Okay. I'll take care of it."

"Why?" The question popped out of her mouth before she could stop it. When he raised an eyebrow, she tried again. "Why are you being nice all of a sudden?"

He made a face she couldn't decipher. Chagrin, maybe. Hadn't he meant to be dictatorial earlier?

"Because I want to do this right. I want… a relationship with you. A long-term relationship."

Jo blinked. A long-term relationship?

"I like you," he said.

A smile tugged at her lips. The SEAL liked her.

She could live with that.

"Stop looking like the cat who ate the canary," Hunter growled.

Jo laughed. She couldn't help it. "I'm not gloating; I'm simply surprised. I didn't know you were… human."

"Too human. I let it slip to the General today Cass is pregnant. He didn't seem to know."

"Oh, God." Cass was going to be furious.

"Should I tell her?"

"Yes. But maybe not until tomorrow morning… and then I'd get in your truck and ride like hell toward town."

He chuckled. "Good plan." He headed for the back door. She thought he was leaving until he jerked his head and indicated that she should follow him.

Outside, Max joined them as they both stood looking at the trailer parked in its spot beside the main house. It was a good location for what would eventually become a guest house, Jo thought as she fondled the puppy's ears.

She couldn't wait for it to be done.

"I WANT TO give you everything, Jo."

She looked up at him sharply and left off fiddling with Max's ears. Max wandered off. "You don't have to give me—"

"I want to," he repeated. "But more than giving you things, I want to do what's right. You're going to need a real house come spring. A big house that someday can hold a family. That's the one we'll spare no expense on. But I'm willing to look for some work, see if we can make up the difference to buy everything you want for the little house. It isn't a lot. Maybe I was being over-cautious."

"It isn't important. Besides, I can afford the tile," she began.

"It's important to me," he cut her off. "I want you to know I…"

What had he been about to say? Jo reached out and touched his wrist. Felt longing, worry, fear—

Loneliness.

Her breath caught in her throat. He was afraid he'd lose her over this. Over doing the wrong thing. The pain in him shocked her. He wanted to stay. Wanted her—

"Hunter, look—I don't need a tile backsplash. I want it, but I don't need it. I know the difference." She gathered her thoughts, still shaken by the depth of his feelings for her, paired with his need. She viewed Hunter as a warrior—a strong man who was complete in and of himself. To sense he was vulnerable made him human. "If the General gave us a budget, we'll work with it."

"It's not him—" Hunter cut off abruptly. Shook his head. "Hell," he added quietly.

He hadn't meant to say that, Jo realized. Why not? What was he—?

It came clear in a flash.

"Hunter Powell, are you paying for my house?" She

faced him, hands on hips.

He didn't answer.

"Why?" She huffed out a breath. "The General refused, didn't he? He'll pay to fix the main house for Cass, and he'll build Sadie a walled garden, but if I want a little place of my own, screw me, is that how it is?" She hated the shrill tone to her voice, but she couldn't recall ever being so angry.

"You've got it wrong—"

"How? How do I have it wrong? That man hasn't given a damn about me since he walked out on us."

"Jo, that's not the way it is." Hunter put a hand on her arm. "He's worried. Afraid of you sleeping in that house alone at night, with what's been going on. He's got a point."

"So then I won't sleep alone," she said wildly. "You can sleep with me!"

His eyes widened, and a corner of his mouth turned up. "Really?"

She opened her mouth but couldn't think of a thing to say. After all, they were already intimate. She wanted to stay that way with him. Didn't he realize that?

"Hell, yeah," he said, although she hadn't asked a question. He pulled her close and, without another word, kissed her—hard.

One kiss led to another, and another, until she found her arms wrapped around his neck, her body pressed close to his.

"I'd be glad to." His voice was rough.

Jo tingled all over. "Then it's a plan. Screw the General."

"I'd rather screw you."

"We'd better start building."

But neither of them moved. Being in Hunter's arms felt far too good.

When he glanced around for somewhere to go, Jo said, "The carriage house."

"Are you sure?"

She knew what he meant; after what had gone down there, it should be the last place she wanted to be. They wouldn't be upstairs in Alice's workroom, though. She led him around the side to the small room she kept for her breeding dogs when a new litter was born. In between litters, she scrubbed the place clean, and while it had a certain doggy scent, that didn't bother Jo, who'd been around animals all her life. She had a few clean blankets in there. It would be rough, but she doubted the SEAL would care. After all, they'd spent the last three nights sleeping in the stables.

"This is private," he said approvingly as she unlocked the door.

"And I'm the only one who comes here."

He sniffed as he walked in. "Dogs?"

"You got it. We don't have to stay—"

He shut the door, circled around her and hemmed her in against it. "I want to stay."

"Good—oh." Jo sighed as he lifted her chin and met her mouth with his own. His first kisses were soft, searching, but then he deepened them, exploring her mouth with his tongue. His hands dropped down to hold her hips in place, and the pressure of him against her abdomen told her he wanted far more from her.

She was fine with that. More than fine—delighted.

Ready for whatever he had in mind.

When he slid his hands up to caress her breasts, Jo murmured her approval. He touched her with an instinct so fine she was dizzy with the sensation in moments. His warm palms covered her sensitive nipples, and his firm strokes teased her until she found herself arching her back and pressing her breasts into his hands.

She helped him off with his shirt, and in turn, he helped her out of hers. He moaned when her nipples brushed his bare skin, and she loved the way it felt when he tugged her closer to him. He tasted good when they kissed. She wanted more.

He must have read her mind.

He spotted the blankets, angled over to them, spread them out—all without breaking off their embrace—and lowered her onto them.

She'd already undone the button of her jeans and began to shimmy out of them, kicking her boots off before thrashing her legs until she was free. Hunter rolled her over to access the clasp of her bra. He rolled her back so she faced him clad only in her panties.

"This all right?" he asked as he undid his belt.

"You're asking now?"

"Better late than never." He grinned at her and she grinned back.

"This is better than all right." Jo got to her knees

and helped him finish the job. When he'd skimmed off his jeans and boots, and tugged down his boxer briefs, she bent forward and, without warning, took him into her mouth.

Hunter groaned, braced himself on his knees, his thighs straining to hold himself in place. Jo wrapped one hand around him and let the other rest on his hip. As she took him in, the taste of his smooth, warm skin made her flush with heat, knowing soon he'd be inside her in a different way. Anticipation curled deep inside her.

First she wanted to tease him and make him want her as much as she wanted him, though.

"Jo—"

Hunter couldn't seem to put his thoughts into words. Jo liked knowing she held that kind of sway over him. Liked making him feel so good he could barely talk. His thickness in her mouth made her buzz with desire, and she imagined how it would feel when he pressed inside her. She moved him in and out of her mouth. Gave attention to every part of him. When she could tell he was struggling to hold back, she let go, lay down and tugged him on top of her. He fumbled in his jeans and pulled out a condom.

"Jo, I'm not going to be able to take it slow," he said as he sheathed himself and tossed aside the wrapper.

"I don't want it slow," she told him. "I just want you. Now. However you want."

"You're killing me."

POSITIONED BETWEEN JO'S legs, pushing into her, watching her close her eyes and open to him was almost more than Hunter could bear.

She felt so good. He wished he could hold on for hours, teasing her like she'd just teased him, but she was so hot and he was so hard he'd be lucky to last a minute.

No—he'd last more than that, he promised himself as he sank into her, pulled out and pushed in again with a long, strong stroke. He had to bring her along for this ride.

Luckily, it looked like she was nearly there, too.

He liked the way Jo liked sex. She was fearless—just like she was in the rest of her life. She took her pleasure and gave it with equal abandon.

She was perfect.

As he worked himself in and out of her, bringing both of them to a point of no return, Hunter knew this wasn't an assignment anymore. He wasn't here because the General had sent him. He was here because he wanted to be. He wanted far more than a short-term thing with Jo. He wanted everything. To be married. To make a life.

To make a family.

Soon he was past all thought, however, moving inside Jo to an ancient rhythm he had to obey. Jo moved with him, her body accepting everything he had to give her—and when they crashed over the edge together, coming in unison, their cries intermingling, he was far too lost to the pleasure he felt to worry about the future.

But afterward, as they lay entwined on the rough

blankets, Hunter wondered if he could make Jo happy as a husband.

Maybe some other man would make her happier.

He hadn't realized he'd tightened his embrace until Jo wriggled in his arms. He loosened his hold on her again.

"Sorry."

"Don't be. I had fun."

"So did I."

"Hunter, why are you really here?" she asked.

He wished to God he could tell her the truth. Maybe he could.

"I'm here to love you."

HE WAS HERE to love her?

Jo wasn't sure what to make of that. He'd already become more to her than any man she'd dated before, but surely it was far too early to talk about things like love.

He must have read her thoughts in her face.

"Look, I'm not saying I'm fully there or that you have to be. But I feel—something. And it feels big," he said.

She nodded. She wasn't sure what else to do. "I'm not ready—"

"I'm not asking you to be." He took her hand and she read his emotions. There was far more certainty in him than he was letting on. She was humbled by that. Why would this man—this warrior who'd seen the world—be interested in her? Love her?

She wondered if he could read her insecurity the way she read his conviction. She hoped not. Finding herself wanting to meet his strength with her own, she was almost ready to say more than she really felt, but that wouldn't be honest, and she prized honesty.

Jo tugged her hand away. She felt something, too, though. Something that presaged the kind of emotions he had brought to the table. She simply needed time to learn more about him—and herself.

"Take all the time you need. I'm not going anywhere," Hunter said, and she blinked again. *Could* he read her the way she read him?

"We should both go have some lunch," she told him, trying to restore normalcy.

"Sure thing." But instead of heading inside, he reached for her, and she found herself leaning toward him, ready for his kiss.

"I can wait," he told her when he pulled back, leaving her breathless with want.

She wasn't sure she could.

Chapter Eleven

S EVERAL DAYS LATER, Hunter handed Jo a drill. "Be my guest."

Jo surveyed the wooden cladding they were applying to the outside of the house, set the screw in place and screwed it in expertly. She picked another screw from a nearby box and kept going. They'd framed in the house, gotten help with the plumbing and wiring, and were working on the exterior and the roof today. Max came and went on his explorations around the grounds. Tabitha had checked in earlier and gone her way, too.

Hunter watched Jo patiently. She'd made it clear from the beginning she didn't intend to stand around and let him do all the work. She wanted to learn every aspect of building her house, and since he was learning it at the same time, he didn't see any reason not to let her—even if sometimes he ached to take the tools out of her hands and do it himself.

During the days he'd lived at Two Willows he'd observed all the women carefully and noticed a pattern he was pretty sure had led to Jo's current state of mind. On the one hand, all her sisters deferred to her on matters pertaining to the care of the critters on the ranch. Jo might not talk about her ability to read feelings and emotions, but her sisters intuitively grasped she had a special connection with them. On the other hand, everyone from Cass on down interfered in Jo's life in all kinds of ways. Cass mothered her—constantly. Reminding her to eat breakfast, telling her to take a sweater, commenting if she looked tired and possibly sick. Alice didn't comment actively, but she kept a watch on her younger sister he was sure stemmed from the early days when she would have acted as Cass's deputy. Lena ran the cattle operation without ever consulting Jo. She merely ordered Jo around, and he thought Jo was so used to it she didn't think to step up and demand to help make decisions. Sadie was still on her honeymoon, so he had to wait to learn more about her, but Jo had already told him several times about the way Sadie liked to dose her with herbal remedies and all the tricks Jo made use of to fool her sister into thinking she actually consumed them.

Four older sisters made for a harrowing existence, as far as Hunter could see. Jo needed a break. She needed space. She needed to be the master of her own destiny. This was her house. And even if he meant to share it with her, he knew he had to let her build it.

As she worked down the length of the house, he cut boards and handed them to her, passed her screws, put a hand on the cladding to hold it in place while she drilled guide holes. Whatever it took to get the job done.

"You're quiet today," she said finally.

"Thinking."

"About what?"

"You."

She rolled her eyes. "Not much to think about there."

"You'd be surprised." He hadn't meant it to sound lascivious, but somehow it did and he could see her exasperation. Jo boxed up her experiences, the way some people did. Romance was for romantic times. Work was work.

"Cass seems to be talking to you again." She returned to the job.

"Amazingly." Cass had been furious at first when she learned what Hunter had done, but then she'd simmered down and thanked him for telling the General she was pregnant.

"I've been putting it off, and that's ridiculous," she'd said. "I want to heal this family. Having this baby is the first step."

Hunter hoped she was right. As much as all the women held a grudge against the General, Hunter thought they missed him, too. Someday the man would have to come home to his ranch. He'd have learned about his grandchild one way or the other.

When his phone rang, he pulled it out absently but quickly accepted the call when he saw who it was.

"Hey—where've you been?"

"I don't have time for that. I need money, Hunter."

"Money? For what?" It didn't take any kind of hunch to know Marlon was in trouble. His voice was rough. He didn't sound together. "Where are you?"

"Look, you going to help or not? I can't talk."

"How much?"

Marlon named a sum that made Hunter whistle. "What do you need that for?"

"I don't have time." Marlon cut through his words. "Stop fucking around and answer the question."

"What the hell are you on right now?" Marlon's anger was palpable, and it had a reckless quality to it Hunter didn't like. Had he been drinking? That wasn't like Marlon. His friend prided himself on keeping his head on straight.

"I'm not on anything. I've got pictures, Hunter. Photographs. Her with *him*."

"Him?" He knew Marlon was talking about May, and he could only guess where this was headed. He gripped the phone more tightly.

"Yeah—him. The guy May's shacked up with. No wonder she doesn't want me coming by. She's not leaving me because we've grown apart. She's leaving me because she's fucking someone else!"

Hunter's heart sank. Marlon was furious, and this wasn't going to end well.

"The asshole detective I hired knows exactly where this dude lives, but he wants more money. He says there's more to tell me, but he won't say what until I pay him."

"Jesus." This wasn't good. "Where are you?"

"That doesn't matter."

"Are you at Coronado?"

When Marlon hesitated, Hunter swore. If he wasn't—he had to be in Alabama.

"Marlon, you need to get back to your team. This guy sounds like a total prick. He's playing you."

"He's not playing me. These photos are real!"

"Maybe. Maybe not. But you're AWOL again and you're going to screw everything up—"

"I'm already screwed. I need money. At least… send me enough to buy a plane ticket home."

Hunter stared at the phone. Marlon wasn't making sense. "Use your credit card."

"He won't take credit!"

So this was about the investigator again, not about plane tickets.

"He's got pictures, Hunter. I need to know who this guy is."

Marlon's voice cracked and Hunter winced again. He couldn't let his friend get anywhere near May—or the man she was with. The investigator, whoever he was, sounded like a piece of work, and Hunter wondered if a guy like that was already working out how to extort money out of May and her boyfriend, too.

"You need to get back to California. Now, Marlon."

"You're supposed to be such a good friend. Isn't that what you said when you were bossing me around? So give me the fucking cash!"

He was slurring his words. Drunk. High. Something. Screwing up big time after Hunter had put his whole future on the line to buy him another chance.

Hunter would do anything to shield Marlon. He

would hop on a plane and go to sort things out. He'd get Marlon to a motel. Give him time to dry out. Fly with him back to Coronado. He knew how much Marlon valued his family. Knew how terrified he was of losing his kids. This wasn't who his friend was.

But he was blowing it.

And there was no way Hunter would forward Marlon cash.

"Hunter? Come on, man. Make up your damn mind."

Hunter heard the desperation in Marlon's voice, but he held firm.

"I'll come and get you. Tell me where you are." He'd be putting his own future on the line—again. Risking the General's anger—and Jo's. He couldn't afford the expense right now, either, not when he'd promised to build Jo a house come spring. Couldn't afford to put off building her temporary home for a single week with winter bearing down on them.

"Just send the—"

"No money. I'm coming to take you back to San Diego."

"Fuck you!"

Marlon cut the call. Hunter leaned against the porch railing, gripping it hard enough he thought the wood would splinter in his hands. There was no other way he could have played that, he told himself. Marlon was a SEAL. Trained to kill. Out of his mind with rage and anguish at his wife's betrayal. The last thing he needed was her boyfriend's address.

And he couldn't keep Marlon's secrets anymore, not when things had gone this far. It killed him to know how angry Marlon would be, but he didn't think he had a choice. He made two more calls. One to Sue-Ann Frank. One to Marlon's home phone number, just in case May was checking their messages. Someone had to stop Marlon.

He was searching for a flight when his phone rang again a half hour later. It wasn't a familiar number.

"Powell here," he said when he took the call.

"Hunter?"

"Yes." The voice was familiar, but he didn't place it at first.

"It's Abel Frank."

"Abel." His gut tightened. Marlon's oldest brother.

"Mom told me what's going on."

"Yeah?"

"Why the hell did you wait so long to fill us in? We had no idea about the divorce—or about May stepping out on Marlon. Didn't you think we should know?"

"That was for him to decide."

"Yeah, right. The guy whose life was falling apart." Abel's voice rose. "And now he's AWOL. What's with you guys?"

Hunter didn't know how to answer that, either. It was bad enough he'd broken Marlon's confidence. Abel swore.

"It was Marlon the last time, too, wasn't it? He made a run for it, and what—you followed him? Brought him back? What'd you do? Take the fall for him?"

"Something like that," Hunter admitted reluctantly.

"Christ, what a mess. Hunter, I think I know where he lives—May's boyfriend. And I'm afraid if I was able to find out that fast, Marlon will, too, pretty soon."

Hunter's grip on the phone grew tighter. "How did you find him?"

"I asked around. No one was going to tell Marlon, but someone spilled the beans to me. Wasn't that hard to track him down once I had a name."

"What's the plan?"

"That's what I'm asking you. Marlon won't listen to me, you know that."

Hunter did know it. Marlon still resented the way Abel had lorded over him the whole time they'd grown up. He'd see any interference from his brother as a reason to dig in deeper.

"I don't even know where he's staying," Abel went on. "You need to go get him. Take him back to base."

"Hunter? What's wrong?" He turned and found Jo right behind him. "Is everything all right?" she asked.

"It's fine." He raised a hand to warn her off. He needed a moment to figure this out. He had to get everything under control—

But that's what he always did, wasn't it? Tried to control things, just like Jo had said.

He was trying to control Marlon, and it wasn't working for shit, was it? He'd handed Marlon a perfect way out of the mess he'd made for himself, but Marlon had gone and screwed up his second chance.

Even if he did manage to find the man and get him back on base—if he somehow miraculously saved Marlon's ass again—who was to say Marlon wouldn't screw it all up a third time?

Maybe he kept choosing this path because he needed to walk it.

"Are you going to say no, Hunter, after everything my family has done for you?" Abel asked.

Hunter closed his eyes, helpless against that line of attack. "Fine. I'll go," he growled.

"I'm texting you May's boyfriend's address. If Marlon's trying to find him, he's got to be around here somewhere close. You know all his old haunts. Hunt him down. Get him back to California safe and sound. We're counting on you."

Hunter cut the call and turned to face Jo.

"What was that all about?"

"Marlon. I need to go after him." He was already figuring out the logistics.

"Go after him? How long will you be gone?" Jo glanced at the tiny house and he knew why; fall was progressing. The rains would come soon and make it difficult to get anything done. His leaving now meant they might not be able to finish the house in time.

"I really don't know."

"YOU REALIZE YOU'RE going AWOL, too," Jo said when she pulled into a parking space at the Chance Creek Regional Airport early that afternoon. Hunter had found tickets to Alabama, and they'd rushed to get him packed and ready to travel. They'd told the others it was a family emergency, which her sisters had accepted without question. Brian had eyed Hunter thoughtfully, though, and Jo wished Hunter had simply told him the truth. She understood why he was trying to keep the details to himself: he was protecting his friend as best he could. Trying to contain a situation that didn't seem to Jo to be containable. Still, it bothered her he couldn't say when he'd be back.

In her experience, when someone left like that, they didn't come back at all.

Jo touched him briefly and was only partly reassured. There was that loyalty again, blazing strong. She felt deep worry, some of it directed at her. But a far deeper worry aimed at Marlon.

She tried to pull herself together as she parked the truck. Hunter had a past. Friends. Family. She didn't own him.

Hunter pulled his bag from the backseat and grabbed the door handle. "I'm sorry I'm asking you to cover for me if your father calls."

"Of course I'll cover for you." Lying to the General was the thing she and her sisters did best. The General tried to control them from afar—what was the harm in thwarting him once in a while?

"I'll be back just as soon as I can."

Jo swallowed, hard. How many times had she heard that before? In the first months after her mother's death, the General had pretended it was his job keeping him away. She remembered phone calls and video chats during which she'd begged him to come home before her sisters convinced her that showing weakness wasn't the way to deal with their father. It had broken her heart that he'd never come home, but she'd learned over time not to show it.

She hoped she wasn't showing her disappointment now.

"Jo, I don't want to do this," Hunter said.

Then don't. She didn't say the words out loud, but she didn't have to. Hunter's face pinched with concern.

"I'd much rather be with you."

Jo knew she was being unfair, but what was it about men that their other concerns always outweighed their love for you?

Love.

Hunter had been the one to bandy the word about first. Far too early to really mean it.

"I've got to go; I can't miss my flight." He leaned in to kiss her, and Jo closed her eyes as his lips brushed her cheek. She couldn't help the way she felt. This cut too close to the way men had treated her in the past. Hunter sighed. Glanced at his watch. "I'll be back. Soon. I promise."

She nodded. She wanted to believe him, but as he climbed out and closed the door behind him, she wondered if she'd ever see him again. Was she being dramatic?

Maybe.

But who could blame her in the circumstances?

Back at the ranch, she tried to lose herself in work,

but later that afternoon, when Alice asked if she wanted to ride along to the fabric store in town, Jo jumped at the chance. Anything to stop brooding over Hunter. In the truck, Alice hummed as she drove, and it dawned on Jo she was excited about something.

"What's going on?" Jo asked.

"Can you keep a secret?" Alice asked with a little bounce.

"Of course."

"I got an email today. From a costumes manager working for a major movie producer. He's got a project for me."

"What kind of project?"

"A Civil War movie. A saga." She took her eyes off the road briefly and met Jo's gaze. "Hoopskirts!"

Jo laughed despite herself. Hoopskirts were Alice's passion. She knew Alice enjoyed all kinds of period costumes, but the ones she loved the most were the ones with the most complicated undergarments. She was happy as a clam creating the Regency-era corsets for the ladies at Westfield who ran a Jane Austen–style bed and breakfast, but they were nothing compared to hoopskirts in Alice's eyes.

"Too bad it isn't a movie about the French Revolution," Jo teased, knowing the extravagant dresses of that era would send Alice over the moon.

"Stop it! Civil War gowns are just as good." Alice drove on. "Okay, not quite as good, but who knows? This is a big commission. If I get it and I do a good job, almost anyone might hire me. This could be the start of something huge!"

"You already get Hollywood commissions," Jo said. Wasn't that unbelievable enough? She didn't know how her sister managed it without leaving the ranch. Alice was just as devoted as the rest of them to their mother's property, and was as determined as they were to stay here. Only the quality of her costumes could force people to accept such a constrained arrangement.

"But not like this. He'll want dozens of costumes. Think of it; one of the scenes is a ball!"

Jo could see why Alice was so excited. "Of course you'll get it. What do you have to do?"

"Three introductory costumes. He sent the specs this morning. I'm looking to see what I can find in town before I place an online order."

Jo realized she'd signed onto a longer trip into town than she'd expected. She'd planned a quick trip to the grocery store and maybe a coffee at Linda's Diner while she waited for Alice to pick out her fabric. "I'll stop and see Megan if she's not too busy."

"Why don't I drop you off there? I'll want to hit the grocery store on our way back if you don't mind."

"Perfect."

A minute later, Alice pulled in and parked.

"There's Megan now." She pointed to the front door of the real estate office from which Megan had just emerged.

"Come say hi," Jo said and quickly got out of the truck.

Alice joined her, and when Megan spotted them, she

visibly brightened. "Hey, I'm off to get a cup of real coffee. Want to come?"

"Sure." Jo's spirits lifted. She could tell Megan what had happened with Hunter, and get her friend's take on it all.

"I'll join you for a minute, but not long. I need to keep moving," Alice said.

Settled into a booth at Linda's Diner fifteen minutes later, they had just been served their coffee when the door opened and Jo lifted her head to see a familiar man walk in.

"Don't look now, but that jerk is here," she interrupted Alice, who was telling Megan an anecdote from their childhood. She nudged Megan, who glanced up, took in Mr. Ramsey and sighed.

"I can't find anything he likes, but that doesn't stop him from coming around all the time. My boss probably told him where I was."

"He's spotted us," Alice said with a smile. "Too late to hide."

The man was making his way over to their table. Jo's spirits sank again; now Megan would have to leave and they wouldn't get a chance to talk.

But Mr. Ramsey slid into the bench seat by Alice without even saying hello. Alice, stuck, made a face, but gamely shoved over and made room for him.

"Paul, meet Alice and Jo. Paul Ramsey is a client of mine. Jo, you've met him before."

Jo knew Megan well enough to understand her friend felt trapped into making pleasantries. Her job was on the line.

"I remember," Jo said pointedly.

Ramsey leaned forward. "What about your ranch? Is it for sale?" he asked abruptly.

"No." Jo didn't offer any more of an explanation. She wasn't going to play games with this man.

"Sometimes people change their minds about that. Decide there are greener pastures somewhere else."

Jo couldn't believe the guy, and she was about to tell him to go shove his observations where the sun didn't shine when Megan said, "Alice? You all right?"

Alice had gone rigid. Her eyes were closed.

"Fire," she said. "Horses. Your house." She opened her eyes and stared at Jo. Turned to the man beside her. "Jail."

Jo went cold. So she'd been right; this man did plan to do them harm.

"What about the horses?" she asked at the same time Ramsey twisted around to get a better look at Alice.

"What the hell do you mean, jail?"

"I've got to go," Alice said, standing up. "I've got to go right now. So do you, Jo."

Jo stood as well.

"Now, wait a minute. We just started talking—" Ramsey cut off as Alice hopped up on the bench seat without another word, stepped up onto the table and hopped down into the aisle that ran the length of the restaurant. Megan pushed out of her seat quickly so Jo could get by, and followed them toward the door without a backward glance at her client.

Jo took Megan's arm. "Don't go anywhere alone with him. You heard Alice. Not alone. Not anymore."

Megan nodded, her face pinched with fear. She'd known the Reeds long enough to take Alice's predictions seriously. Jo didn't know how she'd manage to evade the man, though, considering her job. "I mean it, Megan."

"I won't." Megan leaned in closer, despite the fact Ramsey still sat in the booth where they'd left him, staring after them like he couldn't figure them out. "I know how to handle this. We've got a protocol if a guy gets forward when we're showing him houses. We pass him on to Mike."

Jo smiled despite the seriousness of the situation. She knew Mike. She doubted Ramsey would like him. "I'm sorry you'll lose the commission."

"I don't think I was ever going to get one. I don't know why Ramsey's here, but it isn't to buy a house."

"We've got to find Cab," Jo said on their way out of the diner, after settling the bill for the coffee they hadn't even consumed. "We've got to tell him everything."

THE ALABAMA HEAT was the first thing that struck Hunter after his time in the much drier, much cooler Montana town. He rented a boxy sedan he normally wouldn't be caught dead in, the better to be able to search for Marlon without drawing attention to himself.

Abel was probably right; maybe he should start looking for his friend in the usual places, but some instinct told him to drive straight to May's boyfriend's house. He had a feeling if anyone knew where Marlon was, it would be her.

She hadn't returned his earlier call, not that he thought she would. He and May had a complicated history—one that extended as far back as her relationship with Marlon. He'd known Marlon too well to believe his marriage to May was going to work out, and she'd known he'd felt that way. And didn't like him for it.

He pulled out the address Abel had given him, punched it into the sedan's GPS and got on the road. Time to stop Marlon before he did something he'd really regret.

He waited nearly three hours parked outside May's boyfriend's house before a black GMC truck pulled into the driveway, and May got out, circling the car to pull out a bag of groceries. The home was nothing special, a 1950s-era bungalow with a yard devoid of landscaping except a few leggy begonias by the front stoop. Hunter wondered if May would want to spruce the place up. Was she serious about this guy?

He got out of the sedan and strode across the yard to intercept her before she reached the front door.

May yelped and put her hand to her chest when she recognized him. "Hunter? What are you doing here? Did Marlon send you? Is he here, too?"

"No, and he doesn't know I am, but you should know he's somewhere close. He found out about your boyfriend and he's pissed. Where are the kids?"

"With my mom."

Up close, May looked tired. Her hair, usually her pride and glory, was caught back in a sloppy bun, a large plastic clip holding it askew. Her makeup was minimal, her lipstick chewed off.

So she was suffering, too.

Then she shifted her groceries and put a hand to the small of her back in a way he recognized. His eyes dropped to her belly. She looked like she'd put on weight—

"Oh, God." Hunter took another good, long look at her. "You're pregnant."

"That I am," May said tiredly. "And no, it's not Marlon's."

"You're going to kill him."

He thought she'd protest, but for once May seemed stripped of her usual snappy answers. "I know. I honestly didn't mean for it to happen like this, Hunter."

Hunter didn't know what to do. "You realize he went off the deep end when you filed for divorce. You realize—" He cut off. He couldn't spill Marlon's secrets. "He loves you."

"Does he? Really?" May challenged him. "Because I don't think so. I think when this is all over he'll be just as relieved as I am. We were never right for each other; everyone knew it. You said so from the start. We rushed into a marriage and it didn't work. We're not the first and we won't be the last."

"But you've got kids."

"Yeah, we do. And it's been rough on all of us, but

Marlon's not making it better."

"Couldn't you have waited until he was out of the military to do all this? It's just another month and a half. He wouldn't be facing a court martial for deserting his team if you had."

She looked down at her belly pointedly. "No. I can't wait for another month and a half. My life has moved on. He needs to realize that. So do you. I brought up divorce months ago. He could have worked with me and made this a done deal. He's the one dragging it out. I want to marry Arthur. Before I have this baby." She shifted the bag of groceries again and frowned. "Did you say court martial?"

"As far as I can make out, he's on his way here."

May's shoulders slumped. "So he's AWOL again? He's making it worse for everyone."

"Then help me find him. Help me get him back to his team. Because I don't know where he is." Hunter held his breath. Would May know where to look? It would make all of this so much easier.

"The Douglas Point Motel," she said immediately. "I'll bet anything he's there. We used to slip away…"

Hunter turned on his heel and walked back to the sedan.

"MY PROBLEM IS I can't arrest anyone on the basis of a hunch," Cab said.

"Alice's visions are way more than hunches, Sheriff. You know that." Jo leaned forward in her chair. She and Alice sat in front of Cab's desk. They'd dropped Megan off at her real estate office with admonitions to keep far away from Ramsey.

Cab shrugged. "Doesn't change anything. I still can't arrest anyone. I'll do my best to keep an eye on things, though. I'll send a cruiser by your place several times a day, and we'll keep an eye on Ramsey as best we can.

"You aren't taking this seriously enough." Jo sat back in defeat.

"I'm absolutely taking this seriously. Rest assured all my men will be on alert. I want all of you to be on alert, too. You tell Brian and Hunter everything you've told me. They'll set up a watch on the ranch, too. When's Conner getting home?"

"Not for another few days."

"He shouldn't have gone for so long."

"India's a long way off," Alice pointed out. "It's his honeymoon; he deserves a break, and so does Sadie. I just wish Hunter was here."

Jo nudged her. Alice looked down. "I mean—"

Cab frowned. "Where'd he get to?"

"Alabama. Family business," Jo rushed to say. No sense hiding his location now that Alice had spilled the beans.

Cab swore. "Does the General know that?"

"No. And you're not going to tell him."

"As far as I know, Hunter's still in the Navy," Cab said. "Which means he's AWOL right now. He's supposed to be guarding you."

It was Jo's turn to frown. "He's not supposed to be guarding me; he's supposed to build me a house."

Cab turned to Alice. "What about those hunches of yours? Will you get one when the trouble starts?"

"It doesn't work that way. I can't predict my predictions." Alice sighed and stood up. "But thank you for doing what you can, Sheriff."

"This isn't a large department," Cab said apologetically as he ushered them to the door. "We're thin on the ground, and we have to patrol the highway as well as all of Chance Creek County. I'll do whatever I can, you can count on that. But all of you down at Two Willows need to do your part. Stay vigilant. And tell Hunter to get his ass back where he belongs."

Jo didn't know whether to feel better or worse after they'd left the building. "You shouldn't have said anything about Hunter."

"It slipped out. It didn't occur to me he was still in the Navy. That he's gone AWOL." Alice was quiet a minute. "Do you think… are we… a mission?" Her pretty face was twisted in concentration.

"What do you mean?" But Jo thought she knew exactly what Alice meant, and it didn't make her feel a bit better.

"Brian, Connor, Hunter… is the General ordering men to marry us?"

THE DOUGLAS POINT Motel was about as inspiring as he'd predicted, Hunter thought sourly as he pulled in and parked in an empty spot. In fairness, there wasn't anything wrong with it. The paint looked new. The planters were planted with cheerful annuals. It was cared for.

It also housed a man whose life he was about to turn on end.

Hunter was tired, and more to the point, he was discouraged. Seeing May had made it clear there was no hope for his friend's marriage. He thought he'd already understood that, but some part of him must have been holding out for a happy ending, after all. If Marlon had been desperate when May had served him divorce papers, he'd be distraught when he learned she was pregnant with another man's child.

He didn't know how long it would take to get Marlon back on his feet, and he needed to return to Montana before Jo lost faith in him. He knew she felt he'd abandoned her—just when she needed him. Time was passing; winter was on its way. They didn't have any days to spare where building the house was concerned.

Telling Marlon about May wasn't going to get any easier, though. Might as well get it over with. He stopped in the main office, where a teenage clerk gave out Marlon's room number without needing to be asked twice. Marlon popped his head out of room nine before Hunter even reached it.

"Get over here, Hunter."

Hunter bit back a chuckle. Of course the SEAL had been keeping an eye out for trouble.

"Nice to see you, too, Marlon."

"Did Mom send you?" He tugged Hunter into the room and shut the door. They faced each other over a worn green carpet. Hunter swept his gaze around the place. Tidy but tired, just as he'd expected.

"Abel did. And so did May."

The bravado went out of Marlon just like that. He sat down on the orange-and-brown coverlet of the bed. "May sent you?"

"I paid her a visit. Had a little talk with her."

"So people helped you but not me. I had to pay an investigator to find her, and he turned out to be a crook. He still hasn't given me the address of that guy she's with."

"People were afraid to help you," Hunter said bluntly. "You're supposed to be one of the good guys, remember?"

Marlon opened his mouth to retort, then waved their talk away. "I can see you've got news. Spill it."

Hunter took in the case of beer on the table and the empty cans piled around the trash can. He wished he could think of a way to sugar-coat what he had to say, but there was nothing for it but to tell him the unvarnished truth. "May's pregnant. It's not yours." Pull the Band-Aid off quickly. Wasn't that the usual advice?

Marlon surged to his feet. Covered his face with his hands, then threw them down. His fingers balled into fists. "Hunter—"

"Easy there. I know you want to hit something. Don't hit me."

Marlon paced, first one way, then the other. He kept pulling back to throw a punch—at the wall—at something—

But he held himself back. Hunter was gratified to

see his friend could exercise self-control. Maybe this wouldn't be as bad as he thought.

"What did she say to you?" Marlon finally asked, anguish tightening his voice.

"She didn't mean for it to happen this way. She loves the baby's father. She wants to marry him."

Marlon rocked on his feet, taking each sentence like a blow. He sat down abruptly on the bed again. "Then she's really gone. May's gone."

"I know, buddy." Hunter kept his place. Waited.

When his friend dropped his head into his hands and began to sob, Hunter crossed the room, sat beside him and braced himself for a long night.

"HE'S COMING BACK," Jo said several days later to Cass, replying to Hunter's text with alacrity. Relief made her giddy and she realized she'd half expected him to disappear from her life. She shouldn't have been so worried—he'd been texting her daily. Giving her updates. Now that she knew he had plane tickets, she could relax.

"Of course he's coming back," Cass said. "Did you think he wouldn't?" She stopped halfway to the cupboard, in the middle of preparing a chicken dinner. "Jo, did you think he'd left for good?"

Jo shrugged, not wanting her to know it had kept her awake every night since he'd gone. Paired with her anxiety about Alice's vision, she'd struggled to rest for more than an hour at a time. Brian had tried to mount a one-man guard duty after calling Hunter and chewing him out. Lena had insisted on helping, and Jo had taken her turn, too. That meant broken nights of sleep had piled up until she was hardly sure if she was coming or going.

"Anyone could see that man's head over heels for you," Cass assured her. "When will he get in?"

"Tonight. Late. He said he'll take a cab home."

"Better take a nap so you're ready for him."

Jo didn't think she'd sleep a wink tonight either. She was far too excited, which was almost as unnerving as anything else that had happened recently. Since when did she care so much?

She nearly rolled her eyes. She couldn't pretend she didn't care for Hunter anymore. She did. Even if the General had sent him to marry her. Even if she should refuse to even speak with him on principle, let alone make love to him. Life was weird. There was no getting around that.

She decided to go with it.

The rest of the day she did her chores with only half her mind on them, until that evening Lena thumped her on the arm and told her to go back to the house since she was useless in the barn.

Jo went willingly, wanting to shower and spruce up before Hunter got home, and Cass was right; maybe she should shut her eyes for a minute so she could be awake for their reunion. When she was ready, she grabbed the book of Hunter's mother's poetry she'd ordered off the internet and curled up on the living room couch under a throw blanket. She'd found the poems slow going so far, packed with dense imagery of nature juxtaposed against human angst. The word 'choices' popped up a lot.

"I'm heading up to bed," Cass told her. "Brian's keeping watch outside."

"Hunter and I will take the second shift," Jo said. It wouldn't be any hardship to stay awake through the early morning hours with as much to catch up on as they'd have.

After reading a poem or two, she'd only closed her eyes—or so it seemed to her—when she woke up, hearing a thump on the back porch and Brian shouting.

"Someone's stealing the house!"

Jo thrashed around until she got free of the blanket, staggered to her feet and lost precious time getting her bearings as Max, who'd appeared from nowhere, ran in circles and barked. The clock on the old VCR under their ridiculously outdated television set told her it was 1:30 in the morning.

Where was Hunter? He was supposed to be home.

Jo spotted her phone on the couch beside her, grabbed it up and raced toward the back porch, Max following. Somewhere outside a truck's engine roared past. A door slammed. Another truck started up and roared after it.

There were two texts from Hunter.

Plane delayed. Leaving at 11 instead of 9.

Plane delayed again. Not sure when I'll get there. Go to bed—see you in the morning.

She shoved the phone in her pocket and yanked open the back door, careful to shut Max in the house as she went outside. Brian was nowhere to be seen, but the porch told a story. The wicker seat he must have been sitting in—and possibly sleeping in—lay overturned. His truck was gone from the parking area. Jo clattered down the steps in her bare feet and paced a few yards out to try to see what might have happened.

Someone's stealing the house. Brian's nonsensical shout replayed through her mind. She'd been in the house. How could anyone steal—?

The tiny house.

Jo raced toward it but she already knew what she'd find. Brian was right; it was gone. Who would steal her house when it wasn't even done?

Instantly, an image of Ramsey filled her mind.

It had to be him. And he had to be connected to the group in Tennessee who seemed determined to punish them for blowing up their drugs.

Jo paced, not knowing what to do, before grabbing her phone again to call Cab.

But as she turned, something caught her eye. A flash of orange in the distance.

Flames.

"Fire!" Jo screamed. "Lena, Cass, Alice! Fire!"

She sprinted down the dirt track that led to the out-buildings, the hard earth cold under her bare feet, but even before she reached them she heard the sound she'd dreaded all the way.

Horses whinnying. Screaming with fear and the

need to escape.

She remembered Alice at the restaurant. *Horses. Fire.*

Jo reached the stables in record time, but already flames shot skyward, the building half-engulfed.

Jo heard the frantic whinnying of the horses, heard their hoof beats pounding on the wooden walls of their stalls. She didn't think twice before she dashed into the building as a horse raced out and nearly ran her over.

That was Button, she realized as she leaped out of the way. He must have knocked down his stall door. That left four more, including Bright Star. She made another attempt and got into the stables this time, smoke instantly swirling around her in a thick soup that was impossible to see through and even harder to breathe in.

Remembering what she knew about fires, Jo dropped to her knees and crawled, keeping as low to the floor as she could. She knew this building like the back of her own hand. She didn't need to see—just needed to get to the stalls. Which should be right—

Here.

Her hand hit the corner of the first stall and she felt the reverberation of Priscilla's hoofs clattering against the door. She wouldn't need to guide the mare out. All she needed to do was open the door.

Which meant she had to stand up. Jo held her breath and did so, her eyes watering in the acrid smoke. It took two tries to force the bolt open, but as soon as she did, Priscilla flung past Jo and raced for the stable door.

Jo didn't hesitate. The next stall's door was off its hinges, but the following one was bolted tight and she struggled to open it, her chest constricted in the heavy smoke, dizzy and light-headed from breathing it in. When she finally got it open, River hesitated, unhappy with the dark conditions. Jo had to feel her way in, keep from being stepped on and slap River's rear several times to get him going. Luckily he bolted for the door when he got going.

Two more.

A creak above her head made Jo look up. The entire roof was on fire. Conditions were getting dangerous; she had to work fast. Flames crawled up three walls, and if she wasn't quick, the thick beams supporting the building could give way. She moved as quickly as she could to the next stall, feeling her way, and got that bolt open, too.

"Come on, Bright Star," she cried. "Time to go."

Bright Star seemed to agree. She danced and side-stepped a moment before racing past in the right direction, snorting and whinnying in distress.

Only Atlas was left. Lena's stallion. She could do this.

Jo dropped to her knees and rested a second, wind-ed. Her chest burned. Eyes stung and watered so badly she could barely open them. She knew she had to push forward, but the heat and lack of oxygen were getting to her. She needed to rest.

When her head snapped forward and she nearly fell over, Jo realized she was about to make a deadly mistake. She couldn't rest. Couldn't slide into unconsciousness.

Another groan from the timbers above her gave her the impetus she needed to push to her knees, reach up, feel for the bolt on the last door and pull herself up. She tried to slide it open, but unlike the others, this one always caught. You had to push against the door before it moved correctly. Jo leaned into it, pushed against the door—

And screamed as a beam gave way above her, crashed down, glanced off her shoulder and knocked her to the ground.

Jo writhed around in an agony of pain. Her shoulder felt as if it had exploded. She realized it had been knocked out of its socket. Every movement hurt enough to nearly push her into unconsciousness.

Dislocated shoulder. Dislocated shoulder…

Jo tried to remember what she knew of such an injury. She had to shove it back in or she'd be useless; no way she could get the stall open without two hands.

Forcing herself to her knees, wavering there, then forcing herself to her feet, Jo tried to orient herself. She found the nearest solid post, stepped back, turned sideways, braced herself—

And slammed against it with all her might.

Her shoulder popped into place as Jo staggered around, her mouth open but no sound coming out. She sobbed, the pain nearly toppling her again.

Horse. Atlas. She had to get him out. She couldn't let Lena down; her sister loved that stallion. It meant everything to her.

Where was everyone? Hadn't they heard her?

As if on cue, a shout came from outside, and Jo blinked, coming to herself.

Looked around her.

Nearly slid to her knees in shock. She was inside an inferno—

Flames crawled over every surface, on all sides, above her, too—as if she inhabited a cinder, the glow and snap and heat everywhere she looked.

No one could help her in here.

Atlas threw himself against the door of his stall, rattling it, bringing Jo back to action. She reached for the bolt. Burned herself. Wrapped her hand in her shirt and tried again, bracing her good shoulder against the door and pushing hard.

It sprung free—just as Atlas slammed his weight against it again—and knocked Jo to the floor. Atlas crashed right over her as he raced toward the stable entrance.

Jo heard a man shout—fought against the darkness closing in on all sides.

Lost.

HUNTER WAS IN the back of a cab when his phone buzzed. Finally—it must be Jo, who hadn't acknowledged his texts that his plane was delayed. Was she pissed? He worried she might be; he'd tried to keep her in the loop, but watching over Marlon had been a full-time job.

He'd finally turned his friend over to the Franks, who'd already started smoothing things over with the Navy. Hunter had no idea how that would play out. He could only hope there'd be leniency for a man with only weeks to go in his term of service.

It wasn't Jo calling, though; it was Cab, and when he answered, the sheriff was gruff.

"You in town yet?"

"Almost home."

"Glad to hear you remembered your mission."

Hunter wondered what bug the man had up his ass. "I remember my mission."

"Then get home. I just got a call from Two Willows—that ranch you're supposed to be protecting? There's a fire there. Thought you'd want to know."

"Fire?" Hunter dropped the phone. Leaned forward to yell at the cab driver. "Hit the gas. Now! Two Willows is on fire!"

The cabbie hit the gas, throwing Hunter back against the seat, and all he could do was hold on for the last few miles before they reached the ranch.

Hadn't anyone been keeping watch? What the hell was Brian thinking? He wanted to kick himself for ever leaving Jo, wanted to pound his fists together for having taken a chance and gone after Marlon. But he needed to save his strength. He needed to be ready for whatever came next.

It took forever to reach Two Willows, the country highway twice as long as it had ever been before, but at last they turned the corner into the lane that led to the house. All the lights were on, but he saw no signs of smoke, and he breathed a sigh of relief. The fire must've been small.

"Maybe they put it out already," the cabbie said.

"Wait—"

A flash of orange caught his eye as the cabbie pulled around to the back of the house, slowed to park the truck, then gunned the gas again, swerving onto the track that led to the outbuildings. Was that the barn? No, the stables.

Engulfed in flames.

"Hurry!" But the cabbie already had the pedal to the floor.

There were figures moving around in front of the fire. Female figures. Cass, Alice, Lena—

Where was Jo?

The cabbie brought the car as close as he could to the stables, and Hunter jumped out of the truck before the engine died.

A stallion charged out of the door. Lena lunged to grab it, but it flew past her, nearly knocking her to the dirt.

As Hunter sprinted toward them, Cass shouted, "She's in there! Jo's in there!"

Hunter didn't stop to think. He snatched the robe Alice had wrapped loosely around her shoulders, dashed to a horse trough, where he dunked it under the surface of the water and pulled it out again. He wrapped the soaking cloth around his neck, pulled it up over his nose—and ran straight into the burning stables.

He heard Lena's shout as he ran by, thought she might've reached out to grab him to prevent him from entering, but Hunter moved past her so fast she didn't stand a chance. Inside, the stables were an inferno, and Hunter knew his chances of finding Jo alive were slim.

That didn't matter—he had to try. He had to find her; couldn't leave her in here. As he battered his way through the flames, the rafters overhead groaned and he spared a glance upward, cursing when he took in the woven flames that made up the roof.

"Jo?" He coughed, the smoke choking him through the cloth he'd wrapped around his face, making his eyes water, making it impossible to see. "Jo!"

He couldn't hear anything over the roar of the fire. He was risking immolating himself by staying here. It was too late—he'd arrived far too late. Everything was on fire. Soon he'd burn, too.

Something collapsed ahead of him; the wall of one of the horse stalls. He made his way toward it. Jo would've come to save the horses. If she was in here, she had to be somewhere nearby.

"Jo!" Where was she?

He stumbled forward a few more feet, knowing that soon the heat, smoke and lack of oxygen would bring him low. He was going to die in here if he didn't get out soon.

He couldn't leave without Jo.

He stumbled over something, crashed to his knees, felt around himself, his hands bumping into something lumpy, not quite solid—

Flesh and bone.

"Jo?"

A groan answered him. It had to be her. Hunter didn't waste any time trying to figure out her condition. He scooped her up, her feminine curves reassuring him he'd found what he was looking for. He had to get her out of here, now. The building was going to come down on them any moment.

Disoriented, Hunter searched for the door in the dim light, through the thick smoke. He couldn't see anything except flames. He staggered forward not knowing if he was heading in the right direction, trying to rely on instincts that had become confused by the circumstances and his fall.

"Hunter!"

Hunter didn't answer Lena's call, he simply followed the sound of her voice gratefully. He had to be close to the exit—nearly outside.

"Hunter, watch out!"

Lena's warning was almost lost in the bone-grindingly loud sound of the stables collapsing. Hunter threw himself forward, trying to cradle Jo on the way down, but he landed heavily on her, the two of them tumbling from the impact. Behind them, the stables caved in with a crash that shook the ground. Someone screamed. Hunter tried to get up but found he couldn't move. He couldn't breathe. His wrists ached as if he'd broken them.

And Jo, on the ground next to him, lay perfectly still.

Chapter Twelve

"I DON'T THINK you'll do that again," Amelia said.

As she lay between the crisp, starched sheets of her childhood bed, the sun streaming in a nearby window, Jo gazed at her mother. Her throat felt like she'd swallowed an ashtray, and she stifled the urge to cough, still not wanting to admit what she'd done.

Caught smoking. No one at Two Willows smoked. She was in for it.

"I'm not angry," her mother went on. "Some lessons you have to learn for yourself. Some infractions have their own punishments."

"Will I have to stay home from the fair?" she croaked.

Her mother was right; she'd hated the taste of the cigarettes the minute Katie Hemley had handed her one, but she'd gone on smoking it because the other girls had said she couldn't hang out with them if she didn't.

"All you Reeds, so high and mighty, barely leaving your ranch," Katie had said. "If you're one of us, act like it."

She'd smoked that cigarette, and she'd smoked three

more, even though she realized now everyone else had made their first ones last quite a bit longer. They'd tried to make her sick intentionally. Her mother was right; some transgressions had their own punishments.

Now she'd ruined everything. Her father was coming home from USSOCOM for the weekend and taking them all to the fair. She didn't want to miss that.

"I'll never smoke again," Jo promised. "And I'll never do anything with those stupid girls again. I'll stay at home. Forever. I don't need friends."

"Just because you chose unwisely once doesn't mean you should give up on everyone." Amelia laughed. "I'm sure there are other girls who'll help you make good choices. And of course you'll go to the fair. In this family we stick together. No one gets left behind."

Jo only half heard her. She was looking down at the bed she was tucked into. At the sheets.

Sheets imprinted with hundreds of tiny horses. Sheets she hadn't slept between since she was eleven.

She wasn't eleven. She was twenty-one. And her mother—

Her mother was—

Amelia squeezed her hand again. Leaned forward to brush a kiss against Jo's brow. "Remember, no one gets left behind. I love you. Always."

"Don't go," Jo said. "Mom!" Panic filled her lungs.

"I'll never be far away. Open your eyes, Jo. It's time to wake up."

"Mom—"

Jo opened her eyes. She was lying in bed, between crisp clean sheets, but they were stark white, not dotted with horses. Sitting on the edge of the bed, leaning over, holding her hand, staring down with worried eyes, was Cass, not her mother.

"Mom?" Jo whispered.

Cass's eyes shone with tears. "I'm sorry, honey. She's not here."

Jo tried to sit up, but Cass urged her to stay lying down. "I saw her," Jo said. "She said—she said she loved me."

"Of course she loves you. She always will." Cass smoothed Jo's hair away from her brow. "We all love you."

Jo looked around. Pushed up on her elbows. "The fire—"

She hadn't been smoking. That was an old memory. She'd run to the fire—the stables—the horses—

"What about the others?"

"Lena and Alice are fine. The horses all got out. You saved all of them, Jo. Brian's furious with himself for being fooled by the men who stole your house. Alice is in the waiting room. Lena's at home, of course."

Of course. One of the Reed women always had to be on the ranch. Even at the worst of times they'd follow Amelia's precedent. Their mother had made that bargain with God to keep the General safe, and despite everything they'd keep it—for her sake.

Jo collapsed back on her pillow with relief, but it was short-lived. Someone had rescued her. Someone strong. Someone—

She scrambled up again. "Hunter—"

Cass pushed her gently down again, arranged the sheets to cover her. "Hunter's fine, too. I don't think you'll have to wait long to see him."

"I'M FINE," HUNTER growled for the third time and pushed away the oxygen mask the nurse was trying to refasten over his mouth and nose. "I don't need that and I don't need to be in bed."

"Doctor's orders," the nurse said sternly. She was obviously losing her patience. "You need to rest, and you need to give your lungs a break. You put them through quite a workout."

The door opened, and Alice poked her head in. "Jo's awake. She's doing just fine. I thought you'd want to know."

Hunter threw off the covers, lurched out of the bed and was out the door before the nurse could stop him. Hardly aware of the hospital gown flapping where its ties were loose behind him, he strode off down the corridor before Alice yelled after him, "Wrong way, sailor."

She was grinning when he turned on his heel and moved to follow her, and Hunter relaxed a little. Alice wouldn't smile if Jo was in any danger. When they got to Jo's room, he waited for Alice to open the door, then pushed past her and crossed to Jo's bed. Without a thought for her bumps and bruises, he gathered her up in his arms and kissed her.

"Ouch!" She did her best to kiss him back, wincing and laughing.

Hunter pulled back and tried to be gentler. "I thought I'd lost you. When I saw the flames—heard the horses—"

"Not yet. It'll take more than a burning stable and a

couple of unruly horses to get rid of me."

She looked pale, though. Her hands and feet were wrapped in gauze and her hair singed. There were bandages on several other parts of her, too. She'd taken such a risk saving the horses. He really could have lost her.

Hunter's chest tightened, and this time he hugged her far more gently. He couldn't do without this woman, and it left him breathless to think he might have had to.

How could he have gone on with his life knowing what he'd lost? No woman had ever touched his heart like she had. He didn't think he could ever feel about someone else the way he felt about Jo.

He had to let her know that right now. Hospital be damned. Maybe it wasn't the most romantic setting, but he couldn't wait another moment.

"I don't want to get rid of you. I want you with me always. I want to share your life. Jo Reed, will you marry me?"

Jo gaped at him, and Hunter couldn't blame her. His question must seem to her to come out of nowhere. They'd never discussed marriage at all. But the events of the preceding night had cut through any doubts that tangled in his mind. This was the woman he wanted, and he wanted her now. Forever.

"Say yes," Alice stage-whispered.

Hunter watched Jo's gaze rest first on Alice and then Cass before coming back to him. "Yes," she said hoarsely, cleared her throat and tried again. "Yes, I'll marry you."

Hunter pulled her into another embrace and never wanted to let her go. "You won't regret this. I swear."

Jo pressed her cheek against his. "I've never regretted a minute I've spent with you."

SEVERAL DAYS LATER, Hunter and Brian sat across the kitchen table from Cab Johnson at Two Willows. Max had parked himself by Hunter's feet. Tabitha sat on top of the refrigerator where Alice liked to perch.

"We got lucky," Cab told them. "We caught the thieves heading for Bozeman. Idiots were still trailing the house. If they'd ditched it, we would've never found them. I don't know if they planned to sell it or wanted it for a garden shed."

"Who were they?" Hunter demanded.

"Couple of local small-time criminals from Bozeman. They work as bouncers at a club there and hire their muscle out for other, more lucrative jobs, apparently. Not the sharpest tools in the shed, though. They were paid well to provide a distraction while Ramsey set the fire. They were supposed to take their money, head back to Bozeman and lay low for a while. They got greedy. Took one look at that beautiful little house the two of you were building and decided they could probably sell it for a pretty penny if they carted it off. It slowed them down. Took a bit of work but we got them to talk. They spilled everything they knew. Unfortunately, that's not much."

"Can't find good help these days," Brian said sarcastically.

"That's my line," Cab said. "Anyway, they confirmed Ramsey comes from Tennessee. Admitted they took the potshot at your horse to see what kind of defenses you had in place. They said setting fires is Ramsey's specialty, but it won't surprise you to find out that Ramsey is an alias. We don't know who he really is, but I've got contacts in Tennessee working on it. We'll get him and throw him in jail for arson if I've got any say in the matter. There's got to be a reason one of the crime families down there is so interested in Chance Creek, and when we find him, I hope we get an answer to that. Anyway, I don't think you have to worry about the idiots who tried to steal your house. They'll show up for court and pay their fines. They don't want this kind of heat on them."

"But this is the point where you tell us it's not over yet," Brian said tiredly.

"You stole my line again."

When he had gone, Brian turned to Hunter. "So there's more trouble coming sooner or later."

"Most likely."

"And we've got something else to sort out. I got a call from Logan a while back. He's pretty choked. He said you got sent to USSOCOM for going AWOL from your team. Want to tell me about that? I've been holding him back for weeks, although he's simmered down after the way you saved Jo, but I got to admit, we're all pretty curious. None of this works unless you're the kind of man who sticks around."

"I am the kind of man who sticks around," Hunter said. "I'd have told you all about it if there wasn't someone else involved who could get hurt."

"I think at this point either we trust each other or we don't," Brian said.

"I could turn that right back around on you," Hunter pointed out, then sighed. Brian was right; he couldn't hold secrets back from these men. "It all started when I was a junior in high school. No, scratch that." He paused. "Hell, it started before I was born. Guess you could say my mom fell for the wrong man." Telling his story a second time wasn't nearly as hard as it had been the first time, and when he was done, Brian nodded.

"Thought it had to be something like that. Not your fault," he clarified. "I couldn't have come up with the rest of that story in a hundred years," he added with a chuckle. "I'm glad to hear you aren't the type to cut and run at the first sign of trouble. Because I think we've got a ways to go."

"I think so, too."

"I'll talk to Logan."

"Talk to Jack, too, while you're at it."

Brian lifted an eyebrow.

"I'm pretty sure he knows most of it," Hunter said.

Brian chuckled again, ruefully. "Yeah, I'm pretty sure he knows just about everything."

Chapter Thirteen

CONNOR AND SADIE arrived home from their honeymoon on a blustery afternoon that made it all too clear winter was fast approaching. Hunter thought the time away from Two Willows had done both of them good. He enjoyed hearing their stories about their travels in India, and the photos they'd taken were spectacular. Max was overjoyed that his master had come home, and Hunter sighed, knowing he'd miss the companionship of the little dog.

"I'm so happy to be home," Sadie said, after they'd sat around the dining room table and talked for a while. "The garden looks good," she said to Cass.

"I did my best," Cass said, "but when you get out there and see how many weeds there are, you're not going to thank me."

"Your customers are going to be happy to see you back," Alice said from her perch on top of the refrigerator. "I did my best to match their ailments with the proper tonics, but some of them I had to send away until you came home."

"I can't wait to see your house," Sadie told Jo.

"When will it be ready for you to move in?"

"It's still going to take another couple of weeks," Jo said. "There's lots to do on the interior. And it got damaged a little bit when it was stolen."

"Not too badly, though," Hunter said. "We'll get it done before the real weather moves in, I hope."

"I'd be happy to help out," Connor said. "I enjoyed building the walled garden. I wouldn't mind another project."

"I'll help, too," Brian said. "If you want me."

Hunter looked to Jo for confirmation before he answered. She nodded. "Sure, we'd be happy to have some help."

"Seems like this would be a good night for pizza and margaritas," Alice said. "And a movie or two, of course," she added.

"I was hoping somebody would say that," Sadie said. "Don't get me wrong; the food in India was to die for, but I've been looking forward to some old favorites."

Cass and Brian headed to town to pick up the pizzas and movies. Sadie and Connor went upstairs to unpack. Alice stayed in the kitchen to assemble the rest of the meal, while Lena headed for the back door to check on the animals. Jo followed Lena, and Hunter was about to follow her when his phone buzzed in his pocket. He pulled it out automatically and stiffened when he saw the number.

"Marlon?"

"Yeah, it's me. Got a minute to talk?"

"Of course. Where are you?"

"On base. Just wanted to give you a head's up. I signed the divorce papers. May and I are sharing custody. We've worked out the visitation schedule. The Navy knows everything. And I mean everything."

Hunter leaned heavily against the counter. "You told them—?"

"Yeah, I told them about what you did for me," Marlon repeated. "Told them you didn't deserve to be taken off your team. They're being lenient to me. I guess this isn't the first time someone's gone off their rocker over a divorce."

It wouldn't be the last time either, Hunter figured. Military life could be brutal for those left at home. And for those in the service, too.

"I wish it had turned out different."

"Me, too. But it didn't. And I'll survive this. Maybe it's for the best, really. I want May to be happy, and she wasn't happy with me. Truth be told, I haven't been happy with her, either. Not for a long time." Marlon took a deep, ragged breath. "I know I've let you down, Hunter. You did so much for me, and I just kept blowing it. I hope you'll get another chance to get back to the career that you loved. The career you gave up for me."

Hunter didn't know what to say about that. It was a relief to think his name might be cleared before too much damage was done, but on the other hand he'd made a series of choices that had led him to a different life. If he was going to marry Jo, he didn't want to return to the SEALs. He wasn't sure he could keep a clear head if he was worried about what might happen to her at home.

"I'm getting married," he blurted and wanted to kick himself. Marlon had just lost his wife. It wasn't fair to crow about his happiness under the circumstances.

"You're... what?"

"Married," Hunter repeated. "To Jo. The woman I told you about."

There was a long silence on the other end of the phone. "That's... terrific. Ironic, but terrific. Really, man. I'm happy for you."

"I know you don't want to hear this now, but there'll be someone else for you."

"Maybe. I don't know. Someday, I guess."

Hunter could tell Marlon had something else to say.

"Why the hell are you still talking to me after all I've put you through?"

That was easy. Hunter owed Marlon so much he could never repay the debt. "Because if you hadn't screwed up, I wouldn't be here—about to marry the best thing that's ever happened to me."

"I'm glad something good came out of all of this."

"You know, I wouldn't be surprised if someday you look back on this and see that it's pushed you in the right direction, too."

"Maybe. First I've got to sit in the brig for a month. The Navy's being lenient, but not that lenient. I'm actually considering re-upping."

"Oh, yeah?" Hunter wasn't surprised. Marlon loved

being a SEAL.

"You might not believe this but it sounds like they might actually take me back. If I do some counseling. I guess I'll lose rank…"

"Might be worth it."

"Yeah. Might be."

"Sounds like you might miss the wedding, though." Hunter would've liked to have his friend there. He and Jo had decided to marry before winter set in.

"I'll be there in spirit, even if I'm not there in person," Marlon said. "But I won't lie to you, man; it's going to suck not to see you take those vows. I guess I always figured I'd be there for that. I'm letting you down again."

He sounded so discouraged, Hunter stepped in to deny it. "You couldn't let me down if you tried, you got that? All I want is for you to be happy, too. Do your time. Figure out what comes next."

"Sounds like a plan. Good luck with your wedding. I'll see you as soon as I can."

Hunter had barely hung up from his call with Marlon, his heart heavy with the knowledge of all his friend would have to go through before he put his life back together again, when his phone rang a second time. It was the General.

They'd spoken after the fire, the General berating him for not being there when Jo ran into the burning stables. Hunter had accepted the blame. He thought the same thing. They'd spoken about what might happen next, about Connor being back soon. The General hadn't given him a chance to say that he'd proposed to Jo, or what her answer had been, and in truth he'd been grateful to hang up without having that conversation on that particular day. Better to give the man a chance to calm down. He knew the General was worried for his girls—and rightly so.

"So you thought that was smart, huh?" the General said without preamble. "Lying for a friend. Taking the fall for him?"

"At the time I did," Hunter answered truthfully.

"Lucky for you, I didn't call you to give you a hard time," the General said.

"You didn't?" Hunter couldn't keep the surprise from his voice.

"No, I didn't. I called to say as far as the Navy is concerned, you're off the hook, although you will get a reprimand for lying to a superior officer."

"What exactly does that mean?" Hunter asked slowly. "I'm still a SEAL?"

"Of course you're still a SEAL," the General said. "You're still in the service. You always were."

"But my mission here—at the ranch—your daughter—"

"You mean your failed mission at my ranch? I don't suppose that matters anymore."

Hunter straightened, alarmed. "But—"

"Like I said, you're off the hook. You can go back to your unit."

"I don't want to go back. I want to stay here. With Jo. I'm marrying her—in about three weeks. And you're going to pull whatever strings it takes to terminate my enlistment. Because once my ring is on her finger, and she's taken my name, I'm not leaving this ranch again. Do I make myself clear?"

Too late he realized he was shouting at the General, but the man only laughed. "I'd say you've made yourself perfectly clear. Sounds like your mission wasn't so unsuccessful after all. Jo said yes?"

Hunter relaxed a little. "Yes, sir, she did. I'm sorry—"

The General spoke over him. "Good." He sounded mighty satisfied, Hunter thought. "That's three down; two to go," the General went on. "Looks like the lot of you aren't a bunch of fuck-ups after all."

"Sir, about that wedding? Are you going to be here? Jo would like that, more than anything. She misses you a lot, you know."

"Nah, it's her mother she misses. Amelia should have been here for this."

"But she can't be, sir," Hunter said, knowing he had to stick up for Jo. His father was out of the picture for good, but she and the General still had a chance for a relationship. "That's why Jo needs you there to walk her down the aisle. It isn't fair to make her walk alone."

The general was quiet for a long time. "Not much is fair in this world, is it, Powell?"

"No. But most of it we can't control. This you can. Come to Two Willows. For Jo. For all your girls."

Hunter held his breath. Would the man finally give in? He hadn't for Cass's wedding, nor for Sadie's.

Would he for Jo's?

The General sighed. "It's not... possible," he said curtly.

And hung up.

ALL OF THE horses except Atlas had found temporary homes in neighbors' stables until they had a chance to rebuild theirs. Atlas remained skittish from his ordeal in the fire. He'd gotten somewhat singed and had cut his leg in his struggle to break out of his stall. Hunter and the other men had managed to build a makeshift stall for him in the main barn, and while he preferred Lena's company, he allowed Jo to brush him. Jo found the exercise soothing to her nerves.

Animals were better than humans at rolling with the punches. Already, Atlas was calming down, forgetting what had happened. Jo wasn't sure if she'd ever forget. Coming so close to losing her life a second time, she found most things simply didn't feel important any-more. All she wanted was to get back to doing what really mattered—caring for the animals on the ranch. The people she loved.

Hunter.

When she'd woken up in the hospital, and didn't know what had happened to him, she'd been so scared—it had been like climbing out of her own body. Now she found herself checking constantly to make sure he was still around.

Luckily, he stayed close for the most part, as if he sensed her need for him—or maybe to quench his own need for her. She saw the way he looked at her. Hungrily.

Desperately.

She was so lucky to know a love like this. Jo felt that down to her bones. To be understood—and thoroughly desired. To feel she knew the man she was going to marry. To be secure he'd always come to her aid if she needed him.

She didn't sleep alone anymore, hadn't since the day she'd left the hospital. They hadn't needed to talk about it. Hunter packed the things in his room, came to her door, and she'd let him in.

Soon they'd move into their little house.

Jo couldn't wait.

When Hunter had told her about his call to the General, and the General's refusal to come home for the wedding, Jo had found she wasn't as hurt as she'd thought she'd be. She realized she'd always miss the way things were in the past, but she'd grown since then.

She'd changed.

She didn't need to moon after a father who couldn't force himself to be near her. She had better things to do.

Other men to love.

"Ready?" Hunter asked, coming into the kitchen, where she was waiting for him.

"Ready."

"Where are you two off to?" Sadie wandered in and opened the refrigerator. "God, I'm starving."

"To town. To buy a ring," Hunter answered, linking

Jo's arm with his own.

Sadie straightened. "Pick a good one, Jo. Get exactly what you want. You only get to do it once."

When they arrived at Thayer's, Jo was uneasy. She didn't wear much jewelry and wasn't sure what she wanted. She knew some women kept up to date on styles and probably picked out their rings years in advance. She'd never really paid much attention to that kind of thing.

Rose Johnson greeted them and indicated the glass cases where the engagement rings were stored. "Take your time," she told them. "Give me a holler when you're ready for me."

Jo was grateful when she moved away again.

"See anything you like?" Hunter asked.

She found it hard to answer. What if she chose wrong? What if—?

"There are a lot of them," he added, and he sounded as bewildered as she felt.

"This is going to be boring for you," Jo said apologetically. "It might take time for me to decide."

"Hey, listen." He cupped her chin in his hand and bent down to kiss her. "I'm never bored when I'm with you. Never. Take all the time you want. Do we need to come up with a method to figure this out?"

Jo smiled, falling in love with her fiancé all over again as he motioned Rose over. "I think we're going to need to see all of them," he went on. "Jo needs to try on every single one."

Jo's mouth dropped open. "I don't need—"

"A woman after my own heart," Rose said happily. She opened the case and began to bring out trays. She put a small silver salver beside them. "Put any contenders on here. We'll keep comparing them until we've got one left."

She went away again, leaving Jo and Hunter to it, and the next hour and a half was one of the happiest times of Jo's life. Hunter made her try on every single one, even the gaudiest, most hideous ones that Jo figured were left over from when Rose's predecessor owned the store. She laughed until she cried at the monstrosities Hunter added to the little silver tray, but in the end there was only one that truly caught her heart.

It was a very refined, very grown-up silver ring with a single diamond in a simple setting.

"Are you sure? There are fancier ones," Hunter asked her.

"This is the one. I'm sure of it." It was feminine, but it was strong, too, and that's how she felt. It was the kind of ring worn by a woman who knew her worth shone forth from her actions, not her wardrobe.

Jo handed it to Rose, and Rose held it a moment, then smiled a smile that was so warm, so full of happiness and genuine respect, Jo knew she'd chosen wisely.

"You two are going to have an amazing life together," Rose told them, and Jo took Hunter's hand. He squeezed hers in turn.

"Yes, we are," he said.

IT HAD BEEN over a week since Marlon's last call. Hunter wondered how he was faring in the military prison. He'd hoped the Navy would commute the sentence given the circumstances, but it seemed like Marlon was going to serve his full time.

He knew he couldn't control any of that, and none of his worrying would change anything. It was up to Marlon to live his life now. To figure out how he wanted to proceed.

Meanwhile, he had a call to make he'd been putting off. He was due to wed in two weeks, and he still hadn't invited his mother. He wasn't sure if he wanted to—or if she'd want to come. It would mean leaving Alabama, for one thing, and she only did that on her monthly trips to see her aunt.

Speaking of which, was he supposed to invite Great-aunt Minnie, too? He hadn't seen her since he was a child. His mom had always waved off his half-hearted offers to join her on her visits, saying Minnie rarely spoke much anymore and there was no sense having the two of them sitting in silent vigil while she rested.

Still, he probably should issue that invitation. Grateful for the excuse to put off the call to his mother, he looked up the number for the Southern Skies Care Facility, punched it in and waited until a receptionist answered his call.

"I'd like to find out how to address a letter to one of your residents," he said. "Her name is Minnie Powell."

"Minnie Powell," the woman repeated. "Hold one moment." She came back after a few seconds. "I'm sorry; we don't have anyone by that name here."

"Yes, you do. Check again," Hunter told her. She probably was new to the job, he thought as she put him on hold again. When she came back, she was apologetic.

"Sorry for the delay, sir. I asked the office manager and we had to search the old files. Minnie hasn't lived here these past nineteen years, but once she saw the photograph the office manager remembered her. Says Minnie was a hoot."

"Nineteen years? Where'd she go?"

"The office manager? She's right here. Do you want to speak with her?"

"No, I mean—" It was too late. A new voice came on the line, low and husky with age.

"This is Sarah Dunsworth. How can I help you?"

"I'm trying to find my great-aunt, Minnie Powell. Do you know where's she's gone?"

A long silence greeted his question. "I'm sorry," Sarah said finally. "Minnie passed away nineteen years ago."

Hunter was still reeling when he called his mother. He didn't bother with pleasantries when she picked up.

"What the hell do you do when you go to Georgia?" he demanded.

The sound that escaped her told him she knew she'd been found out. "I go to see Drake," she said simply when she spoke. "We spend the weekend together."

Everything he thought he knew—about his mother, about his relationship to her—crashed down around him. "You spend—what about Aunt Minnie?"

"I used to visit her, too. Until she died. Now I stop by the cemetary."

"You never said—"

"No. I never did. Those were the terms. That's what Drake and I agreed."

"But he—he wouldn't even acknowledge me." Hunter couldn't believe this. His mother had carried on a relationship with Drake all this time? "He practically threw me out of his house when I confronted him."

"No, he didn't. He asked you to leave," she said in a measured voice. "And I'm sorry you couldn't have more than that from him."

"I didn't have anything from him!" He tried to get himself under control, but he knew he was failing. This was too much. Didn't she understand what his child-hood had been like? Didn't she know how often he'd longed for a father to complete their family? And she'd been seeing him all along?

"You had a living from him, until you walked away from that. He paid child support like clockwork. You really think we afforded our house on a stenographer's salary? You think my income paid for Scouts? Sports? Restaurants?"

Hunter couldn't find an answer. That was supposed to make up for the father he'd never had? For the shame he'd always felt?

"How could you—?"

"Love someone? A man who wouldn't ditch his wife when he fell in love with someone else? Is that what you'd have had me do—force him to ruin someone else's life when it wasn't her fault?"

"You think you've made things better for Drake's wife by sleeping with him once a month?" Hunter was incredulous. He couldn't believe they were even having this conversation.

"Do you think I'm the kind of person who would think that?" his mother retorted. "Life is complicated. You should know that by now."

He did know that, but he still couldn't understand. "I couldn't hang around and wait for stolen weekends with the woman *I* love—the woman I'm going to marry. If she had a husband, I'd leave her alone. It wouldn't be right otherwise."

"Hunter—" His mother broke off. "You're a man, and things are so black and white for you. I don't know if you can understand it. I hardly understood it myself when it all started. That's why I never talked to you about it."

"Try me," Hunter growled. There was nothing she could say that would make this situation acceptable.

"Drake's wife, Melissa—she's the one who found me."

He stopped pacing. "Found you? What's that supposed to mean?"

"She's the one who hired me—for the stenographer position in Drake's court. She's the one who arranged for Drake and me to be together."

She waited, and Hunter didn't know what to say. "Why would she do that?" What had his mother been involved in? Did he even want to know?

"Do I have to spell it out for you?" his mother said exasperatedly. "Not everyone enjoys sex, Hunter," his mother said bluntly. "She put up with it until she had her girl and her boy. Then she drew the line. Told Drake she was done. Told him he needed to make arrangements. That's what I was supposed to be. An arrangement. We spent the weekend together once a month when the two of them were supposed to be visiting their vacation home in Orange Beach. She went and had fun with her family at the shore. He met me in Georgia. It was all supposed to be neat and tidy, except I was young. I screwed up. Missed a couple of pills." His mother sighed. "There was hell to pay for that, but then Melissa decided it was the best thing for all of us. It tied me to Drake. Tied him to me, too. She didn't want a scandal; didn't want her husband carousing with a string of women over the years and she didn't want to leave him, either. She wanted the life he gave her—a nice house, the chance to be a stay at home mom. A position in the community. She came up with a generous figure for child support. We kept all the other aspects of the arrangement the same. But now I knew the rules. No more children."

"And you put up with that?" Hunter was so flabbergasted, he didn't know where to turn. His mother had always seemed so self-contained. So utterly impervious to the passions that ruled other human beings. Now he was supposed to believe she'd arranged her whole life to be a good mistress to a married man?

"You know what? None of that makes me feel embarrassed," his mother told him. "Here's the only thing that does. I learned something about myself. Something that doesn't fit with the way other people think I should be."

"What's that?"

"I don't want a husband. Never did." She let that sink in. "I made no bones about it. I'd had a proposal before, you know. My high school boyfriend wanted a traditional wife. I knew I couldn't do it even back then. Maybe Melissa had heard about that. I don't know. I'm a loner, Hunter. I don't like to do all those things other people like to do. I don't like groups. I don't like big family gatherings. I don't want to tailor my activities to what everyone else wants to do. If I had to live with Drake all the time, I'd... I don't know what I'd do."

Hunter was staggered. He didn't know what to think of any of this. The way he felt for Jo—he couldn't get enough of her. The idea of seeing her once a month would kill him "Mom—"

"Sweetie, I know. This is hard to hear. But it shouldn't come as much of a surprise. I let Sue-Ann Frank practically raise you. Most women wouldn't allow another woman to co-opt her child like that."

"She didn't co-opt me," Hunter protested.

"No, she saved us. Both of us. I have loved you every second of your life—with every fiber of my being. I tried so hard to be a good mother to you. I also saw right away that the Franks could give you everything Drake and I couldn't. All those boisterous dinners and fun times you craved. Not to mention all the things you learned from working with them on their ranch. I don't know how to ride a horse, or care for cattle, or anything like that. They stepped in and gave it all to you without me even asking." His mother was silent for a moment. "I have thanked God every day for the last thirty-four years he put me next to Heartfelt Acres when I moved home to Finley. I'm very aware of everything good that came from that. I knew I couldn't give you a father, or be exactly the mother you deserved, so I let the Franks fill in the gaps. I'd hoped it would be enough. I see now that it wasn't."

"No, it wasn't." Although Hunter had to admit he'd felt like part of the family over at Heartfelt Acres, still it wasn't the same thing as having a family of his own.

"I can just about hear the gears turning in your head. Try to remember that everyone is different," his mother begged him. "Melissa loves everything about Drake that I don't. She wants him there in the morning when she wakes up and there when she goes to bed at night. She wants to hear about every part of his day and talk to him about everything to do with their kids. That's not what I want. I want my home life to myself. I want time to pursue my own quiet passions. I want to be able to dream and think and write poetry without interruption. And when I'm with Drake I want to have fun. I want it to be separate from the cares of my day-to-day life. Does that make sense?"

"What about me?"

His mother sighed. "You got the short end of the stick in every way, didn't you? I am sorry for that. More than I can say."

Hunter didn't know what to say. Didn't know what to think.

"None of us were anticipating a child when we started our arrangement. I know this isn't easy to hear, and I know you'll have some thinking to do before you can come to terms with it, but I think you'll understand in time. We all did the best we could," his mother said quietly. "Now, this woman. The one you love. The one you're going to marry—"

"I've got to go." Hunter hung up.

He needed to go find Jo. She'd know how to make sense of this.

"THE CABINETS ARRIVED," Jo said to Hunter when he met her out back. A crew from Renfrew's was unloading their truck and she paced around them, hardly able to wait to finish the tiny house kitchen. "Do you have time to help me install them?"

"Sure." He seemed distracted, though.

"Something wrong?"

"Yeah—no. I don't know." He pressed both hands to his temples, then dropped them to his sides, shaking them out like he needed to shake off something disgusting. Jo became concerned.

"Hang on," she said. He really didn't look good at all. Jo thanked the drivers and pocketed the invoice they gave her, and when the truck trundled off up the driveway, she turned her full attention on him. "What's going on?"

Hunter gave her a brief rundown of the phone call he'd had with his mother, and Jo didn't blame him for looking shell-shocked. "So she's been seeing Drake all this time?"

"And she never breathed a word of it; not to me, not to anyone, as far as I can tell. Why did she do that?"

"Because she loved him," Jo said without hesitation. It was clear to her—especially after she'd read Gwen's poems. "She loved him, and she loved you, too. She was willing to accept what she could get in the circumstances. She made a choice. A hard choice."

"I don't see how any of them could agree to a setup like that." He seemed to find it hard to stand still. She'd never seen him so agitated.

"It's not ideal, and I don't think it was easy for her," Jo said, wishing she could soothe him. "That's what her poetry is all about. Have you read any of it?"

He made a face. "Some. When I was younger. I didn't get it."

"It's about… nature," Jo said slowly, finding it easier to understand now. "Nature in both senses of the world. What's out there and what's inside of us. How nature is beautiful and fierce and we are, too. How we like to pretend we have this veneer of society, but when the hard times come, that falls away and reveals who we really are. It's about choices. Choosing the path that aligns with who you really are. I think that's what she tried to do—be herself. Not what society wanted her to be."

"Why didn't she ever tell me the truth?" he demanded.

"Because she probably never wanted to hear what I'm hearing in your voice right now. Anger. Disgust. She loves you, Hunter."

"Of course I'm angry." He ignored the second half of what Jo had said. "I grew up without a father!"

"So have a lot of people," she pointed out quietly.

Hunter rubbed a hand over his mouth. "That doesn't make it any better. I don't know what to do."

Jo thought about that. "I'm not sure there is anything to do," she said slowly, running a hand along the top of one of the cabinets the men from Renfrew's had unloaded. "She's your mom, Hunter. That hasn't changed. None of the circumstances have. She still wants to be in your life."

"But my dad doesn't."

"No. Because he doesn't want to hurt his wife. He made an agreement with her and he's sticking to it."

"His wife chose my mother to be his mistress. So what gives her the right to dictate whether or not we talk to each other?" Hunter shook his head. Lifted his hands. "I should be angry."

"You just said you were."

"Angrier." He sounded fed up. Tired.

"It doesn't help," she blurted. Unexpected pain welled inside her because it was true. Being angry hadn't ever helped. She still wasn't any closer to the General despite all her rage. Nothing had changed or gotten better. Quite the contrary. The distance between them had grown, if anything.

When she looked up, Hunter's gaze was resting on her. "We can't change our parents as much as we might want to," she went on. "We can't control anyone but ourselves. All we can do is make a decision. Do we want the people we love close to us or not?"

"Do you want the General close to you?" he demanded.

That was hard to answer. She was so angry with him for not being there when she needed a parent. On the other hand, she understood now in a way she hadn't when she was young how much her mother's death had devastated him. And he'd sent Hunter to her. Had he been trying to make amends?

"I'm… open to giving him another chance," she said finally. "Maybe. But I won't fight for his attention. Now he'll have to fight for mine. How about you? Do you want a relationship with your mother?"

"I don't know. I shouldn't. But… yeah," he said raggedly. "I do. I can't see shutting her out. No matter what she's done. But as far as I'm concerned, I don't have a dad."

"I can understand that." Jo took both of his hands and faced him. "Maybe the important thing now is you and me. Maybe it's time to focus on our family, and leave everyone else to sort themselves out."

Hunter moved to pull her into an embrace. "That makes a lot of sense to me. No matter what anyone else does, you've got me from now on. I hope you know that."

She knew that. Every touch confirmed his determination on that front. "You've got me, too. Whatever happens, we'll be here for each other. We'll stay strong."

He smiled suddenly. "You're right. Who gives a damn what anyone else does as long as I've got you."

"You've got me." She went up on tiptoe to meet his kiss. This was enough for her. He was enough for her.

He was everything.

WHEN HIS PHONE rang early the next morning and he recognized the number as the Franks', Hunter was reluctant to answer it. He hadn't heard from any of them in weeks, and he wasn't sure what they thought of him now. After yesterday's revelations, he wasn't sure he was ready for any more drama, either. He'd decided he'd call his mother later and formally invite her to the wedding. It would take some time to repair his relationship with her fully, but keeping her from the celebration wasn't any way to start the next phase of his life. He'd try to be adult about this. Try to see her side.

As difficult as that was.

"Hunter Powell, you idiot," Sue-Ann said without preamble when he picked up. "How could you be so stupid?"

This was worse than he'd imagined. Hunter told himself he deserved it; he hadn't managed to keep Marlon out of trouble, after all.

"How could you throw away your career for my son when my son was doing his damnedest to ruin everything?" she went on. She was in full-on scolding mode, mothering him like she'd always used to when he was young.

"I wanted to give him another chance—"

"When someone is that determined to undermine himself, there's nothing you can do to stop it. Don't you know that?"

"I do now," he admitted. "But this is Marlon we're talking about. You know everything he did for me—that you all did for me."

"Your mother lives next door to me," Sue-Ann said as if she hadn't heard his objections. "How am I supposed to hold my head up when my child has tanked your career? She's going to blame me for that. You know she will."

"She won't blame you. Besides, Marlon didn't tank my career. I'm leaving the SEALs voluntarily." Hunter didn't think his mother would have much to say to anyone just now, anyway.

"Thank you for everything you did to help him," she said, softening. "You went out on a limb. I know this is all on Marlon. He took a wrong turn. Married the wrong girl. We all knew it. It took me days to brace myself for this phone call," she admitted. "When I think of everything I said—"

"Don't mention it. You were worried about me. Besides, I think Marlon will recover—now that the hard part is over."

"I sure hope so."

Hunter wasn't sure what to say next. He wanted to tell her about the wedding, but it seemed callous to talk about something that made him so happy when Marlon was still in the brig.

As if she'd read his mind, she added, "He told me about Jo. I'm so happy for you both. I can't wait to meet the woman who's won your heart."

"You know I'd like you all to be at the wedding, but I understand—"

"Hunter Powell, we will be at your wedding, you can depend on that. It'll be a good reminder there'll be more happy times ahead. We could use that," she added.

"I'm glad you're coming. That means a lot to me."

He only wished Marlon could be there, too.

ALL THE DAMAGE had been repaired in Alice's carriage house studio, and with the large windows letting light spill into her sewing room, Jo was able to keep her mind on their childhood romps in the large space instead of the unpleasantness that had happened here recently.

She had tested herself coming up the stairs. Only weeks ago, she'd fired a shot that had helped kill a man here on the upper landing, but Alice must have used some of Sadie's sage to clear the space of bad vibrations. Jo felt no trace of that horrible encounter; only the light and life that had always imbued Alice's studio.

"Where's Alice?" she asked Cass when she entered the main room to find her sister holding up their mother's wedding dress. Cass had worn it to marry Brian. Sadie had worn it to marry Connor. Now it was Jo's turn. How would she look in it?

Ridiculous?

No, she wouldn't look ridiculous, she told herself;

Alice would see to that. Still, she remained curious and a little unsettled when she tried to picture herself at the altar, pledging herself to Hunter.

"Alice will be here in a minute." Cass carried the dress over and held it up. "You're going to look beautiful. Put it on."

"You don't think I'm rushing things?" Jo asked lightly as she stripped down to her bra and panties and pulled the gown over her head. She was glad she'd cleaned up after another morning of working on the house. It was really coming together now that the other men were pitching in.

"No. Oddly enough, I don't. I think Hunter is one in a million, and the way the two of you are together is a revelation," Cass admitted. "Sometimes I think I don't know you at all."

Jo, midway into the dress, stopped, confused, before fighting her way through until her head was clear of the fabric. "What do you mean?"

"It's my fault," Cass said. "I see that now. I've tried to keep you young. I've treated you like you never got past seventeen. I think… I think I was afraid to let you grow up. Because that meant it would be over."

"What would be over?" Jo slid the gown the rest of the way down and turned around so Cass could do up the back.

"Our childhoods," Cass said softly. "I think I hoped… that if I could just hold on… maybe Mom would come back. Or Dad. But they never did."

Jo turned to face her. Took her sister's hands. "But

we've got each other. That's what matters. That's what you always told us."

Cass blinked rapidly. "If you only knew how many times I didn't know what to say—didn't know what to do. I was so scared, so much of the time. So terrified I'd get it wrong. I couldn't be her. I tried—"

Jo caught Cass in her arms and held her.

"What if I'm a bad mother to my own child?" Cass said, gulping back tears. "What if I mess everything up?"

"You won't. You did a fantastic job. I mean it, Cass; I couldn't have asked for a better mother, even if you were my sister."

"But I didn't protect you from Sean. I didn't stop Grant—"

"I didn't need you to." Jo realized she was speaking the truth. "I needed to stand up for myself. I needed to be myself. You couldn't do that for me."

Cass pulled back and searched her face. "You mean that? You're all right, after everything? You don't hate me for the times I've gotten it so wrong?"

"You're my sister. That means everything to me," Jo said fiercely. "All I remember is the times you got it right."

"We have to make things safe before I have this child." Cass lay a hand on her belly. "I don't know how, but we have to."

"We will," Jo told her. "Somehow we will."

Alice appeared at the top of the stairs, a phone in her hand. "It's for you," she said to Jo. "It's the General," she added in a whisper.

Jo took the phone reluctantly, remembering what she'd said to Hunter. "Hello?"

"Jo. Heard about the wedding." The General's voice was gruff. She recognized this tone. All business, as if they spoke all the time.

"Heard you're not coming," she retorted.

Silence greeted this. "Look," he said finally. "This job—"

Jo meant to scoff, but the sound that came from her mouth was more of a sob. "This… job?" Was he for real? Did he think she was still a child to be fooled by a lie like that?

As if he'd heard her thoughts loud and clear, the General fell silent again. When he spoke again, his voice had changed. Grown thin. He sounded… old. "Look, Jo. I'm… trying."

Jo held her breath. She didn't have to touch her father to know he was finally telling the truth.

"Your mother," he went on. "I… miss her."

"I miss her too."

"I've let you down—so many times."

Jo swallowed, not knowing what to say. She couldn't deny it.

"You're still my soldier. My little soldier. My girl. I'm still so proud of you. I wish—"

He cleared his throat—a strangled sound. Jo waited for him to finish. She barely heard the quiet click. She didn't realize he'd ended the call until the dial tone sounded.

Jo clutched the phone, tears streaming down her

face. Alice moved to take it from her hand, then wrapped her in a tight embrace. Cass joined them, encircling both of them in her arms.

Sadie and Lena, who'd just clattered up the carriage house stairs to join them, came to a halt. When they took in the scene, they quickly moved to join them.

"We've got each other," Cass said firmly, as if she'd heard everything the General had said—and didn't say. "We've got each other and we always will. No matter what."

"FINISHED. WITHOUT A moment to spare," Hunter said several days later. He put away his tools and stood next to Jo, both of them surveying the small house they'd built together. The board and batten exterior was painted a weathered gray, the windows trimmed in white. They'd built a brick walkway from the dirt track to the front door and put up a square of picket fencing around the yard. Sadie had already planted shrubs and bulbs inside its perimeter and promised to put in a full garden come spring. It looked snug and tidy, and Hunter was proud of it. He had to admit Jo had done a great job designing the interior and they'd managed to work together to iron out the difficulties that cropped up during the building of it.

"I can't believe it's done. I was beginning to think it never would be." Jo pushed the hair that had escaped her pony tail out of her eyes. She'd been quiet the past few days and Cass had filled him in on her phone call with the General. Hunter had made sure to stick close to Jo and she'd shared more details with him when she was ready. She seemed calm. At peace. "He misses my mom," she'd said simply. "I think I understand that all the way now."

"Think you'll have the stamina to build a bigger house in the spring?" Hunter asked Jo.

She hesitated long enough he laughed long and hard.

"By spring we'll have forgotten how difficult this was. Right?" she asked.

"Yeah. And we'll probably be so sick of stepping on each other we'll be ready for more space."

"We haven't even moved in and already you're complaining?" She elbowed him.

He was happy to see her good humor returning. "I won't be complaining one bit when we move in. I'm looking forward to a little privacy. You and I can make some noise tonight."

"We could make some noise right now."

"Hell, yeah." Hunter was all over that. With a hammer tucked through her belt loop and a smudge of dirt on her cheekbone, Jo looked delicious. He held open the door. "After you."

Jo tossed her hammer aside and hurried up the two front steps and inside the little house. Hunter quickly followed. Inside, they stopped to admire the wooden cabinetry, the hand-hewn slab countertops, the tile backsplash and crisp, new stainless-steel appliances.

"We could do it right here," Hunter said. "Or we could go up to the bedroom."

"Or we could do it everywhere." She looked up at him from under her lashes.

"Sounds fine to me." He pulled her close, leaned back to shut and lock the door, then began to undress her. He'd gotten good at that the past few weeks. Jo got to work on his clothes, too, but both of them soon lost patience, and his jeans were still tangled around his ankles and her bra still on when he pulled on a condom, lifted her on the kitchen counter and she wrapped her legs around his waist. Her back was angled awkwardly against the upper cabinets, so when he'd filled her, and tried to pump into her a couple of times, Hunter decided they needed to find somewhere else.

He held her as he kicked his boots and jeans the rest of the way off, keeping up a rhythm as best he could to keep both of them happy in the meantime, then lifted her up and walked toward the back of the house to lean her against the ladder that led to the loft.

He'd only meant to pause while picking their next spot, but he couldn't help himself. Bracing her there, he pumped into her again, one hand gripping her bottom, the other cradling her to shield her back from the hard rungs.

Jo dug her fingers into his shoulders and pressed her mouth to his neck, her soft moans music to his ears as he moved inside her. God she was hot. Slick with need for him. Urging him on with the movement of her hips.

This couldn't be comfortable for Jo, though. Hunter glanced around. Should they try the couch? He picked her up again and lurched over to it, nearly dropping her as he tried to lay her down. All the while, Jo kept her legs wrapped around him—kept urging him to keep up his rhythm.

This was easier.

Sort of.

He thrust into her again.

The couch was a little short for his tall frame, and Hunter found himself half crouched on the floor, half perched on the cushions trying to get leverage he needed. For her part, Jo did the best she could, but now she was clinging to the back of the couch as well as his shoulder, as if afraid they'd slide off it altogether. Her positon brought her breasts up near his face and he took the opportunity to lavish them with attention. He loved Jo's breasts. Love the heft of them in his hands.

Not that he had a hand to spare—he was holding on to the couch, too.

"Don't let me fall!" Jo shrieked as they began to slip.

"Upstairs?" he gasped. She felt so good, he wasn't sure how much longer he'd need no matter where they were.

"Yes. Hurry."

Hunter didn't need to be told twice. He scooped her up again, steadied himself, took two steps to the ladder and began to climb.

Carefully.

"Faster!" Jo rocked against him. "God, you feel good."

"I know what you mean." He finally made it to the top of the ladder and crawled forward, Jo dangling underneath him like a sloth hanging from a branch. She began to shake and Hunter realized she was laughing. "What?" he demanded.

"Would you pick a place and make love to me?"

"You said you wanted to christen the whole house."

"Not in one go. You need to focus—oh." She sighed as he set her down and stroked into her.

This was better. Now they were on their bed, in their loft. At night they'd be able to see the stars out of the skylights in the roof. For now the autumn sun shone through and warmed his skin. As he pumped into Jo, he felt the rightness of it.

This was where he belonged. This was their home.

The one they'd built together.

He picked up his pace and Jo clung to him. She lifted her hips to meet his thrusts.

Nothing felt like Jo. He could do this all day, every day.

"Oh, you feel good. So good." She arched back and moaned.

Hunter thought he'd never seen anything as sexy as Jo giving herself utterly to him. Never heard anything as sexy as her cries as she came. For once they didn't have to be quiet. Overtaken by his own release, he thrust into her again and again, until he collapsed on top of her, absolutely drained.

"I love you," he whispered into her hair. "Jo Reed, I love you. I want to spend my life with you. Every day of it."

"That's what I want, too."

"DO YOU WANT children?" Jo asked later, after they'd made love again, more slowly this time. They were still lying on their bed, watching puffy white clouds drift past in a sky so bright blue it made her eyes hurt to look at it. She wasn't sure where the question came from, except that they were marrying soon. It would be good to know.

"I think so."

"You don't sound sure."

Hunter twirled a strand of her hair around his finger. She could see him considering what to say.

"Neither of our fathers are anything to write home about. I don't want to be like that. But what if I am?"

"Do you think you'll be like that?"

"No," he said. The corner of his mouth tugged up. "But does anyone think they'll be a failure as a parent?"

"Probably not. Here's the thing, though. We've both been on the receiving end of absentee parenting. We know what it feels like. Don't you think that'll keep us in line?"

"And if that doesn't work, we can keep each other in line." He kissed her.

"I know how to be loyal. So do you. We've both proved that."

"That's true." He gave her a considering look. "So when do you want to have kids?"

She felt her cheeks heat. "I don't know."

As he gathered her close, Jo sighed, so in love with her husband to be.

"Now?" he asked her.

"Maybe." She kissed the underside of his chin. Hunter rolled her over until she was astride him. She could feel the stirrings of his interest underneath her and she smiled, anticipating taking him inside again.

This time would be different.

No condom for one thing.

"That was fast," she said as she rocked against him. He'd grown hard already.

"You're damn sexy."

As she leaned forward to kiss him, he palmed her breasts in his hands and Jo murmured her approval against his mouth. She lifted up to allow him to move into a better position, then eased down until she felt him nudging against her.

He felt wonderful—like he always did, no matter how many times they made love. When he palmed her breasts again, and leaned forward to take one sensitive nipple into his mouth, Jo groaned.

She settled down over him as he pushed into her, sighing as he slowly eased inside. Hunter filled her perfectly, and as soon as she'd taken him in, she couldn't help but begin to move rhythmically. She lifted up and down in time with his thrusts, arched her back to give him access to her breasts, and closed her eyes, loving his touch, loving the way he moved inside her.

Soon she'd lost track of everything except the way Hunter was making her feel, and she was so close to the brink that every stroke of him inside her was liquid fire. She couldn't get enough of him. Couldn't get close enough to him. She wanted more.

More—

Jo cried out as she crashed over the edge, pulsing with ecstasy, her body thrumming with waves of feeling. Hunter picked up his pace, thrusting into her until he came, too, his grunts echoing her cries.

Jo held on through his orgasm, her body revving up until she shuddered through a second one of her own, surprising her with its intensity.

By the time she collapsed on top of him, they were both panting.

That… was… incredible," Hunter said.

She could only nod.

"We'll have to do that a lot," he went on. "Takes a lot of work to make a baby, you know."

"Sounds good to me."

Chapter Fourteen

O N THE DAY of his wedding, Hunter watched the guests settle into the folding chairs that were arranged in the front yard of Two Willows. The morning had dawned clear, and after a brief scare when a squall had run through the area, the skies were clear again. It was a cool day with a hint of a breeze. It was a good day to be alive, Hunter decided.

A good day to marry the woman he loved.

They'd taken a chance scheduling an outdoor wedding, but Jo had wanted one and it had all worked out. Hunter was glad.

In the past week, they'd made love in every corner of the small house and he wondered how long it would take for Jo to get pregnant. He wasn't in too much of a hurry. He was having far too much fun now. After the wedding, they were headed for a short honeymoon in New England. They were going to see the fall colors and tour the quaint towns and scenic byways of Connecticut, Vermont, New Hampshire and Maine, which would give them plenty of opportunities to work on that baby. Hunter looked forward to seeing a part of the

country he hadn't spent time in before. He thought Jo
felt as he did; that stepping out of their lives for a few
weeks would give them a chance to simply be together
and start their time together as husband and wife right.

His mother took her seat in the front row and ges-
tured to Sue-Ann and Jessie Frank to join them. The
rest of the Frank siblings sat beside them and in the row
behind them. It was good to be surrounded by the
noisy, happy family again.

All but Marlon, who hadn't gotten in touch since
their last conversation. Hunter knew he was serving his
time. He hoped Marlon was on his own journey—
toward healing. Toward a future where love could touch
him again.

"You ready?" Connor appeared by his side.

"Yeah, I think so."

"Let's get 'er done."

They walked out together to take their places by
Reverend Halpern. Hunter shook the man's hand,
suddenly nervous, although he didn't know why.

This was his home. These were his people.

And somewhere in the house, waiting for her cue,
was Jo.

Emotion constricted Hunter's throat when as he
watched first Sadie, then Lena, then Alice, then Cass
step out of the doorway in their spring-green bridesmaid
gowns and walk sedately up the aisle between the rows
of seats toward him. When Jo stepped out, however, on
Brian's arm, he only had eyes for her. Slim and beautiful
in her mother's wedding gown, she held her head high

and kept her gaze on him as she walked to stand beside him.

There was no doubt in Jo's eyes. They were clear, untroubled, shining with the same love he felt for her.

When she drew near, he held out his hand and she took it. Hunter had to keep himself from holding on too tightly. He was overcome with love for this woman.

Overcome with gratitude for every step—no matter how hard—that had brought him here.

"Dearly Beloved," Reverend Halpern began, and Hunter swallowed, joy beginning to burn in his chest. This was everything he wanted.

He had a wife. A family.

A true home.

JO THOUGHT SHE'D never been so happy. As Reverend Halpern spoke the words that would bind them together, she couldn't keep from clinging to Hunter's hand. She wondered how she could ever have been fooled by another man; this love was unlike anything she'd ever felt before.

Hunter understood her in a way no one had since her mother died. He'd seen her true assets—her strength, courage and loyalty—and fallen in love with them.

She'd seen him for what he was, too—a man who did the right thing even when it was hard. Someone who'd be there for her, talk to her, help her weigh her options. Someone who might be bossy from time to time but who would listen in the end.

She was determined to be a true partner to him. She couldn't wait for their honeymoon—to spend time with Hunter alone, away from the cares and worries of Two Willows.

But she knew she'd be just as happy to come home and inhabit the little house they'd built together. All winter long they'd make plans for the real house they'd build come spring, but for now a cozy home built just for two seemed like the perfect place to spend the first months of their marriage.

As Hunter slid her wedding band on her finger, then bent to kiss her, Jo rose up on tiptoe to meet him and thought her heart would burst with joy.

"I now pronounce you man and wife," Reverend Halpern intoned.

She wrapped her arms around Hunter's neck and laughed when he spun her in a circle.

"Ready for the rest of your life, Mrs. Powell?" he asked when they faced the congregation again.

"Ready, Mr. Powell."

And she was.

KITCHEN DUTY. THERE wasn't anything Lena hated as much as kitchen duty, but it was better than simpering around among the guests in this travesty of a dress.

It was a green, full-length gown with a hem she'd stepped on and torn at each of the weddings she'd worn it to so far. After Sadie's wedding, Alice had held up the pieces in exasperation. "At this rate I'll need to sew a whole new one before everyone's married!"

Lena slammed a pile of dishes into the sink and ran water over them. Outside, people were still dancing, the music and laughter sliding in the open windows.

The night was cooling down, however, and already the men were building a bonfire to keep folks warm. Soon they'd be in for another hard, cold Montana winter.

Lena didn't mind. She loved every season at Two Willows. Coming home from the barns on a cold, crystal winter evening, every star a bright pinprick in the sky—

Those were moments to live for.

She could almost enjoy herself if there weren't so many damn men around the place these days.

Not that any of them were bad in themselves. She'd come to respect Brian and Connor, and even held some admiration for Hunter after the way he'd saved Jo.

But three were enough. She'd have to work hard to keep on top now that they could gang up on her.

Someone knocked on the front door, and Lena groaned but dried her hands and made her way across the kitchen.

This was her ranch. Hers. Not Brian's or Connor's—or Hunter's, for that matter.

Her cattle operation.

She hoped they understood that.

The knock sounded again.

She hoped the General understood that, too. Two Willows wasn't Reed land. It had belonged to the Griffiths—her mother's family.

He didn't get to call the shots here.

She had almost reached the door when the knocking became a thunderous pounding.

Lena yanked the door open in irritation—saw a tall man, with the shoulders of a fullback and biceps as big as cantaloupes, his hazel eyes flashing with humor, mouth tugging into a smile as he took her in—

"Hello, baby girl. I'm Logan Hughes. The General sent me," he began.

"Oh, hell no!" Lena slammed the door shut.

And locked it.

Want to know if Logan ever makes it inside the house?
Read on for an excerpt of Volume 4 of **The Brides of
Chance Creek** series—*Issued to the Bride One Marine.*

Be the first to know about Cora Seton's new releases!
Sign up for her newsletter here!
www.coraseton.com/sign-up-for-my-newsletter

Other books in the Brides of Chance Creek Series:

Issued to the Bride One Navy SEAL
Issued to the Bride One Airman
Issued to the Bride One Marine
Issued to the Bride One Soldier
Issued to the Bride: One Sergeant for Christmas

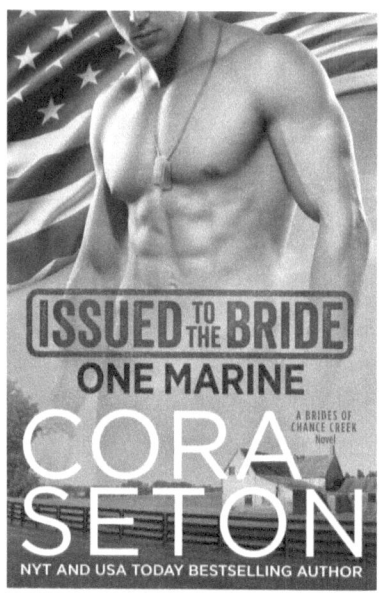

Read on for an excerpt of Volume 4 of **The Brides of Chance Creek** series—*Issued to the Bride One Marine.*

LOGAN WALKED INTO the large rectangular office that was the home of the Joint Special Task Force for Inter-Branch Communication Clarity, crossed the room, whistling, and sat down at his desk, dropping his bag on the ground beside him. He thunked a tall take-out cup of coffee near the monitor of his computer, kissed the palm of his hand and slapped it against the photograph of a dark-haired young woman with blue eyes that hung on the wall nearby. "Hello, baby girl!" he said, then pulled a breakfast sandwich out of a paper bag and began to eat.

"Don't let the General see you do that," Jack Sanders said in a voice as monotone as a robot's.

Logan didn't care; it had taken him weeks to wear the man down enough to make him say his line. He'd started this gag the first day he'd arrived at USSOCOM. First Connor O'Riley had played his straight man, then Hunter Powell had taken over when Connor headed to Two Willows. Jack Sanders had hated every damn day of it, so when Hunter had left just over a month ago, Logan made it his mission to force the man to play his part.

Luckily, *relentless* was Logan's middle name. It had taken persistence, though. One day he'd said, "Hello, baby girl" over a hundred times before Sanders broke down and answered correctly. These days, Sanders resorted to the monotone voice to register his protest over the whole thing, but as long as he said the words, Logan was satisfied. Doubly so, since usually Sanders— a soldier with the Special Forces—was as cagey as a ferret.

"Don't let him see me eat?" Logan said, with as much innocence as he had that very first time all those months ago.

"Don't let him see you slap the woman you're supposed to marry." Jack looked up for the first time. Pointed toward Lena's photograph. "Haven't you left yet?"

"Not without saying goodbye. And eating breakfast." Logan made short work of the sandwich and took the framed photograph of Lena Reed off the wall, unzipped his bag and shoved it in.

"The General will notice that."

"Let him. He's giving me his daughter, isn't he? He can't be pissed if I take her photo, too. Now, if I took Alice's—"

He ducked when Jack snatched a stapler from his desk and hurled it at him. The stapler bounced off Logan's shoulder and fell to the ground.

Jack went back to work, but Logan knew his words had hit their target with as much accuracy as Jack had pegged him with the stapler. Jack was supposed to marry Alice, but the man would have to wait until Logan fulfilled his mission and married Lena before he could try to make that happen.

"Come on, you're going to miss me. Admit it."

Jack snorted.

Logan picked up the stapler and put it on his desk, suddenly reluctant to leave. He had no idea why the General had picked him to marry Lena. From everything he'd learned about the woman, she was going to hate him on sight. She'd hate any man the General sent on sight. And if he failed—

The consequences wouldn't be pretty.

"Well, keep up the good work here at the Joint Task Force."

This time Jack swiveled around in his chair. They both knew the task force was a waste of time—desk work conjured up by the General to bore them so silly that traveling to Chance Creek and marrying his daughters came as a relief.

"Want to know what I'm wondering?" Jack asked.

"What?" Logan was surprised. He didn't know Jack wondered about anything. The man made it his business to know everything there was to know.

"Three men sent to Two Willows. Three marriages."

"So?"

"What are the odds?"

Logan sat back. What *were* the odds? Shouldn't one of the General's daughters have balked by now? "That's a damn good question," he admitted.

"I looked it up online. Matchmaking services have a horrible record as far as success is concerned. You might as well toss names around in a paper bag and draw them two by two—it would work as well. So how is the General—General Augustus Reed, who wouldn't know a thing about romance if it bit him on the ass— scoring a hundred percent?"

Logan had a feeling the General knew more about romance than Jack was giving him credit for. There were photographs of his late wife everywhere you looked here at USSOCOM. Still, he understood what Jack was trying to say.

"I don't know. Divine order?" Logan supposed those successes made his failure with Lena all the more likely.

Statistically speaking.

Or maybe not. Was it like flipping a coin? Each new coin toss still had a 50 percent chance of coming up heads—no matter how many other coins had been tossed previously.

"Divine order?" Jack repeated incredulously. "Who the hell believes in divine order?"

Logan's parents did, with a conviction that made it hard for him to follow a path of his own. So did his brothers, who were both in the priesthood. Logan had spent a lifetime trying to escape the calling his family saw for him. He'd thought he'd done that when he joined the Marines—trading a religious calling for a patriotic one.

Then he'd screwed up.

"Does the General have some kind of predictive technology we don't know about yet?" Jack mused.

Logan cocked his head, glad for the distraction. He didn't want to think about the past he'd run from. "Are you worried you're out of the loop on some new kind of spook software, Sanders?" It had been a running joke among the rest of them in the task force that the soldier might be Intelligence.

Jack sighed. "Just trying to make sense of something that doesn't make sense."

"I've stopped trying to make sense of anything." Logan got to his feet. Unlike his parents and brothers, he'd rebelled against the idea you could be directed toward your fate by something outside yourself. He'd left home. Joined the Marines. Escaped any divine order that might be leveled at him.

And then, eight months ago, the dreams had started.

He touched the medallion he wore on a cord around his neck, then shook his head at the gesture. He wasn't going to be a priest, no matter what his parents wanted.

Not even if St. Michael himself kept charging into his dreams at night.

When he'd messed up, he'd thought he was on a one-way ticket back to Idaho. Back to the pressure to conform to a calling he'd never had. Now he'd been saved again by the General. Here he was, on his way to Chance Creek to get married and put to rest forevermore his parents' wish for him to become a priest. To hell with the dreams.

"There's something else," Jack said, interrupting his thoughts. He pulled a document out of a file folder and handed it to Logan. A photograph, but of what Logan couldn't make out.

"What is it?"

"Drone footage. Of Two Willows. I finally got one there this morning to do a flyover. See, here's the house and the carriage house."

"Oh, yeah. There are the outbuildings." Logan could see it now. Everything lined up with the maps on the walls of their office. It had taken them a while to realize why the General had surrounded them with intelligence about his own ranch.

He wondered who Jack had in Montana to put the drone in the air. Was he working with one of the other men already at the ranch? Somehow, Logan doubted it. Jack liked to keep secrets. Logan leaned in for a closer look. "But what's this smudgy part in the middle?"

"Near as I can figure out, that's the hedge maze. Thing is, I can't get a clear image of it. I tried several times. See?" Jack handed him more photographs, and

Logan examined them. From what he'd heard, the maze was one of Two Willows's most distinctive attractions. Planted by the General's wife when she was a girl, it had grown so high you couldn't see into it from the ground—or from the second-story windows of the house. Brian, Connor and Hunter had all reported back that there was something uncanny about the huge standing stone at its center. He couldn't pretend he wasn't as curious about it as Jack seemed to be. Which made it interesting that Jack was right; the maze was blurry in each of the photos.

"How do you explain that?" Logan asked. "And who have you got on the ground at Two Willows? Brian?"

Jack shrugged. "I can't explain it; that's the problem. How the hell are those women scrambling my drone?"

"I don't know." Logan noticed Jack had evaded his question. Just like he thought; it wasn't Brian—or any of the others, he'd bet. He didn't have time to stand here and grill Jack, though. He gave his desk a last once-over, then lifted his bag. "I've got to go. See you on the other side, man."

Jack got up and faced him. Held out a hand.

Logan, surprised again, shook it.

"Good luck. I think you're going to need it," Jack said.

"Thanks a lot," Logan said wryly.

But Jack was right, and therein lay the problem. He needed to get married and settle his future once and for all, but like the General had hinted, Lena was a capable, independent woman—a fighter in her own right. Uninterested in marriage. How the hell could someone like him change her mind?

As LENA SURVEYED the tables and chairs set up on the back lawn for Jo's wedding reception, she couldn't help thinking she and her sisters should stop renting the damn things and just buy a set of their own. They seemed to host a wedding every other month here at Two Willows. First Cass had married, then Sadie, now Jo.

The outside weddings would have to stop, though. Colder weather was drawing in. Jo was lucky it looked like the rain would hold off for a day or two. And besides, no one else in this family was getting married.

Certainly not her.

"You look stunning," Brian Lake said, joining her on the back porch and trying to take the stack of tablecloths out of Lena's arms. Cass's husband had been at Two Willows for months now, and Lena had gotten used to him, but she wasn't used to compliments and she shrugged this one off. Jo had insisted they all go to a beauty salon in town that morning and have their hair—and their nails—done for the wedding. In shifts, of course, since they all couldn't leave the ranch at once. At least one Reed had to be on Two Willows land at all times. Her mother had made that promise when the General first left Two Willows to serve his country—not because he asked her to, but because she somehow thought it would guarantee his safety—and now that she was gone, they'd fulfill it for her.

Lena swore Jo had paid the hairdresser off to make her look as girly as possible. Her dark, straight locks had been pulled back and twisted into a complicated updo, and her angular face was framed by tendrils the woman had curled into corkscrews. Lena had nearly gagged when she looked in the mirror afterward. But then things got even worse. Jo had decided they'd all get makeovers, too. Lena had to submit to being plucked, moisturized, buffed and made up like a beauty queen, rather than the rancher she was.

The final indignity was the fake nails and the layers of polish another worker at the salon had shellacked onto her. She couldn't do a lick of work like this, and how was she going to tackle the evening chores when the time came? She'd spent an hour walking around with her fingers fanned out, afraid to touch anything, before exasperation overcame her caution. If only she could rip the fake nails off—

But Lena suspected they'd been glued into place with an industrial-strength substance that required an equally industrial-strength solvent to dissolve.

Worst of all, she couldn't carry her pistol, and these days she preferred to be armed. Her sleek shoulder-holster was normally easy to hide under a loose shirt or light jacket, but this darn dress didn't come with one. Cass, her older sister, told her she didn't need a firearm today, but to Lena's way of thinking that was a reckless assumption. Three times Two Willows had been attacked by drug dealers who wanted to establish a foothold in Montana. Three times they'd fought them off—with weapons of one sort or another.

"I got this," she said to Brian, refusing to give up the tablecloths. This much she could do, at least. She walked down the steps and began to spread them on the tables, grateful it was a day without wind.

"Really, Lena—you're beautiful." Brian followed her and reached for the rest of them. "You'll be fending off suitors left and right at the reception."

"I don't want suitors, and I don't need any help," she snapped. Why was it the minute she put on a dress, guys like Brian thought she became incapable of doing anything? She spread another cloth on a long rectangular table.

"That won't stop men from trying," he told her. "They'll be falling all over themselves."

Was he laughing at her? She'd have punched him if she wasn't afraid of breaking one of these damn nails.

She spread the final tablecloth and turned on her heel, her ankle-length, spring green bridesmaid dress swishing around her legs in an annoying way as she walked up the steps to the back porch. Inside, she found Sadie and Connor organizing the tableware. When Sadie approached with a stack of plates, Lena quickly lifted a tray of glasses to move it to the other end of the large plank table. Just as quickly, Connor moved to try to take it from her.

"I got this," she said and set it down in a better position.

"Can't help wanting to ease the way for a lovely lass

like you," Connor said brightly. "Never seen you in finer form, Lena."

Lena rolled her eyes. Connor wasn't nearly as Irish as he liked to pretend sometimes, and she wasn't in the mood for his theatrics today. "Everything ready in here?" she asked—as if she was running this show. Which she wasn't; weddings weren't her thing.

"We're ready," Sadie said.

"Come on, lass. Give a man a little twirl," Connor continued with his overblown Irish accent. He reached out, took her hand and spun her around before she could stop him. "Lovely sight. You should dress up more often."

Lena snatched her hand away.

Sadie nudged her husband, but she was grinning. "Stop riling up my sister. He's right, though, Lena. You should let your girly side out once in a while. It's fun, isn't it?" Like Lena, she wore her green bridesmaid gown and was done up to the nines. Only Sadie seemed to enjoy it.

"It's ridiculous." Lena stalked out of the room, her anger building. Being girly wasn't fun. It was dangerous. She'd learned that the hard way. Once she'd let her guard down around a man. Once—

The memories crashed over her, and Lena, in the front hall now, braced herself against the staircase railing, fighting to push them back. She'd never forget the way Scott had drawn his arm back. The way he'd smashed his fist into her face so hard she'd nearly blacked out. She'd always thought herself an equal to any man.

He'd proved her wrong.

Lena pushed off from the railing, straightened and stalked down the central hall to the front door. Yanking it open, she stepped outside to where the ceremony would be held and pushed the memory to the back of her mind, where it belonged. Scott was gone, and she wouldn't replace him with any other man. She'd keep her distance from them from now on.

Out front, Hunter Powell was setting up chairs in rows. Jo, her youngest sister, was already upstairs getting ready for her big day. Her husband-to-be looked nervous to Lena. She grabbed several chairs and lugged them over to add to the rows, happy to finally have found something to do.

Hunter hurried over to her, his hand outstretched to grab the chairs from her. "Well, look at you," he said in his honey-smooth Southern drawl, pausing to look her up and down. "You're a knockout, Lena. Didn't know you had it in you. Those Chance Creek cowboys aren't going to know what hit them tonight. Let me help you."

"I've got these." Lena was past all patience. She turned her back on the former Navy SEAL sniper and began to unfold the chairs one by one. Hunter grabbed them to line them up, and she bit back a frustrated groan. "I said I didn't need help."

"Darling, you're too beautiful to lug chairs around. You'll ruin your dress."

Lena let out a frustrated groan and gave up. She stalked off around the house, heading past the little cottage Jo and Hunter had built together toward the barn, ignoring Hunter when he called after her. They could all make fun of her if they wanted to. She wasn't beautiful. She wasn't feminine. She didn't care at all about dressing up—

And she didn't care about men.

Bunch of idiots, if you asked her. Assholes. Got in your way. Slowed you down. Shot at you once in a while.

Knocked your lights out if you let them.

Lena stumbled on the uneven ground, caught herself and picked up her pace.

Now they were invading her ranch, wooing her sisters—and marrying them.

So far, they hadn't wrestled control of the cattle operation from her. Brian, Connor and Hunter listened to her when she told them how things should be done, but how long would that last? When would they join forces against her? Overrule her?

If she couldn't take on one man, how could she take on three?

She kept walking, her throat aching with the vicious unfairness of life. She should have been six feet tall. She should have had muscles and strength, and the cutthroat personality Scott had. The kind of personality that let you tell a woman you loved her—just before ramming your fist into her face.

Lena balled her hands to stop their trembling, her fake nails digging hard into the flesh of her palms. She didn't want to think about Scott. And she didn't want to think about Brian, Connor and Hunter, either. She had dreamed for years of finally getting to run Two Willows—her way. But that dream was fading fast.

She didn't know where that left her. She'd never given thought to a life that didn't include living on this ranch, tending these cattle—protecting this land. She'd fought the General tooth and nail for years for the control of it.

Now he was winning by sending husbands.

It had to stop.

WHEN LOGAN PULLED into the long lane that led to Two Willows, he found it lined with cars and trucks, and had to park almost out at the street. He grabbed his bag from the passenger seat, and the small box the General had sent along with him, and walked the rest of the way, taking in the lovely old white-clapboard house the General's wife had grown up in and made the family home. It was a large, generous old Victorian that immediately tugged at Logan's imagination. He'd grown up in Idaho in a town with plenty of houses like this.

His childhood home had been of much newer construction, though, built during an era that didn't prize grace and architecture. A four-bedroom, two-bath structure without much to recommend it except its location on his uncle's large spread. His uncle's place had been the original home on the ranch, of course, and it was old and charming, like Two Willows was. Logan had always felt a sense of relief when he'd entered it. His aunt and uncle, while Catholic, weren't as devout as his parents were. They worked hard but didn't take things so seriously. He'd grown up in a loving home, but the difference between his parents' expectations and his own dreams was so large he never felt quite as at ease there.

Neither of his parents worked the ranch; his mother had been a librarian and his father worked at a hardware store. They'd taken the house on his uncle's spread because family was important to the Hughes—and because the price was right. His father pitched in during the busiest seasons, but once Logan had grown able to do a man's work and could take his place, he'd stepped back from even that.

Logan had spent most of his time helping his uncle and the hands. By the time he'd left for the Marines, he'd known just about everything there was to know about working with cattle, which was part of the reason the General had chosen him for this role.

When his phone buzzed in his pocket, Logan stopped, pulled it out and took the call. It was his brother. "Hey, Anthony."

"Hey, yourself. Mom said you hadn't gotten in touch in a while."

"Been busy." Busy hiding the mess he'd gotten himself into. He didn't want to give his parents any ideas that he might come home.

He still couldn't believe how stupid he'd been, rushing into the Major's house—busting down his door— like an avenging angel ready to save a damsel in distress.

"Busy, huh? Too busy to call your mother? She worries, you know."

"Stop playing parish priest with me."

His brother chuckled. "Sorry. It's hard to step out of character, you know?"

Logan did know. He'd worked hard to break out of the character his parents had wanted to cloak him with and become a Marine, instead.

"I'll call her—soon as I can."

"Call her today."

"If I have time. I'm… busy."

"Where are you? Can you at least tell me that? Still in Florida?"

Logan always found it hard to lie to Anthony. Ten years older than him, Anthony had always held the upper hand in their relationship and was a man of the cloth now, like their much older brother, James. James was a missionary in Ethiopia. No one expected him to call home all the time.

"No—I'm in… Montana."

"Montana? What kind of mission are the Marines running in Montana?"

"You wouldn't believe it if I told you. And I can't tell you, so don't ask."

"Already did," Anthony pointed out. "You know, if you had to join the military, the least you could've done was be a chaplain. It would have eased Mom's heart to know—"

"That wasn't my path," Logan snapped. They'd gone over this a thousand times. His mother had two priests for sons. Wasn't that enough? Why harp on the one that got away? "You can tell her that next time you two talk."

"I know you don't think you have a calling—"

Seriously? They were going to do this again? Logan shoved his free hand in his pocket. "I *know* I don't have a calling."

He had no desire to be a priest. Didn't think God would have him after so many years in the service, anyway. Surely he'd broken far too many commandments to make that even possible, if he'd ever had an inkling that way.

Which he hadn't. Not ever.

So how to explain his dreams?

He wasn't a priest in them, either, he reminded himself. Normally he wasn't one for dreaming much at all.

Which made them even more—

Weird.

"You ever think about St. Michael?" he asked Anthony as casually as he could.

"St. Michael? What about St. Michael?"

Logan couldn't tell his brother he'd been dreaming about the saint. Anthony would have him home and in a collar before he could finish the sentence.

"St. Michael carries a sword." He touched the medallion again. His middle name was Michael—for the saint. His first name represented a touch of whimsy his mother seemingly hadn't had before or since. "He's supposed to be a protector. Like me," he asserted, unsure why it seemed so important to clarify the connection.

"Not exactly like you. He was a saint. You're a Marine," Anthony said.

"I protect people, just like he's supposed to." That's what the dreams had to mean, right? In them, St. Michael descended from the heavens and handed him that radiant sword he was always depicted with. In the dreams, Logan took the sword, held it firmly and wielded it like he knew what it was for.

He always woke with the sense he was supposed to protect—someone.

Which was why, when he'd heard the Major's wife yelling, he'd gone charging in like a white knight.

Unfortunately, she wasn't the damsel he was looking for.

And now he'd skunked his career.

He knew Anthony—and his parents—would interpret the dream very differently. "It's symbolic," his mother would say. "The sword is the word of God. You're meant to protect your parish. Come home and take up your calling."

Logan fought the urge to rip the medallion from his neck and toss it away. "Look, I've got to go."

"Call Mom—"

Logan hung up. He'd call his mother.

Just as soon as he caught himself a wife.

KITCHEN DUTY. LENA hated nothing more than kitchen duty, but it was better than simpering around among the guests in this travesty of a dress. Like Brian had predicted, she'd been fending off male attention ever since the reception had started. Jo's wedding had been beautiful, and now her sister was glowing like she'd reached some stage of nirvana. Lena was happy for her. Really. But all this romantic love stuff was pissing her off.

As were her fake nails. Maybe if she scrubbed some dishes, they'd fall off.

Lena slammed a pile of dishes into the sink and ran water over them. Outside, people danced, music and laughter sliding in the open windows to fill the kitchen.

The night was cooling down, however, and already some men were building a bonfire to keep folks warm. Soon autumn would really make its presence known and they'd be in for another hard Montana winter.

Lena didn't mind. She loved every season at Two Willows. Coming home from the barns on a cold, crystal winter evening, every star a bright pinprick in the sky—

Those were moments to live for.

She could almost enjoy herself if there weren't so many damn men around the place these days. She'd come across Brian, Connor and Hunter having a chat about how to handle security on the ranch once Hunter left with Jo on their honeymoon. They hadn't even bothered to add her to their little conference, although she'd always guarded this property with her life. When she'd burst in to add her two cents, they'd all looked guilty, like they'd been caught doing something wrong.

Which they had.

They'd underestimated her again. Just because Scott had gotten the drop on her didn't make her useless.

She'd been caught off guard once and only once. It would never happen again.

"We didn't want to bother you—it's your sister's wedding," Hunter had said.

"It's *your* wedding!" she'd cried back at him. He'd exchanged glances with the others, as if he hadn't understood the distinction. Apparently, men were supposed to handle things like security. Women were supposed to slither around looking sexy. She would bullwhip the lot of them if she could get away with it without upsetting her sisters.

Instead, she'd given them a piece of her mind and left them to it. They could make all the plans they wanted; she was the one who knew Two Willows like the back of her hand. She could keep it secure. When her mother died eleven years ago, and the General refused to come home, she'd pledged to keep her sisters safe.

Although lately she'd been failing on every front.

But that was the past, she told herself sternly. She'd learned her lesson.

Someone knocked on the front door, and Lena dried her hands, relieved to get away from the dishes—and her ugly thoughts. She had to get things back in hand. No more self-defeating thoughts. No backing down from the job she'd worked toward her whole life.

This was her ranch. Hers. Not Brian's or Connor's—or Hunter's, for that matter.

Her cattle operation.

She hoped they understood that.

The knock sounded again.

She hoped the General understood that, too. Two Willows wasn't Reed land—it had belonged to the Griffiths—her mother's family.

He didn't get to call the shots here. Much as he thought he did. He'd sent three men, and her sisters had married them. He'd better not think he could—

She had almost reached the door when the knocking became a thunderous pounding.

Irritated, Lena yanked the door open—saw a tall man, with the shoulders of a fullback and biceps of an MMA superstar, his blue eyes flashing with humor, his mouth tugging into a smile as he took her in.

"Hello, baby girl. My name's—"

"Oh, hell no!" Lena slammed the door shut.

And locked it.

End of Excerpt

The Cowboys of Chance Creek Series:

The Cowboy Inherits a Bride (Volume 0)
The Cowboy's E-Mail Order Bride (Volume 1)
The Cowboy Wins a Bride (Volume 2)
The Cowboy Imports a Bride (Volume 3)
The Cowgirl Ropes a Billionaire (Volume 4)
The Sheriff Catches a Bride (Volume 5)
The Cowboy Lassos a Bride (Volume 6)
The Cowboy Rescues a Bride (Volume 7)
The Cowboy Earns a Bride (Volume 8)
The Cowboy's Christmas Bride (Volume 9)

About the Author

With over one million books sold, NYT and USA Today bestselling author Cora Seton has created a world readers love in Chance Creek, Montana. She has twenty-eight novels and novellas currently set in her fictional town, with many more in the works. Like her characters, Cora loves cowboys, military heroes, country life, gardening, bike-riding, binge-watching Jane Austen movies, keeping up with the latest technology and indulging in old-fashioned pursuits. Visit **www.coraseton.com** to read about new releases, contests and other cool events!

Blog:

www.coraseton.com

Facebook:

www.facebook.com/coraseton

Twitter:

www.twitter.com/coraseton

Newsletter:

www.coraseton.com/sign-up-for-my-newsletter

www.ingramcontent.com/pod-product-compliance
Lightning Source LLC
Chambersburg PA
CBHW030315200626
46816CB00006BA/1790